A DESPERATE MEASURE

A DESPERATE MEASURE

A Novel by

DICK REYNOLDS

ISBN-13: 978-0692390238
ISBN-10: 0692390235

Water Forest Press
PO Box 295, Stormville, NY 12582
valentinepress.com
waterforestpressbooks.com

Printed in the United States of America

DEDICATION

To my bridge partners,
Karen Briggs, Ethel Kolbor, Pat Lieppe,
Ken Rubenstein, Ed Shinholser,
Jo-Anne Skinner, and Donna Wortham
With gratitude for your friendship, good humor
and infinite patience.

And to independent film producer and dear friend,
Stephanie M. White, for gracefully allowing me to use
her name in this book.

CHAPTER ONE

Detective Sharon Hardcastle slid quietly out of bed and instantly began shivering. Totally nude, she found her discarded flannel pajamas and dressed quickly as the early morning sun seeped into the room.

After putting on her sweat suit, she looked across the bed at Eliot, sound asleep and looking like a little boy instead of Colorado's Lake County Sheriff. She walked to the other side, gave him a soft kiss on the cheek and padded out to the kitchen.

The coffee maker had been set up last evening. She had only to push a button and have a steaming cup within a few minutes. Since Sharon had been sleeping over on weekends, Eliot had gotten into the habit of grinding coffee beans the night before so the noise wouldn't wake whoever was sleeping in.

A glance at the back door thermometer revealed a chilly forty-five degrees, typical for an early June morning in Leadville. The cloudless blue skies made her feel good. She and Eliot could enjoy their Sunday together by doing something outdoors before she had to leave that night for Pueblo and tomorrow's work.

She took her coffee out to the back porch. Though the sun

was up, mountain ridges to the east blocked her direct view. She inhaled the heady pine scent and enjoyed gazing at numerous blue spruce and quaking aspen bordering Eliot's modest cabin. A pair of large blue jays fought noisily for seeds he'd left on a feeding platform in the backyard.

She daydreamed about yesterday's wedding, the marriage of Sarah Dolan and Andrew Krag, held outdoors on a large grassy slope surrounded by fourteen-thousand-foot peaks. The music was performed by a string quartet from Pueblo with the familiar strains of Lohengrin echoing Rocky Mountain majesty. Leslie Krag, Andrew's ex-wife, had been relentless with her revengeful tactics, trying to destroy Andrew and Sarah's relationship, but she had failed. Leslie's anger had only resulted in crippling herself, both emotionally and physically, and paralyzed for the rest of her life.

Sharon didn't hear Eliot sneak up behind her. He put his arms around her waist and planted a noisy smooch on her neck.

"Morning, sweetheart," he said. "Thought you deserted me."

She broke his embrace and turned halfway around to see him in his undershirt and boxer shorts. "Eliot, you'll freeze out here."

"I love it. Sharpens the smeller and perks up the brain."

"Coffee's made. Grab a cup and come join me."

He came back and stood next to her, carefully sipping the hot brew. "What've you been up to out here?"

"Enjoying the peace and quiet. Thinking."

"About what?"

"Oh . . . stuff."

"Stuff. That's profound."

After a few moments she said, "Wasn't it a beautiful wedding? I've never seen a happier couple."

"Giving you some ideas?"

"I always have ideas, Eliot, comes with being a detective. But those two deserve each other. And I mean that in a nice way, especially after all the trauma and aggravation they've been through."

"Agreed," he said. "A happy ending to the Sarah and Andy story. I thought it was a nice touch, them walking down the aisle and back out under the ice ax arch."

"The only outdoor wedding I've been to. Where did that gazebo come from?"

"Andy's buddies from work made it. They even did the decorations, flowers, balloons, and all kinds of construction doodads."

"I need another cup," she said. After she came back she continued, "I actually do have an idea, a pretty good one."

"I thought so."

"Relax, you'll love it."

"Then lay it on me."

"Had a little chat with Sarah last night at the reception. She told me about a place they went on their first non-date, a snowshoe hike in the White Forest up to a spot overlooking Turquoise Lake. That's the same lake we saw when I came up for your fish hatchery tour."

"A non-date? What's that?"

"Just something they did as friends before they started real dating."

"So you'd like to go up there?"

"Yeah, are you up for it?"

"Sure, sounds like fun. Should have some nice weather today and we can pack a picnic lunch. And, if you play your cards right . . ."

She patted him smartly on the cheek. "You got lucky last night, cowboy."

The state of Colorado operates twenty-two prisons, most of them with the euphemistic title of Correctional Center or Correction Facility. All are located in rural settings away from large population centers and vary in both size and degree of security provided. For example, the Rifle Correctional Center in Garfield County is eight miles from the town of Rifle and about 160 miles west of Denver along I-70. It's a minimum security facility with 192 beds. At the other end of the spectrum is the Colorado State Penitentiary, a top level security institution located at Canon City along U. S. 50, some sixty miles west of Pueblo. On eighty acres with a capacity of 756 inmates, it houses the most violent and dangerous offenders incarcerated in the state's penal system.

On the same Sunday afternoon Eliot and Sharon were enjoying a picnic lunch and the view of Turquoise Lake, Assistant State Penitentiary Warden Travis Wilcox was in his office, holding a serious discussion with inmate Chance Cullen while a uniformed guard stood near the door.

"I have to give you credit," said Wilcox, "for working hard the last couple of years and staying out of trouble. Not easy to do around here but you've certainly earned parole and still have plenty of opportunities to build a good life for yourself."

Cullen massaged his red beard's stubble and shifted nervously in his chair. "Yeah, and I'll bet you tell the same bullshit to the other cons when they leave. What about the ten years of my life spent in this shit hole that I'll never see again? How do I get them back? You tell me that, warden."

"I can't. But you're damned lucky. You could have served the entire fifteen years of your sentence. Did you ever think of that?"

"Should've never been sent here in the first place," groaned Cullen. "That damn public defender deserved a jail sentence for all the damage he did. You wanna know what a nice life would be for me? Settling a few scores with the people that got me here in the first place."

"Haven't you learned *anything?* That kind of attitude will only land you back here again." Wilcox handed Cullen several sheets of paper. "You have an appointment tomorrow at nine o'clock with your parole officer, Mary Jane Acosta."

"Is she hot? Maybe she can get me laid."

Wilcox ignored his question. "The parole office is on Abriendo Avenue and you'll be billeted at a hotel close enough for walking. You'll be a guest of the state of Colorado but it's only for a week."

"In what town would I find all these things?"

"Pueblo, about an hour from here."

A wide smile spread across Cullen's face but he didn't say anything.

Wilcox asked, "What's so funny?"

"Nothing. I hear Pueblo's a nice town."

Wilcox handed him an envelope and slid another paper across his desk. "The balance of your earnings," he said, "cash amounting to $432.85. Sign the receipt."

Cullen signed it and stuffed the money into his pocket. "Is that it, warden?"

"The guard will take you back to your cell. Change your clothes, pack all your belongings and be ready for the transport van at five o'clock." Cullen got up to leave but the warden wasn't finished. "And for God's sake, Chance, don't do anything stupid out there. I don't want to see you again. Ever."

"Don't worry about me, warden. I won't do anything *stupid*."

Eliot and Sharon got back to his cabin just before six o'clock. She collapsed on the living room couch and moaned a loud, "Hoo boy."

"You OK?" he said.

"That was some workout. Think I'll just sit here a few minutes and get my battery recharged."

"I'm having a beer. Would you like one?"

"No, thanks, but a soft drink would be good."

Eliot brought her a bottle of root beer and a glass full of crushed ice. He came back into the living room with a bottle of Coors and sat next to her. He clinked his bottle against her glass and said, "Great weekend. Let's do it again."

"That it was," she said. "Hope this week goes by quickly so we can."

"How's your case load holding up?"

"Too well, unfortunately. No shortage of fraud, embezzlement, and all kinds of thefts. Did you know the crime rate in Pueblo is higher than the national average?"

"That's surprising. Something the casual visitor probably wouldn't appreciate."

She took a long drink of her root beer. "Do you ever get discouraged, Eliot, thinking about our line of work? About the people we have to deal with?"

"Sure. Wouldn't be human if I didn't. But somebody has to do it. Think about what life would be like if nobody stepped up to enforce the law."

"Good point."

"And sitting in a courtroom when the jury comes back with the right verdict, seeing the victims or their families hugging each other when justice is served. That helps a lot when you have to face the next day's duty."

They were silent for a few moments until several musical notes came from another room. "Sounds like your cell phone," she said.

Eliot took his beer to the kitchen counter and picked up the phone. Caller ID on the screen listed Clayton Burke, one of Eliot's deputies. "Waters," he answered.

"Sorry to disturb you on a Sunday, sheriff, but there's a *situation* developing out here that I thought you should know about."

"Go ahead."

"I'm at the moly mine near Climax. Got lots of bikers out here, having a big party with plenty of booze, loud music, pot and pills no doubt."

"Are they causing any trouble?"

"Not yet, but it has plenty of potential."

"You got any help?"

"Touched base with Deputy Stewart and he's on his way."

Sharon made hand and arm signals to alert Eliot she was heading for the shower.

"They could have permission from the owners. Have you talked to them?"

"Not yet. Who owns this place now?"

"Not sure. Have our duty dispatcher do a database search. If that doesn't work, call Roscoe Bartlett. His outfit's been doing cleanup work on that site. He'd probably know who to call."

"I'll get right on it, sheriff."

"Play it low key, Burke, and let me know if the situation gets any worse."

Eliot busied himself around the kitchen until Sharon came out of the bathroom. "How about something to eat," he called, "before you head out?"

"I'm not hungry right now, thanks to the trail snacks I gobbled on the way back. I've got plenty of food at home."

"Late night ice cream sundae, eh?"

"Not before bed," she said, slapping one of her hips, "or I'll be wearing it right here in the morning."

"All packed up?"

"Sure, but get over here close."

He enveloped her with a tight hug and a long tender kiss. "Sure will be nice when we don't have to say goodbye anymore."

"Amen to that."

Neither one was anxious to break the embrace but a beeping sound from Sharon's pocket caused her to back away. "*My* phone this time."

She stared at the screen for a few moments and shook her head. "Weird."

"What?"

"A text, some guy named Brian wants me to drop by his office tomorrow."

"Who's Brian?"

"The only man I know with that name is the mayor, Brian Mansfield. But what would he want with me?"

Eliot made a nervous grin. "Oh, several things come to mind. Like a medal, maybe a commendation, or better yet, a meritorious pay raise."

"Ha. In your dreams."

"What are you going to do about it?"

"First, find out if this is for real."

"And if it is?"

"Get a heads up from someone in his office. Don't want to go in there without any preparation."

"Suppose this Brian guy is not the mayor. Then what?"

She held up her phone to eye level. "Use the DELETE key."

They had more hugs and kisses next to her car before Sharon got behind the wheel. "Drive safely," he said.

"Love you," she replied, starting the engine.

"Back atcha. Call me when you get home."

"Will do."

After she pulled out of the driveway Eliot went back to the kitchen and made a ham and cheese sandwich. The message from the mysterious Brian nagged at him. He wasn't worried about Sharon. She had proved herself several months ago when they had pursued Leslie Krag in a fast-moving gun battle. But if the sender of that text was indeed the mayor of Pueblo, then the matter didn't pass the smell test. If he wanted to see Sharon on official business, the mayor would have used the chain of command and passed the word through the city's police chief.

He finished his makeshift dinner, tidied up the kitchen and glanced at the wall clock. Too much evening left before bedtime, he thought. Think I'll take a drive out to the moly mine and see how Deputy Burke is getting on.

Chapter Two

Chance Cullen woke up early Monday morning with a headache, a foul taste in his mouth, and sticky eyelids that wouldn't open. He carefully pried open each eyelid and saw the ceiling fan lazily turning its black blades with a scraping sound suggesting imminent self-destruction.

He was momentarily disoriented until the woman next to him made a snorting noise, allowing him to piece together what had happened last night. He'd been dropped by the prison's transport van at a flea bag hotel somewhere in downtown Pueblo, gone out looking for drinks and dinner, and found a place where he'd consumed more booze than food. After two margaritas at the bar he became cozy with a woman sitting nearby. One thing led to another and somehow she was now in bed with him. *What the hell is her name? Did I give her any money? I better check my wallet and make sure she didn't rip me off.*

The woman rolled to one side, facing away from him, but in the process she threw off much of the light sheet which had covered her. Chance gazed at her long black hair spread across the pillow, the alluring curves of her naked light brown body, and soon had a large erection. He reached under her elbow and grasped a large, artificially enhanced breast. When she moaned softly, Chance took this as an encouraging sign.

He pulled her towards him, threw a leg across her body and got on top. She soon awoke and began to struggle. "What the hell are you doing?" she cried.

"Trying to get inside. What else?"

She broke free and slid out of the bed onto the floor. She struggled to stand up and let loose a loud tirade. "What is wrong with you? Didn't you get enough last night? We did it three times so you can't be horny. "

"It's been a long dry spell. Think I told you that."

She gathered up her clothes, which had been scattered around the room, went into the bathroom and slammed the door.

"Don't be all day in there," he called out.

Cullen's demand only increased her anger and made her spend a long time getting dressed. She finally came out and said, "Don't bother calling. And if you see me around town, don't even think of talking to me."

He looked at the excessive makeup splattered across her face and had a thought. *She sure looked prettier last night, especially after I'd had a couple of drinks.* "No worry about that," he said. She walked out and slammed the door even harder.

Cullen dragged himself out of bed and looked around the room for a coffee maker but none could be found. Instead, he gobbled three aspirin, put on jeans and a polo shirt, and left his room in search of breakfast. Going down on the elevator he recalled one advantage of being incarcerated; breakfast with coffee had been served every day at the Colorado State Prison mess hall.

Cullen reported to the parole office shortly after nine o'clock, a short walk from his hotel on Jackson Street, wearing the best clothes he had. When a short, heavyset woman about sixty came out to the reception desk and introduced herself as Mrs. Acosta, he smiled and said, "Chance Cullen, but you can call me C.C." *Warden Wilcox would probably like to know that she's definitely not hot.*

"Come with me, Mr. Cullen," she said, turning abruptly and walking away.

He followed her and muttered, "Guess this is going to be all business."

Acosta sat behind her desk and Cullen sat across and facing her. She opened a folder and spread a thick sheaf of papers on her desk. "I have your prison history here so you're not a total stranger. The term of your parole, as you know, is one year and we're going to get better acquainted with each other over time. My job is to help you reenter society and your job is to stay out of trouble and be a productive citizen. I'm sure you don't want to go back to Canon City."

"Correct."

"All right. First, the state will pay for only a week at the hotel where you're staying. You'll need to find a permanent place to live." She handed him a single sheet of paper. "Here's a list of places around town where you can rent a room."

He glanced at the list. "I don't know this town at all. How do I get around to find these places?"

"I'll give you a map in a minute. Pueblo has a pretty good transportation system so you can take a bus. Which brings me to another necessity, getting a job so you can support yourself."

"Yeah, lots of opportunities out there for ex-cons, I'm sure.

Who the heck's gonna hire me? Grocery stores and fast food joints?"

"It's not as bad as you might think. Those kinds of places are possible but there are others." She folded her hands and rested them on the desk top. "Tell me about your work skills."

He took a deep breath. "Oh, well. Worked at a car wash when I was in high school, then a hardware store for a while after I graduated. That was in Fredericksburg, Texas, where I grew up. Moved on a couple of years later, worked in the oil business on drilling crews and machine shops in the Houston area, making drill bits and things like that. When the oil business went into a slump, I moved on to different places like Phoenix and Las Vegas, construction jobs, building new houses, that kind of stuff. Even bumped around the rodeos, calf roping and Brahma bull bashing, but I wouldn't call that a work skill."

"There's a startup out in Pueblo West, a small company building spec homes. I understand they're looking for some experienced help."

"Do the buses run out there?"

"No, you'd have to drive."

He smiled. "Well, there you go."

"Tell me about the work you did in prison."

"Kind of lucked out there," he said. "Landed a good job in the hospital and did that for six years. Doc Wilson taught me a lot about medicine and nursing. Not much about bedside manner, you know. Not around a bunch of guys like me."

"I might be able to place you in a hospital here in town. Parkview Medical Center." She found a map in one of her paper piles and pointed at two spots. "This office is here on Abriendo and the hospital is right here. It's about two miles away and you could probably walk there from your hotel. What do you think?"

He shrugged his shoulders. "Might as well give it a try."

"I'll call them and arrange an interview. But first, there's a few more items we have to discuss." She passed him the map and a packet of papers. "Plenty of reading material there when you get some free time. Look it over carefully. Here are the most important things to remember. You come in here once a week, every Monday morning, unless your work schedule interferes and then we'll work something else out. I want to see your physical presence and make sure you're alive and not in jail. And by the way, I think you already know that if you do wind up in jail, for any reason at all, it's a one-way ticket back to Canon City. I also want to know where you live, your phone number, and how I can reach you if necessary."

"I don't have a phone," he said.

"Buy one of those throwaway cell phones."

"Can I travel?"

"Travel? You just got here."

"True, but I've been cooped up for the last ten years. My feet are getting itchy and I'd like to stretch my legs."

"Where do you want to go?"

"Different places in Colorado. Maybe enjoy some mountain scenery."

"But you don't have a car."

He smiled. "But you mentioned something about buses."

"Forget that. When you get a place to live and a steady job, then we'll talk about it. Until then, you stay within Pueblo's city limits. Understand?"

"Got it."

"We do spot checks on our parolees," she said, "just to make sure you're obeying all the rules. Something to keep in mind."

"Yeah, right."

She picked up the telephone handset and said, "I'm calling Parkview and try to get you a job interview."

The Pueblo Police Department has an Investigation Bureau consisting of six sections and is headed by a deputy chief. Sharon Hardcastle is one of nine detectives working out of the Crimes Against Property Section lead by Sergeant David Hess. This section is responsible for investigating property-related crimes such as theft, burglary, embezzlement, fraud, identity theft and forgery. Earlier this year, Sharon had received a commendation for apprehending a man and woman who'd been illegally renting properties that were already occupied by their actual owners.

Shortly after Sharon came to her office on Monday morning, she went looking for the only other woman detective in the section, Deborah Wasserstein. Darling Debbie, as she was known throughout the bureau, seemed to have the widest network of snitches, gossips and unpaid undercover agents of the entire police force. She found Wasserstein having coffee in the section's kitchen. "Deb, I need to pick your brain."

"Easy picking today," she said. "What's up?"

"I got this text and I'm not sure what to do with it." She pulled her phone out of a trouser pocket and showed her the screen. "What do you think?"

"Who's Brian?"

"The mayor? He's the only Brian I know."

"Hoo ha," said Deborah. "Maybe he wants to put the moves on you." When Sharon quickly scowled, Deborah added, "Course your Leadville lawman wouldn't be too happy about that."

Sharon ignored both comments. "How would *you* deal with this?"

"Me? I'd just stick my head in his office and ask what he wants."

"That easy, huh?"

"Yeah, and don't try to make an appointment. The harpy sitting outside his office is like that three-headed dog guarding the gates of hell."

Sharon chuckled. "Yes, but Cerberus was there to keep people from leaving."

"Just walk in there with your badge held high and say *police business.* Put on your best Clint Eastwood sneer and act like you know what you're doing."

Sharon shook her head. "If he didn't send the text his first call will be to Dave Hess and I'm toast."

"No, you quickly apologize, do an about face and get out pronto."

"This has trouble written all over it."

"Maybe, but think of this. What if the mayor did text you and you ignore it."

"All right, all right. I'll do it."

Sharon's fears evaporated when she entered Mayor Mansfield's office several hours later and his secretary announced, "Go right in, detective. He's expecting you."

Sharon was so surprised that she hesitated for a moment but Mrs. Schrader, the secretary, only turned back to her computer screen. So much for that, she thought, opening the door to the mayor's private office.

He stood up from his desk as she entered. "Ah, Detective Hardcastle. Come in, please." He pointed to several chairs grouped around a small table and said, "Have a seat. Care for some coffee?"

"Thanks, but no." She sat in a plush upholstered chair and watched him walk over and take an opposite seat. About fifty with short brown hair graying at the temples, Mansfield wore glasses with thick black frames and fidgeted nervously with his tie when speaking.

"I'll get right to the point. I need your help with something, a sensitive matter that involves a friend who also works for the city. What do you say?"

"Whoa . . . me? What kind of matter?"

"You have to promise that what we discuss is privileged information and not to leave this room. Do I have your word?"

"Sure."

"All right. There's a man on the city council, a good friend and a loyal supporter of my policies. Frank Streckfus is his name. You've probably seen him on TV or in the newspaper. I'm afraid he's got himself in trouble and, if it's true, he's got to be stopped from getting in deeper."

"You want me to talk with him?"

"No, but dig into everything about him. I see him driving expensive cars and he recently moved into a huge mansion. Just doesn't look right for an elected official having a luxury life style on what the city pays him."

"Maybe a relative died and left him a bundle."

"I doubt it. My wife and I have been friends with him and his family for years. He would have mentioned it."

Sharon took several moments to regain her composure and think about where this conversation was going. "You know, Mr. Mayor, spying on your friend might be considered an invasion of privacy, harassment, and improper use of police resources by elected officials."

He smiled. "A valid point but I've consulted an attorney and I believe we're within the letter of the law."

Sharon squirmed while noting his use of the inclusive *we*. "I'm not sure I have time for this. My case load is pretty heavy right now."

"Not a problem. I've spoken to Sergeant Hess and he knows we're talking."

This was not welcome news. "How convenient."

"Find out all you can about his financials. If he's doing anything illegal, I want the details. If not, I want that too. When we know which way the wind is blowing, we can plan the next step."

"Would you like to meet on a regular basis for my reports?"

"No, this will be our last meeting." He handed over his business card. "My private e-mail address is on the back."

He stood, signaling the end of their meeting. "Thanks again for coming by. Let me hear from you soon."

Sharon went on to work more pressing investigations and got back to her office about six o'clock. Neither Sergeant Hess nor Detective Debbie was there, a bit of good luck that relieved her of answering any awkward questions. She spent another hour updating case files with information collected earlier. After turning off her computer, she thought about her meeting with the mayor and the unofficial spy job he'd given her. She needed to talk with someone about this.

Eliot answered his phone after two rings. "Thought I'd be hearing from you right about now."

"Oh, yeah? Why is that?"

"You'll be wanting to tell me about your meeting with

the mayor."

"Lucky guess." Eliot listened while Sharon replayed the entire dialogue between herself and Mansfield. Afterward she said, "Dammit, Eliot, this business is fishy as an ocean. I saw it in Kansas City when I was on the force and now it's happening again. Using government resources for something they were never intended for. Why should Pueblo's top elected official be concerned about a friend living beyond his means? And why should he get the police department involved?"

"Sounds to me like the mayor is not telling you everything. Have you learned anything about Streckfus?"

"Not yet, I wanted to run this by you first."

"What do you know about the mayor? Do you trust him?"

"I don't trust any politician. I'll start digging on Streckfus but I'll open another mine shaft and see if there's any dirt on Mr. Mansfield."

"Good idea, Sharon. Above all, be careful and protect yourself. Document everything, with a backup, and start with the conversation you had with Mr. Mansfield."

"I'll do that right after this call."

CHAPTER THREE

Chance Cullen did get an appointment at Parkview Medical Center but the job interview wasn't to happen until the next morning. He took advantage of his Monday free time to get more familiar with Pueblo, at least for the near term.

First on his to-do list was opening a bank account. Cullen's father had sent him a cashier's check for $2,500 just before being released from prison to help him get back on his feet. Chance's mother had died of breast cancer while he was in prison, an event which caused a violent reaction and ten days in solitary because he'd not been allowed to attend her funeral. His father had since remarried and moved to San Antonio. Chance now had a stepmother and several new siblings whom he'd never met and was not likely to meet unless he went to San Antonio. When his dad sent the check, there was no invitation for Chance to come visit his new family, the absence of such a request being a sure sign that he wasn't wanted.

The bank was happy to open a savings account for him. A checking account would have to wait until he had a place with a permanent mailing address. He kept out three hundred dollars for his next adventure and a shopping expedition to a Target department store on a main bus line.

That evening, armed with a city map from Mrs. Acosta and Monday's edition of *The Pueblo Chieftain*, Cullen scoured the want ads for places to live. He found several promising candidates in residential areas close to downtown Pueblo and circled them for further investigation.

The next morning, Cullen arrived at Parkview for his job interview with a Mr. John Julian in the employment office. Cullen had shaved his beard, but kept his red mustache, and wore new khaki slacks and a light blue shirt open at the collar. He was surprised to see that Julian was black and approaching sixty, dressed smartly in a white shirt and maroon tie. He wore gold rim glasses and his hair was cut short with tiny gray curls at the temples.

Julian welcomed him with great fanfare. "Come in, come in," he said with a wide smile. They shook hands and Cullen took a seat in front of his desk. "I'm told you want to work here. Tell me why we should hire you." Cullen thought he could detect a faint British accent.

"Well, I need a job for one thing. And I worked in a hospital at the last place."

Julian glanced at a paper. "More like a dispensary than a hospital, wasn't it?"

"Yeah. How'd you know that?"

He smiled and leaned forward slightly. "From a similar experience." When Cullen only stared, Julian continued, "I've been at Parkview for ten years. No doubt I left Canon City about the time you were going in."

Cullen relaxed slightly. "I'll be damned." *Wonder what he did time for?*

"Ex-cons can succeed if they wish. It takes time, hard work

and patience."

"I'm no stranger to hard work."

"Good. We actually have two openings right now. One is a day job in the kitchen. The usual, like collecting trays, cleaning dishes, and getting meals ready for patients. The other is at night in housekeeping."

"Cleaning patients' rooms and mopping hallways, I suppose."

"Correct. The pay is the same for both, twelve dollars per hour, but you are allowed a lunch when you work in the kitchen."

"I'd rather be in housekeeping. What's the schedule like?"

"Three to eleven, Wednesday to Sunday, with Monday and Tuesday free."

Chance thought about it and liked the idea of partying late after his shift was over and sleeping late the next morning. "Hey, I might get lucky and enjoy a nurse after work."

Julian chuckled. "Our nurses are more likely to go out with doctors, but you never know. You *might* get lucky."

"One thing about the hours, I can see my parole officer in the morning."

"Good idea to stay on Mrs. Acosta's sunny side." He handed Cullen a form. "Fill out this application and we'll get you on the payroll."

"You're hiring me?"

"Of course, starting tomorrow afternoon. After we're finished I'll take you to meet Ms. Dawson." He started laughing. "A tough old dear but she's fair."

Eliot stayed late at his office Wednesday afternoon finishing some paperwork. He'd reviewed Deputy Burke's report on Sunday evening's biker rally at the old molybdenum mine and made notes about items that needed further amplification.

He shut off his computer and was about to leave when a woman opened the door. As she came toward him, his first reaction was annoyance at being detained. He had to look upward to see her face because of her height, aided by high-heeled black leather boots which came up just short of her knees. She stopped several paces in front of his desk, flashed a brilliant smile, but said nothing.

Eliot stared, taking in her gray wool dress and black turtleneck, soft dark brown hair falling over her shoulders, and glasses that couldn't conceal her sparkling green eyes. *The eyes and the smile, a dangerous combination which few men could resist.* "Cassie?" was all he could get out.

"In the flesh."

"What are you doing here?"

She put both hands on her hips. "Is that any way to greet an old friend?"

He moved carefully around the desk with an outstretched arm but she wasn't about to settle for a handshake. She moved hard into him, put her arms around his neck and kissed him tenderly on the lips. "Glad to see me?" she whispered.

He grasped her waist and pushed back. "Not sure."

She sensed the awkwardness, not something she expected or hoped for. "Sorry for barging in like this. Thought it would be nice to surprise you."

"You look nice. You always looked nice."

She turned in a sweeping pirouette with arms outstretched. "Wow, you've certainly come up in the world. County Sheriff with a big office, lots of deputies and hired help to boss around."

"Yep, a fine place to live and good people to work with."

She glanced at her wristwatch, one that Eliot noticed was loaded with diamond-like stones. "Is there a nice restaurant in town? I'll spring for dinner, we can have a drink and talk some. Lots of catching up to do."

"Sure, we can do that. Just a short walk to Quincy's."

They were both silent as Eliot guided her down Harrison Street. The quiet time allowed him to take a virtual hike down memory lane, nineteen years ago, and back to the Parada de Sol Rodeo in Scottsdale, Arizona where they'd met. Cassandra "Cassie" Maugham had been living in Scottsdale with her second husband, but Eliot hadn't a clue that she was married. Their affair was passionate, like an Indy 500 race car speeding through a southwestern night at a thousand miles per hour, seat belts unfastened, headlights broken and an unlimited supply of high octane fuel.

After only three months, Cassie left her husband and followed Eliot on the rodeo circuit until that bitter winter day when she had second thoughts. *My husband has money and Eliot doesn't. In a very short time, we're going to be in nowheresville.* Eliot pleaded, shouted in violent arguments about her lack of faith, pledging that he'd quit the rodeo and get a responsible job that paid well. She only laughed, reminding him that he had little education, no real work skills, and he'd best forget about her and get on with his life. For many months after she'd pulled up stakes, Eliot drank himself to sleep every night and woke up in the darkness, wishing he could touch her just one more time. Finally, when New Years Day of 1995 rolled around, he stopped drinking and soon found a job with the border patrol.

They were shown to a quiet table in the back of Quincy's though the place seemed crowded with tourists. "They know me," said Eliot as they sat down.

"Your usual, sheriff?" asked their waitress.

"Yeah, but a double this time."

"A glass of Chardonnay for me," chirped Cassie.

When their drinks arrived, Cassie offered a toast, "To good friends, reunited."

"To friends," he answered, followed by a slug of Jack Daniel's on the rocks.

She matched his sip with a healthy one of wine. "So what have you been doing with yourself all these years?"

"Worked the Arizona border near Tucson for five years but got mighty tired of that, especially in the summer heat. Something about all those Mexicans trying to get into the country and being hunted down like dogs turned my stomach. The worst part was the scammers, packing dozens of people in the back of a closed truck. No food, no water, and sometimes not enough air. I saw some things I'll never forget."

"Then you left and came to the Rockies?"

"Signed on here as a deputy thirteen years ago. Then later the fine citizens of Lake County elected me sheriff. Got another one coming later this year."

"My God, you're a politician."

"Not at all, I'm an elected law enforcer." He paused to sip his drink. "Are you still married to Dwight?" Eliot was referring to her second husband, the one she'd gone back to after dumping Eliot.

She twirled her glass with a thumb and forefinger. "Dwight's history, the ancient kind." She finished her wine and held the glass up high as a refill signal. "I was a very foolish girl, Eliot, thinking that he and I could make it work after what I did. He couldn't stand it, thinking about you and me together. He even had the nerve one night, after we had sex, to ask if he was as good as you. I couldn't lie and he couldn't stand me anymore. Called me all kinds of dirty names, packed up and left. I got a lawyer pronto and made out pretty well in the divorce."

"So you're single again?"

She drank from a new glass of wine. "Not quite."

"Like being a little bit pregnant?"

"It's complicated. I married Winston after Dwight and I divorced, on the rebound you might say. We bought a Scottsdale McMansion and dove right into the social pool. Did I mention he's twenty years older than me?"

"So it's not working out?"

"He's out on the golf course every day, long boozy lunches with his old crony buddies, the afternoon nap, dinner at the club followed by the mandatory bridge game and then early to bed. To sleep. Nothing else. It's *Bo - ring* with a capital B."

Eliot only chuckled.

"What's so funny?"

"I've got some questions for you. First off, how did you find me?"

She brightened. "It's quite a story. I heard about this private detective from a friend, a guy with a good reputation for tracking people down. So I contacted him and told him what I needed. Can you believe it? He knows you."

"What's his name?"

"Clarke Layton. He did some work for a Denver client, finding her husband who was having an affair with the boss's niece. He lived right here in Leadville."

Eliot patted his mustache lightly and gave her a serious look.

"I know Mr. Layton. That case you mentioned didn't turn out so well for his client and he had to leave Denver or get thrown in jail. I've always wondered what happened to him." After a pause he added, "Hope you didn't give him any money."

"Not yet."

"OK, you've found me. Which leads to my next question. Why did you come all this way?"

She brushed the back of her hand across his cheek. "To see you, silly."

"And?"

"Oh . . . whatever."

There was a third question, about what she really wanted, but he knew what her unspoken answer would be so it remained unasked.

Their prime rib dinners arrived, the only entree offered by Quincy's during the week, and the conversation subsided. Cassie ate hungrily but Eliot was slower, still not comfortable with her sudden appearance. They talked about old times and recalled pleasant events during their courtship which made Eliot more relaxed. That is, until she got around to more sensitive matters. "Is there a Mrs. Waters waiting at home?"

"The only Mrs. Waters is my mom and she's in Lubbock with my dad."

"You're so damn clever. You know what I mean."

He sliced off a chunk of baked potato. "I never married."

"That's encouraging," she said, giving him a warm smile. Eliot glanced at her and wondered how many dentists she'd made rich with that mouth.

They finished their meals, declined dessert, and Cassie paid with her credit card. As they stepped out the front door into a dark evening, she said, "Eliot, it's freezing out here."

"It does get nippy at 10,000 feet after the sun goes down." She began walking quickly back in the direction they came from. "Where's your car?" he said.

"In the lot behind your office." When they got to her car, she said, "I haven't found anywhere to stay tonight. You know of a nice place a girl can bunk?"

"Silver King Inn on Poplar Street is good. I can show you where it is."

"No room at your place, huh?"

"Sorry, I don't have a guest room."

"You are so thick sometimes." She got inside, started up the engine and rolled down her window. "See you tomorrow?"

"Good night, Cassie. And thanks for the dinner."

She zoomed from the parking lot with a horrible screech and Eliot only shook his head. Ninety-eight percent of him had no feelings at all for the woman. But the other two percent wanted to throw her into the nearest bed, screw her brains out, and kick her pretty ass all the way back to Scottsdale.

CHAPTER FOUR

Sharon Hardcastle was having a good Wednesday afternoon. So far, anyway. She'd responded to a call from Mrs. Annie Clark, a sixty-eight year old woman who lived in the southwestern part of Pueblo. Mrs. Clark had received a call from her bank saying that a check had been returned and marked *insufficient funds*. In Mrs. Clark's opinion, her bankers were a bunch of crooks and should be thrown in jail.

After calming her down, Sharon took some time to examine Mrs. Clark's bank statements, checkbooks and unused checks. She discovered that five checks had been ripped from the bottom of a fresh book tucked away in a small box. Although Mrs. Clark didn't want to admit it, all signs pointed to her niece who'd recently visited and was now back home in Chicago. Sharon advised Mrs. Clark to call the bank and get copies of all canceled checks corresponding to the ones that were missing. She should also cancel any of the five checks still outstanding. If her niece was indeed guilty of theft and forgery, Mrs. Clark should follow up with Chicago police.

Sharon intended to return to her office but decided first to take a brief detour. Only a few blocks away on Delano Street, she stopped opposite an elaborate two story home, the residence of city councilman Frank Streckfus. She'd checked county property records and learned that he'd bought this house seven years ago for $850,000. She judged it could probably be sold now for close to a million dollars. About 6500 square feet with five bedrooms and five baths, it seemed too much for Mr. and Mrs. Streckfus and their two teenagers. The house also sported two separate garages, each capable of housing two automobiles. I'm surely in the wrong business, she thought.

Sharon got back to her office near quitting time and wanted to harvest more information about Streckfus. Once inside her cubicle, she was about to begin a computer search when she heard Detective Debbie announce her presence.

"Hey, Hardtack, I thought you resigned." The nickname, referring to a hard saltless biscuit sometimes found in army rations, was something Sharon detested but didn't make an issue of it because it would only cause Wasserstein to use it more often.

"Nope, still on the job."

Debbie plopped into the chair next to Sharon's desk. "Haven't seen you in a while. You been avoiding your best bud?"

Sharon turned off her computer. "Not at all. Just trying to wrap up some of my cases."

"How did you *make out* with the mayor?" She accompanied the emphasized words with air quotes and a lecherous grin.

"Just fine. Had a nice chat, very business like. Wanted to make sure I was a happy and productive cop."

"Uh huh. Can't believe he has no ulterior motives."

"Oh, he might. But I made a point to ask about Mrs. Mansfield and his kids. That seemed to squelch any personal agenda."

Wasserstein got out of the chair. "Doesn't ring true, Hardtack.

Still think something's not right."

"Not going to waste time thinking about it. I'll let *you* worry about him."

"Not my type," she called over her shoulder. "Too nerdy looking."

Sharon went off to the kitchen for a soft drink from the fridge. She brought it back to her desk and, satisfied that Wasserstein had left the area, turned her computer back on. From the many news articles in *The Pueblo Chieftain,* she gained an appreciation of Streckfus' activity on the city council. She found a laudatory news article, published in 2008 when he'd been first elected, highlighting a twenty-year career in the U. S. Army. Originally a native of Pittsburgh, he was commissioned a Signal Corps second lieutenant in 1984 and spent almost all of his career in communications and electronics. He received a bronze star for meritorious achievement as a captain in connection with Desert Storm and Desert Shield during the invasion of Iraq in 1990 and 1991. Finishing his military career at Fort Meade, Maryland, he retired as a Lieutenant Colonel in 2004. Before his move to Pueblo in 2006, the article cited Streckfus as a consultant with a company called Informatics International based in Reston, VA, a small town near Washington, D.C.

Sharon found several items about Informatics and learned it offered services and solutions for all manner of requirements and issues related to information processing and security for enterprises both large and small. The company also boasted offices in Tokyo, Berlin, London, Zurich, Ankara, Paris, Tel Aviv and Rome, lending credibility to their claim of being a global corporation.

"Now I get it," muttered Sharon. "Streckfus worked for the National Security Agency at Fort Meade." *With a nice army pension and a good salary from Informatics, he can probably afford the big house and expensive cars. Why shouldn't he indulge himself?*

Burrowing further, she found another article in a Sunday issue of *The Chieftain*. A color photo showed Frank and Gloria Streckfus, both tanned and physically fit, cutting a ceremonial pink ribbon at the grand opening of a new library branch. Frank looked handsome in a tuxedo, sporting a shaved head and politically correct smile. Gloria wore an expensive looking black dress, a triple-strand necklace of turquoise and silver, and had perfectly coifed short blonde hair. Brian Mansfield and his wife, Lillian, were also in the picture, standing close to Frank and Gloria. Interestingly, Lillian stared straight into the camera and appeared like she was having gastric problems. Brian was eyeing Gloria's partially exposed and generous cleavage with a dopey look on his face. *Maybe Mr. Mayor wants Gloria to be a much closer friend than Frank.*

On a whim, she Googled Brian Mansfield. When she found an item about his period of military service, she had an *uh oh* moment. Mansfield had been awarded the Army Commendation Medal as a first lieutenant while a member of the 4th Armored Cavalry Regiment during Operation Desert Shield during 1991. This discovery made her recall a line from *Jaws*. "You're gonna need a bigger boat."

A signal from her stomach caused Sharon to glance at her watch. She closed the document she'd compiled, attached it to an e-mail and sent it to her personal address. She also deleted all of the search results and turned off her computer. *After some dinner and a drink, I'll work on this some more at home.*

Several hours later Sharon finished her search for information on Councilman Streckfus and Mayor Mansfield and felt frustrated with her lack of progress. *Too few relevant facts and too many unanswered questions.*

She called Patricia "Trish" Guinn whose friendship went all the way back to Our Lady of the Pillar grade school and De Smet Jesuit high school in Creve Couer, MO. Both had a keen interest in the law as teens. Sharon became a paralegal but Trish went on to study law, earned her J.D. and was now a twenty year FBI veteran in Washington, D.C. Sharon had asked Trish for help several times over the years and tonight hoped she'd aid her again.

"Sharon," she answered brightly, "how ya been?"

"Busy, busy. Sorry for calling so late."

"No problem. Just sitting here with a glass of wine, watching a movie, and trying to unwind after another day of nonstop crises. What's going on with you and the mountain man?"

"We went to a Saturday wedding up in Leadville. Beautiful outdoor ceremony, lots of fun at the reception. Took a picnic lunch up into the mountains on Sunday."

"Sounds mucho romantic, girlfriend. Like maybe you'll be thinking about another wedding real soon. Huh?"

"You'll be the first to know, but don't hold your breath."

"Nuts. I'll be an old lady by the time you two get it together." Trish paused. "Is this a social call or do we need to talk *business?*"

Sharon laughed. "Well, here I am again with my hand out."

"Always here to help you break up my routine."

She told her everything she knew about Mansfield and Streckfus starting with the mayor's text message on Sunday. At the end of her summary she said, "I'll send you an e-mail with everything I've found so far."

"What's your gut telling you?" said Trish.

"Something's wrong here and I could easily get in trouble."

"I agree. What do you need from me?"

"Anything and everything you can dig up on these guys. One thing I'd like to know about is any foreign travel by Streckfus. Where did he go and for how long?"

"I can probably get that from the ICE people. What else?" Trish was referring to the government organization called Immigration and Customs Enforcement.

"How about their tax returns for the last couple of years?"

"Whoa now," said Trish. "That's dangerous in today's political environment."

"OK, forget it. I don't want to jeopardize your job."

"Hey, I didn't say I wouldn't try. Let me do some snooping."

"Then be careful. Very careful."

"Hey, Careful is my middle name. And Sharon, we never had this conversation. *Capisce*?"

"What conversation?"

Eliot had a terrible night after his dinner with Cassie Maugham, tossing and turning with little sleep. Her sudden reentrance into his life after so many years had dramatically upset his emotional well being, causing him to question not only his relationship with Sharon but what he needed to do, if anything, about Cassie. *Should I tell Sharon about her? Show what a good guy I am by not taking her to bed?*

He sat quietly at his desk Thursday morning, pondering such relationship problems, and wondered if he could sneak off to the jail after lunch and grab a nap. But when Cassie walked into his office and he got a look at her face, he took a perverse pleasure in understanding she must have had a night as bad as his.

"Can we talk?" she said.

"Sure. Want some coffee?" He remained seated.

"No, thanks, I've had some." She stood in front of his desk and said, after an awkward pause, "I need to apologize."

"Not necessary."

"Oh yes it is. I shouldn't have surprised you like I did. What if I'd called and told you I was coming? Would you still see me?"

"All depends. If you were calling from Scottsdale, I'd probably say never mind. But if you were here in Leadville . . . yeah, I guess curiosity would get the best of me."

"You mind if I sit?"

He nudged the chair located next to his desk. "Be my guest."

She made a show of carefully sitting down, unbuttoning her jacket and rummaging through her huge purse before she pulled out a package of tissues and dabbed her tearing eyes. "We left a lot of strings untied when we split and I wanted to see if it was too late to fix them up."

"A lot has happened over those years. To both of us."

"I'd regret it for the rest of my life if I didn't try and there was still a chance."

"Can't blame you for trying."

She sniffled, looked around the room and returned to see him grinning. "What's so funny?" she asked.

"You."

"Me?"

"There *is* someone special in my life. That's what you've been wondering all along. Am I right?"

She sighed. "I see you haven't lost your touch. What's she like?"

"Single, works for a living, and doesn't pressure me."

"Totally unlike me," she said. "Does she live with you?"

"Unfortunately, no. She's a police detective in Pueblo."

"A cop? The woman's a cop? That's crazy."

"Maybe so, but it's true."

"Ha. I'm sure you never run out of conversation topics. I can't believe it."

He just smiled and twisted the end of his mustache.

"So you're a commuter. Or is she? Sounds complicated."

"We make it work on the weekends. Up here or down there."

She sprang from her chair, buttoned her jacket and slung the purse over her shoulder. "I do believe I've overstayed my welcome."

He got up. "Sorry you came all this way for nothing."

"It's not a total loss. I'm going over to Aspen for a couple of days. See some friends there."

He was about to speak but she preempted him with a quick kiss on the cheek. "Goodbye, Eliot," she said softly, followed by a smart about face and a quick march out the door.

CHAPTER FIVE

Chance Cullen was slowly adjusting to his new life of freedom. He'd found a quiet place to live, a side room in a small house on Coronado Street next to the Masonic Cemetery. He figured there'd be no loud parties at all hours of the night in *this* neighborhood.

His landlord, a widower about seventy named Maynard, lived in the main part of the house. He'd wanted a month's rent up front but, when Chance told him about his recent arrival in Pueblo and not being able to open a checking account, Maynard settled for a week's rent in cash along with Chance's solemn pledge to cough up the rest before the week was out. Or else *he* was out.

An awkward moment occurred when Maynard asked for some form of identification. The only thing Chance had to offer was an expired Colorado driver's license. Though he didn't have a car, both men agreed that Chance should get a new license right away. He'd need it to cash checks when his account was established.

Chance walked the dozen blocks to Parkview Medical Center in bright sunlight on Friday afternoon. It was close to ninety degrees and he was quite happy to step inside the five story air conditioned building. He entered a staff personnel area on the first floor, dressed in an off-white cleaning smock, and took his broom and four-wheel cart up to the third floor. Mrs. Dawson had assigned him to work the Rehabilitation Gym and the Oncology Wing, emptying trash bins, collecting soiled clothing in plastic bags, and making sure all therapy items in the gym were clean and stored in their proper places when not being used. There was always the potential for accidents caused by someone tripping over an exercise weight, getting hit by a runaway walker or wheelchair, or slipping on a wet floor.

Chance was sweeping the gym's highly varnished wood floor with a flat dust pad when he paused to watch a woman therapist working with a burly man. In his mid-sixties, the patient had crew cut white hair and wore a gray T-shirt with the symbol of the 101st Airborne on the front. His rugged face was tan and, to Chance's way of thinking, the man had surely served as a paratrooper. *Falling out of planes for a living and being shot at when you land is one helluva way to earn a living.* Chance cringed when he saw long surgical scars running vertically down each knee with crosswise suture marks. *Probably banged up those knees making jumps.*

The woman therapist alternated with each leg, slowly and carefully flexing it by placing one palm under the knee and the other hand pulling back the foot. Cullen was entranced by the look on her face, one of joyful love for the work she was doing. He moved about the gym with his push broom to different areas but periodically stopped to watch her rapt focus on the patient.

The therapist's blonde hair was cut short and brushed back from her face. Though she wore no makeup, Chance thought she was a natural beauty. She wore snug sweat pants and a close-fitting T-shirt which convinced him she was in excellent physical condition. She was also someone he'd like to know better.

She sprang quickly from her kneeling position beside the man's therapy couch, turning at the same time with enough forward momentum to collide directly with Cullen. Chance held himself steady, broom handle out to the right as his left arm slid around her waist.

"Oh, I'm sorry," she said, immediately backing away.

"My fault, should've kept moving." He noticed her name tag said Stephanie and she had blue eyes. "We have to quit meeting like this," he added, instantly regretting coming up with such a corn ball line.

She gave him a brief smile, warm enough to convince him that she wasn't offended or angry and probably had a good sense of humor. "Excuse me," she said, "I've got to play some games with that lady over there."

During the next few minutes he caught glimpses of Stephanie tossing huge green and blue balloons back and forth with an elderly woman. When he spotted Ms. Dawson peeking at him through the open door to the hallway, he knew it was time to move on to the Oncology Wing, an area which had already shown its depressing face to him. But before leaving the gym, he checked the schedule board for the therapist group and was happy to see that Stephanie would be working tomorrow.

Chance got to the hospital just before noon on Saturday, a full three hours before his starting time, and went directly to the cafeteria. As luck would have it he spotted Stephanie sitting at one of the larger tables and eating her lunch. Wasting no time, he picked up a ready-made sandwich and a cold bottle of green tea, paid for them and headed straight for her table.

He sat directly opposite her and said, "Hey there." She looked straight at him with a serious look on her face, betraying no hint of recognition, while continuing to eat her salad. "We bumped into each other yesterday in the rehab gym," he added. He also sensed some bad vibes, like he'd overplayed his hand.

"We *must* stop meeting like this," she said with a straight face.

It took a full second before Chance got it, bursting with a laugh that attracted stares by people around them. His laugh was so infectious that Stephanie finally broke up and joined in, albeit more subdued.

He extended his hand across the table. "Chance Cullen," he said. "You come here often?"

She laughed harder and shook his hand. "Stephanie White. And before you come up with any more silly pickup lines my sign is Libra."

"All right, that's out of the way. Nice to meet you, Steph."

"Is Chance your real name or a nickname?"

"It's real. My dad said he wanted me to have every chance for a good life. Having the right kind of name was a first step in the right direction."

"Interesting. You're new at Parkview, right? Haven't seen you working around the gym before."

"I've only been here for a couple of days. Happy to have a job and it seems like a good place to work. How long have you been here?"

"Coming up on twelve years next month."

"Are you a Pueblo native?"

"Actually, I grew up in Wyoming, a small town you probably

never heard of called Powder River. Moved to Denver with my folks, got a part time job at Colorado Acute, picked up a fizz-ed degree and was hired on by Parkview. I'm the second senior therapist in the department and might get the top job someday if old man Mose dies or ever retires."

"I watched you working with that guy yesterday, the one with scarred knees. You seemed to enjoy it a lot."

She smiled. "I do. Helping people get better gives me a good feeling of accomplishment. I've made some nice friends with the patients here. They send me cards and small gifts at Christmas." She speared the last cherry tomato in her salad and popped it into her mouth. "What about you? I hope you're not planning a housekeeping career in this place."

"Just getting my bearings before pulling up stakes and moving on."

She cocked her head. "Sounds kind of mysterious, Mr. Cullen. Where do you want to be?"

He managed a weak grin. "For now, sitting here and talking to you."

The short silence was broken when she glanced at her watch. "Have to scoot up to the gym and do my thing." She started to get up.

"Wait, how about dinner next week? I'm off Monday and Tuesday."

She stood while grasping her cafeteria tray that was still resting on the table. "Dinner? Yeah . . . sure. Tuesday's good. I live out in Pueblo West but my place is easy to find."

He rubbed his chin and practically mumbled, "My car broke down. Can we meet somewhere downtown? Maybe a nice restaurant near the hospital?"

She pondered his question for a moment. "How about the Pass Key. It's on Abriendo. Do you know it?"

"I know the area. About seven OK?" It was near his parole office but now was not the time to volunteer that bit of information.

"Let's make it six," she said, "so I don't have to make an extra trip home and back again."

"You got it."

The sun was setting when Eliot entered Sharon's house on Friday evening. He called out and she answered, "In the kitchen."

"A vision of culinary cuteness," he said, spying her next to the stove and stirring a pot with a wooden spoon.

"Dinner's almost ready. My chili you like so much along with Texas toast. And wait until you see the ice cream cake I bought for dessert."

He enveloped her with a firm hug, gave her a long kiss, and slipped his hands below her waist, pulling her closer. "You're the dessert I came all this way to see."

She broke free. "Yeah, I can feel you're glad to see me but save it for later."

"Got any beer, darlin'?"

"Sure, and your mug's in the freezer."

He filled a frosty mug about half way, creating an inch of foam, and passed it to her for the customary first sip. "How's your day been?" he asked.

She took a healthy pull and, brushing aside the foam from her upper lip, turned down the flame under the chili pot. "Pretty good, except for Mayor Mansfield."

"What's he done now?"

"Sent me another text, wanting to know what I've found on

Streckfus. It's the third one since our meeting."

"What are you telling him?"

"The truth. Nothing so far but I'm working on it."

"Nothing at all?"

"Well, not exactly. Let me show you something." She led him to the kitchen table where several stacks of papers rested.

They sat down and he took a few minutes to look them over. "Lots of financial stuff here. Walk me through it."

"OK. There's one set of bank statements on Streckfus and the other one belongs to the mayor."

"How the heck did you get these?" he said.

"Had to tell a little white lie." Eliot's eyebrows arched. "Talked to a guy in the city's payroll department. I told him our section was doing an in-depth security check on the city's financial systems to make sure they provided adequate protection. He gave me their social security numbers and the banks where they have direct deposit. So I was able to get their bank statements. Turns out Streckfus and Mansfield have different banks but their financials look about the same." She pointed to one of the printouts. "This is the biggest expense for Streckfus, his monthly mortgage payment. Over here you see his salary deposited, not all that much. This larger deposit is his Army retirement. Then you have the usual small checks for this and that plus visits to Mr. Cash at the ATM. Pretty vanilla stuff."

"You told me about seeing their house and how much it must have cost. But the size of the mortgage payment seems pretty modest for that kind of property."

"True enough. I checked with a real estate broker and she was able to access the MLS data base. Streckfus put down a lot of cash when he bought it, probably to keep the monthly payment at a reasonable level."

"Which makes you wonder where he got the cash." Eliot sipped his beer. "Heard anything from your FBI buddy?"

"Not yet, but I'm sure she'll come up with something. In the meantime, I've gathered up some personal history on both men. Easy to do since they're both public figures. I even did a timeline on each one." She showed him a horizontal graphic for each man with significant events ticked off for each relevant year. "Streckfus didn't move to Pueblo until 2006 but lived and worked in Virginia for two years after he left the Army. Mansfield probably met Streckfus back in the late eighties when they were both in the army or maybe in Iraq in the early nineties. Mansfield was discharged at Ft. Bragg in 1993, moved to Raleigh and worked real estate development in Cary, about thirty miles west of Raleigh. Probably made good money."

"I've heard about that place."

"An interesting town. 135,000 people, mostly transplants, with a median income of $135,000. People in Raleigh call it a Confinement Area for Relocated Yankees."

Eliot chuckled. "So when did Mansfield come west?"

"In 2006, soon after Streckfus arrived. He's been mayor since 2010."

He took several moments to study her timeline diagram. "Here's a question for you. Why did these two fellows give up lucrative careers, move to Pueblo and get active in local politics?"

"Good question. I have no idea."

He drained his beer mug. "Hope this isn't some kind of wild goose chase, Sharon. I'm sure you've got more important things to work on."

She sighed, threw up her hands and said, "Let's eat."

Conversation was light while they enjoyed the chili and Texas toast until Sharon said, "I've been doing all the talking. What's happening up in Lake County?"

Eliot started to speak but hesitated when dinner with Cassie Maugham and their morning meeting flashed through his mind. "Oh . . . it's been pretty quiet all week. I like it that way."

"Nothing exciting?"

"Had a woman walking the centerline of Poplar Street early Tuesday morning. Got kind of belligerent, saying it was her right as a taxpayer."

"You arrest her?"

"Naw, one of our deputies took her home to sleep it off. Then we had a young man on Wednesday trying to cross Twin Lakes Dam on a bicycle."

"Why on earth was he doing that?"

"Said he had to deliver a package to somebody on the other side. Deputy Burke stopped him so the man gave him the package. Said it was his problem now."

Sharon laughed. "Sounds like my kind of town."

Eliot raised his glass. "I'll drink to that."

Chapter Six

Sharon went to bed early Sunday evening. She wasn't sleepy but wanted to watch an *Inspector Lewis* episode on PBS, hoping it would engage her mind. She'd agonized over the Streckfus-Mansfield conundrum and was also missing Eliot who'd left earlier for Leadville.

She had difficulty concentrating on the program's plot and was relieved when her cell phone chimed and she recognized the caller's 202 area code.

"Hey Trish, been thinking about you."

"Hi Sharon, sorry for calling so late."

"No problem, just lying in bed watching TV."

"Alone?"

"Yes, dammit."

"Sorry about that. Anyway, thought I'd give you a progress report. Probably not everything you need but it's a start."

"Let me get something to write with."

"Don't bother, I'll e-mail it to you."

"Great, fire ahead."

"OK. First of all, their tax returns. My friend would *absolutely not* let me have copies or write anything down but he did let me look at the first page of their 1040s going back the last five years."

"Were you able to remember much?"

"Heck yes, I have a great memory. I can even read upside down. But it doesn't matter. Both of these guys filed totally boring returns with nothing that would merit an audit. So they're clean, tax-wise."

"Mmmm. Interesting."

"You don't sound too disappointed."

"No, it's good. I just have to figure out what it means."

"This next bit may help more. Mr. Streckfus is quite the globe trotter. He takes a trip every year in February with his wife to the Cayman Islands, probably their annual vacation. Almost no rain and daily temperatures between 70 and 80."

"Sounds like fun. Any other travel? What about Mansfield?"

"Hardly any foreign travel by the mayor. But Streckfus has also made frequent trips to Zurich for quite a few years."

The line went silent for several seconds. "I'm getting a picture, Trish. Like Streckfus has big money squirreled away in Switzerland and the Caymans."

"You too? Ha, great minds still think alike."

"Well there you go. What else?"

"He's been to Baghdad, Cairo and Riyadh, but that was during his time in the army. He's had some special security clearances during the last couple of years so the picture is very fuzzy."

"That's because he was right up the road from you at Fort Meade. And you know what goes on there."

"Right, super spooksville."

"Find anything else?"

"Yeah, something you probably won't like hearing."

"What is it?"

"You know we have an office in Pueblo, right?"

"Yes, I do," said Sharon. "On Main Street, about ten blocks away from my office. What about it?"

"Streckfus is a *person of interest*. You didn't hear this from me but you need to be very careful and not get yourself caught in a bind."

"What the hell? If you guys are watching him, why am I involved?"

"Can't answer that," said Trish, "except your mayor probably doesn't know Streckfus is under a microscope."

Sharon groaned. "This is way above my pay grade."

"Sorry . . . again."

"It's not your fault. Maybe you ought to come out here and help me."

"That would be fun. Why don't you send me an invitation, like engraved and announcing a wedding or something?"

Sharon made a weak laugh. "Bye Trish and thanks for the heads up."

Sharon marched directly into Sgt. Dave Hess's office the next morning. She was in a bad mood, getting little sleep the night before, thanks to Trish Guinn's report on Streckfus and Mansfield. "We need to talk," she said.

Hess made an exaggerated grin showing a mouthful of glistening teeth, something he did when needing to intimidate a suspect or being put on the defense by another police officer. "Have a seat, detective."

She sat on an uncomfortable metal chair next to his desk. "This job the mayor gave me is *crap*. I've taken it about as far as I can."

"Why should I be hearing this?"

"Because it's important." She launched into a long report on Mansfield's and Streckfus's personal and political history which she'd lifted from Trish's e-mail. She began with their army service in Iraq and frequently referred to her printed notes. She detailed their respective timelines along with Streckfus's foreign travel, concluding with an observation that he was likely hiding money outside the country.

Hess folded his hands into a steeple. "How did you get all this?"

"Friends in high places."

He pushed his chair back and crossed his legs. "Good work. I agree with your take on it. Wonder what his tax returns look like?"

Sharon's eyes widened, prompting Hess to flash his smile again. "Don't even *think* of asking about that," she said.

"You have to wonder," he went on, "with that kind activity by Streckfus, if some other people are eyeballing him."

Sharon only fidgeted in her chair.

Hess laughed. "All right then, what's your next move?"

"*My* next move? I was hoping for some help. This project is like a fish out of water that hasn't been put on ice. It stinks to high heaven and, if there's criminal activity going on, it's way out of our jurisdiction. Politics and police work should never be in bed together."

"All right, detective, just calm down. Here's what I think you should do. Have another meeting with the mayor. Just give him the facts without any opinions and let him draw his own conclusions."

"He doesn't want meetings, just reports by e-mails."

"Then demand one." Sharon started to speak but he cut her off. "I want a full report in writing after you have it. For everyone's protection."

Sharon got up to leave. "I'll take care of it."

"I don't want you spending any more time on this," he said. "Tell the mayor you have to work other things. Have him call me if he gives you any trouble."

"Will do. And thanks for the backup."

Early Monday evening Sheriff Waters responded to a call north of Leadville on Highway 91. A man and his wife had a loud argument which included physical contact and gunshots. A neighbor had called the sheriff's office fearing the wife was in danger.

When Eliot arrived at the feuding couple's house he found a woman standing on the front porch and smoking a cigarette. "Sorry for getting you to come out all this way, sheriff. Wally was just lettin' off some steam after a bad day at work. You know how Mondays can be."

He looked her up and down. "Did he hurt you?"

"I'm all right."

"Where is he now?"

"Inside, sleeping off the booze."

"Mind if I go inside and take a look?"

"Help yourself."

Eliot entered the living room and found an overturned floor lamp, magazines scattered everywhere and pillows on the floor. A window in the side wall had a clean hole with only a few small fracture spokes radiating from its center. Eliot moved through the hallway to the bedroom and found a man on his stomach and spread eagle across the bed. He wore only an undershirt and snored so loud the bed quivered. A small lamp on the dresser allowed Eliot to see a rifle in the corner of the room, resting on the arms of a chair.

Eliot took the rifle out to the front porch and said to the wife, "I'm taking this back to my office."

"Knock yourself out, sheriff."

"Do you want to file charges?"

She flipped her cigarette out to the gravel driveway. "Naw, we'll be OK."

"All right. He can claim his weapon tomorrow when he sobers up."

"I'll be sure to tell him."

"You have a nice evening, ma'am."

Eliot got back into his SUV and was backing out of the driveway when his radio crackled. "Deputy Flint to Sheriff Waters. You copy, Eliot?"

He braked. "I copy. You have something?"

"I'm out here at Independence Pass. A woman wrecked her car, she's banged up a bit and she's asking for you."

"Me? What's her name?"

"Uh . . . Hume. Cassandra Hume."

"Are you sure about that? It's not Maugham?"

"She said Hume. Anyway, she was coming from Aspen and claims some guy forced her off the road and kept on going."

"Have you called the hospital?"

"Yeah, St. Vee is sending an ambulance. Should be here soon."

"OK, Flint, stay with her. I'm coming up to look at the accident scene before her car is towed away. Tell her I'll be at the hospital later on tonight."

Eliot traced his way back through Leadville and pulled into the visitors' parking lot at Independence Pass almost two hours later. There was still enough light to see a small group of people standing next to the asphalt hiking path, looking over the side at an automobile about thirty yards down and lying on its side. Without speaking to the group, he flashed his badge and moved cautiously down the rocky slope with his flashlight. He circled the car, examined the dents and scratches in its chassis, and looked up the slope. He climbed back to the hiking path and, reaching his SUV, paused to get a good feel about the relative locations of the highway, the parking lot, and the final resting place of Cassie's car.

It was 9:30 when Eliot arrived at St. Vincent's, a twenty-five bed hospital with limited care for trauma victims. According to the emergency room's nurse receptionist, Mrs. Hume was lucky that her injuries weren't more serious because, if they were, she would have been airlifted to a Denver hospital.

Eliot was directed to a private room where Cassie had been taken after having a CT scan to check for internal injuries. He approached the room with a slight nervousness, not sure of what he'd find, and with some resentment over having to deal with this woman who'd come back into his life.

She was sitting up in bed when he came to the dimly lit room, looking out a side window into the night's darkness. An IV had been hooked up to one arm and several wires snaked back to wall-mounted electronic devices displaying multicolored lines and numbers while making periodic beeps. A white bandage covered her head and he could make out several scratches on her cheek. Sensing his presence she turned her head and spread her arms wide. "My savior," she called, "come give me a kiss."

Still in the doorway and fumbling with his hat, he moved to the bed, bent over and gave her a quick peck. "How you doing?" he said.

"Much better, now that you're here." She dabbed her eyes with a wad of tissue she'd been holding in one hand.

He pulled up a chair and sat down. "What happened up there, Cassie?"

"Someone's stalking me, Eliot, all the time I was in Aspen and he followed me up that road when I left. The bastard ran me right off that road . . . have you caught him yet? I gave your deputy a full description . . . what he looked like, the kind of truck he was driving. Are you posting a deputy outside my room tonight? I need protection, Eliot, that guy could sneak in here while I'm asleep and—"

"Hold on now," he said. "I'm sure Deputy Flint is following up. Haven't had a chance to check with him but I will as soon as I leave."

She grabbed his hand, sniffled, and dabbed her eyes. "I'm so glad to see you."

"Does your husband know you're here?"

"Hell no. And I don't want you calling him."

"Why not?"

"He could well be the cause of all this. He's the kind of guy who'd hire somebody to keep close tabs on me."

"Why would he do that?"

"Cause he's insanely jealous and very suspicious, even when there's a remote possibility that I may just have a friend who also happens to be a man."

Eliot pinched his hat's brim with his thumb and forefinger, rubbing them back and forth. "Maybe he has good reasons for being that way."

"You don't believe me. I thought you were my friend."

"I've got a job to do, Cassie, and that comes first." She began crying softly and he decided it was time to go. He stood and said, "I'll come by in the morning. Try to get some rest tonight."

CHAPTER SEVEN

Deputy Flint came into Eliot's office Tuesday morning to report on Cassie's auto accident. "I've been to the tow truck lot and retrieved all her personal belongings from the car. Two suitcases, one with clothes and a smaller one for cosmetics."

"What about a cell phone?" said Eliot. "Her purse, a wallet?"

"Nothing else, sheriff."

"Where are the suitcases now?"

"Took them over to St. Vee's and gave them to Mrs. Hume's nurse. Looks like she'll be getting discharged later today."

"I'll be going over soon. She'll need help getting home to Arizona."

"One more item, sheriff. I checked the vehicle registration. It's a rental out of the Denver airport. I called the company and told them what happened to their car. They'll be contacting the towing company to get their vehicle back."

"Good work, Flint. One less thing for Mrs. Hume to worry about."

Eliot left his office and made the short drive to St. Vincent's Hospital. He found Cassie sitting up in bed, her breakfast tray pushed to the side. "Morning, Cassie," he said, taking a seat in the chair he'd left only a few hours earlier. The bandage had been removed from her head and the marks on her cheek were less pronounced.

"Have you found that bastard yet?"

"No, but we're working on it."

She scowled and pointed to a cupboard in the wall. "My makeup bag is in there. Bring it to me, please, so I can repair my face."

He found the bag and placed it next to her on the mattress. "Your face doesn't look all that bad to me."

"Oh yeah? Maybe you should see an eye doctor for some glasses." She pulled out several items and started brushing her hair. "Eliot, I'm missing some things. Your deputy brought my luggage but where's my purse and my phone? I'm sure they were in the car. You think that tow truck driver took them?"

"Highly unlikely, Cassie. Deputy Flint made sure the car was locked. He kept the keys after he searched the inside and got all your things out."

"Dammit, Eliot, I'm screwed. My money and credit cards are in that purse and now they're gone to God-knows-where. They're letting me out of here this afternoon and I've got no way to get home. I'm sure the car is not drivable."

"There's bus service to Denver. You can catch another one to the airport."

She stopped brushing her hair. "Are you serious? You'd put me on a damn bus? I thought you were my friend."

"You have a better idea?"

She threw the hairbrush against the cupboard door making a loud *thwack*. "I can't travel like that, Eliot. I'm just too upset and sick inside right now. I'll never make it home this way and I need help. Besides, that stalker is still out there, watching, probably seeing me get on that bus and following me to Denver. No, it's not right, putting myself in jeopardy like that. You're a lawman, Eliot. Don't you have to take an oath about protecting people?"

"I'm sure we've got some room at the jail. You'd be safe there and could rest up until you're strong enough to travel."

She was silent while looking out the side window. She turned back to look at Eliot, tears in her eyes, and pleaded, "Please let me stay with you. For only one night. I'll call Winston and have him wire me some money. Then we'll figure out something, a way for me to get out of town and back to Scottsdale."

Eliot went to the doorway. He wanted to leave this room, the hospital, and go someplace where he could forget he'd ever met this woman. He wasn't fooled, her coming back this way instead of driving directly to the Denver airport from Aspen. She was still holding on to some glimmer of hope. But if there was even one scintilla of truth in her story about the mysterious stalker, he'd be negligent in his duties as a law officer if he didn't help her. "OK, Cassie, one night. Then you're leaving. Pony express, Wells Fargo stagecoach, or shank's mare. Understood?"

"Yes, Eliot, I understand. Thank you."

"I'll pick you up this afternoon," he said, and walked out of her room.

When she was certain he'd left, she raised both fists above her head, pumped her arms, and whispered in a hoarse voice, "Yes."

After her meeting with Sgt. Hess, Sharon called the mayor's secretary. She was told that Mr. Mansfield would be out of the office all day and wouldn't return until Tuesday morning. She was invited to make an appointment and settled for a five minute slot early Tuesday afternoon. Sharon knew that once she got into his office and talking, he'd want to hear all the dirty details no matter how long it took.

When Sharon entered the mayor's outer office at 1:30 P.M. on Tuesday, Mrs. Schrader glanced at her and said, "Have a seat, he'll be with you soon."

Soon turned into an irritating thirty-five minutes as Sharon fumed, thinking that she could have been doing something productive instead of wasting her time reading last year's magazines. When a trio of female citizens came out of the mayor's office Mrs. Schrader said, "You can go inside now."

Mayor Mansfield closed his door, pointed to a chair in front of his desk and sat in his usual chair on the other side. "Why are you here? I thought I was quite clear about us not meeting again."

"Sorry, Mr. Mayor, but I wanted to give you my report in person. In case you wanted to ask questions or have something clarified. And you won't have to worry about any more meetings because this one will be our last."

"Is that so? Why do you say that?"

"Because I've gone as far as I can with this. And Sgt. Hess doesn't want me to spend any more time on it. He made that point crystal clear."

"Then I'm disappointed in both you and Sgt. Hess." He loosened his tie and unbuttoned the collar of his shirt. "Aw, hell. As long as you're here, tell me what you found out."

"Before starting, I have a question. You and Mr. Streckfus were both army officers. Is that where you first met him?"

He smiled. "Yes, that's right. Got to know him back in 91 during Desert Storm. I later left the service when my time was up but he stayed in for a career. Why do you want to know about that?"

"Just filling in a few blanks." Sharon then proceeded to brief him on the results of her investigations. She told him about her drive-by of the Streckfus home, Frank's foreign travel, and only a general statement about his financials looking extremely ordinary with no cause for worry about any illegal action.

"How did you get his financial data?"

"Tricks of the trade, something our section does every day."

"I know that Frank and Gloria take vacations in the Caymans every year but I didn't know about his trips to Switzerland." Sharon remained quiet and, after a long pause he asked, "Where did this come from?"

"Sorry, but I can't reveal my sources. Just think of me as a news reporter."

"You're a paid city employee, *detective*."

"Yes, sir." Sharon's stomach was causing problems and she felt beads of perspiration sliding down the edges of her back.

He stared at her for several seconds. "Is that it then?"

She handed him a single sheet of paper comprising a report of what she'd learned about Frank Streckfus, a summary which carefully excluded any reference to the mayor as well as her sources. "Yes, sir, that's it."

He took her report and stood. "I'll send Sgt. Hess a note about how well you performed." Sharon could almost see the sarcasm dripping from his mouth.

Once she was out of the building, she collapsed on a park bench, breathed a sigh of relief and said to nobody in particular, "Thank God I don't have to worry about those guys any more."

Chance Cullen made it to the Pass Key well before six o'clock. The outside temperature was still in the high eighties and he wanted to be comfortably cool when Stephanie showed up. He was given a table, told the waitress he'd be joined soon by a friend, ordered a draft Coors and watched a baseball game on TV.

He'd finished half his beer when Stephanie came through the front door. Chance enjoyed noticing her first as she looked around the restaurant, her face becoming happier when she recognized him, and seeing her smile as she came to his table. Dressed in snug blue jeans and a crisply ironed short-sleeve blouse, she'd just applied a light touch of makeup.

He stood, pulled out a chair and she sat down. "Hot out there," she said. "Hope you haven't been waiting long."

"No, just cooling off and watching the Rockies get wrecked by the Cards."

The waitress appeared and gave them menus. "Iced tea for me," said Stephanie.

Chance held up his mug. "Time for a refill on this one."

"So. Here we are. How was your day off?"

"Kind of busy and frustrating at the same time. Spent yesterday and today looking at used cars. I can't believe what these guys are asking for pieces of junk that will probably blow up after you drive them off the lot."

"I know what you mean. I'm giving mine lots of TLC, trying to get a few thousand more miles out of it."

"How was *your* day?" he said. "Any more work on the ex-paratrooper?"

"No, he was discharged this morning. The sweetest man, he gave me a box of candy. His wife said he'll be getting home therapy for a while."

They studied the menu. "It all looks good," he said. "Any suggestions?"

"The Italian sausage is their specialty, known all over town. Whenever somebody mentions having a *passkey* they're talking about that sandwich."

"Just right for me," he said, folding up his menu. Stephanie ordered a chicken Caesar salad, prompting Chance to remark, "You're really into this fitness thing."

She smiled. "True, but it's not a religion. More a matter of a healthy lifestyle and feeling good about myself. Do you work out often?"

"Afraid not. I used to be in pretty good shape but with my work schedule . . . "

"What are you talking about? You have all morning. Every morning."

He rubbed his chin and glanced up at the TV screen, feeling a bit guilty. He turned back and said, "All right, you're the expert. How do I get back into it?"

"Running's good exercise. I do it most every morning before starting my shift. A mile or two makes me feel *so good*. Why don't you try it?"

"I haven't done anything like that since high school gym class. Not sure if I could even do a quarter mile right now."

"You start easy and work up to the longer runs. I do the same for events like the Bolder Boulder race. I even did the Leadville Trail Marathon last year."

"Leadville. I need to be getting up there soon."

"You have a friend there?"

"I wouldn't exactly call him a friend."

An awkward silence followed until she said, "If you're willing, we could run together one morning. I'll give you tips on breathing and how to pace yourself. And I won't push you. How far you go is up to you."

He formed a mental picture of her in a T-shirt and running shorts. "Great. If you're game, so am I. But it would have to be near the hospital, maybe a running track at a school that I could get to easily."

"We've got Mineral Palace Park right next door—does Parkview ring a bell?— and I've got some routes scoped out. Quarter mile, half mile, two miles. Whatever you feel like. How does tomorrow sound? About 6:30?"

Chance made a theatrical groan and emptied his mug. "Sounds like this will be my last beer tonight."

"Then I'll take that as a yes."

The waitress delivered their meals and both ate several bites before Chance put down his sandwich. "Something's bothering me and I need to get it off my chest."

Stephanie laid her fork on the table and clasped her hands together in her lap. "I'm listening."

"Confession time. I just got out of prison and the janitor job at the hospital is about the only one I could get. My future is a big unknown and I think it's crazy for a woman like you to get involved with someone like me." Stephanie held his gaze but said nothing. "So we don't have to do this morning exercise thing and you don't have to talk to me on the job."

"Is that it?"

"Yes. Just thought you should know."

She reached out, placed her hand on top of his and gave him the sweetest smile he'd seen in years. "Now it's my turn. I know about your time in prison."

"You do? How did you find out?"

"John Julian told me."

"You checked up on me?"

"Sure did. Do you want to talk about it?"

"Not tonight. Maybe some other time."

"OK, then relax and enjoy your dinner. As far as you and I are concerned, let's just take it one day at a time. Or, if we start running around together, then one mile at a time. Does that work for you?"

Running around together. I like the sound of that. He squeezed her hand and popped a French fry into his mouth while making a loopy grin. "So you're taking a chance on Chance, huh?"

She rolled her eyes. "Keep that up and I'll run your butt right into the ground."

CHAPTER EIGHT

As Eliot entered his driveway, Cassie, who was sitting in the SUV's passenger seat, squealed in delight. "It's beautiful, Eliot, so cozy and quiet. I'll bet you have some gorgeous views."

"I like it," he conceded.

"I can't wait to see inside. I'll bet you've made it nice and comfortable for yourself. A sheriff's man-cave, am I right?"

He shut off the engine and opened the door. "I'll get your luggage."

She got to the cabin's front door, paused, and looked around the grounds while taking deep breaths. "I love the way Colorado smells. So green, so invigorating. Scottsdale should import some of this."

He dropped her suitcase and cosmetics bag on the front porch and unlocked the front door. "Go right in and make yourself comfortable."

She went into the living room and looked around. "Wow, a fireplace that actually burns wood. Can we have one tonight?"

"Think I can manage that. Follow me and I'll take you to your room."

"My room? *My* room?"

He rolled her bags down the hallway and entered a room on the right. When she came into it she saw a twin bed with side tables and lamps, a chest of drawers and two bookcases filled with both hard cover and paperback volumes.

"I thought you didn't have a guest room. At least that's what you told me. Shame on you, trying to shuffle me off to some cheap motel."

"Must have slipped my mind. There's only one bathroom so we'll have to set up some kind of protocol about who goes where and when."

"I don't mind sharing," she said with a grin.

"Are you hungry, Cassie? Maybe I should start thinking about dinner."

"I'm actually thirsty. You have anything to drink?"

"Beer, wine and the hard stuff."

"Any kind of wine would be great."

"Let's go back into the living room and I'll open some."

She sank comfortably into his couch and he soon came back from the kitchen with a generous glass of Chardonnay and a beer for himself. She chimed her glass against his frosty mug and said, "Thanks for doing this, Eliot. I know it's not your favorite thing right now."

"To your health," he said, "and safe trip back to Arizona."

"To my health."

After taking a gulp of beer he handed her his cell phone. "I want you to call your husband and tell him where you are. He can wire money to any number of places in town and I'll take you down first thing in the morning. You can rent a car and drive to Scottsdale or catch a flight at DIA to Phoenix."

"They'll want a credit card and driver's license for that."

"I'll explain the situation and they'll figure a way to make it work."

She took his phone and got up. "Can I do this in the kitchen?"

"Sure."

Several minutes later she came back. "OK, I called his cell phone and the house, had to leave messages both times. I hope you don't mind having him call me back on your cell phone."

"It's all right. You still have a land line at your house?"

She made a face. "Have to for Winston. He uses the speaker phone because he doesn't hear well and hates his cell phone. Says it makes his hearing aids squeal like a stuck pig."

Eliot chuckled softly and sipped his beer.

"Can I help myself to more wine?"

"Yep, bottle's in the fridge."

"Then I'll take it back to that guest room you don't have—or forgot about—and take a shower. Have to get prettied up for that nice dinner you're cooking for us. Oh, wait a minute. You *can* cook, right?"

Eliot rubbed his chin and thought for a moment. "Why yes, I do believe I have some chunks of buffalo liver in the freezer from last year's big powwow. Should go right nice along with creamed broccoli and my rhubarb puree."

She pulled open the side of her mouth with a finger, made a retching sound and darted into the kitchen.

Eliot made Denver omelets for dinner, accompanied by his own brand of hash browns and small bowls of fresh fruit chunks. Conversation at the table was awkward. Cassie wanted to reminisce about the early days of their passionate affair while Eliot felt more comfortable discussing anything but that. The other problem was Cassie's wearing apparel. After taking a shower she came to the kitchen wearing Grecian sandals and a light blue oversized man's shirt that came down to just above her knees. It was all Eliot could do to avert his eyes from those long tan legs. For one brief moment, he imagined touching her ankle and smoothly slipping his hand up her leg until he reached underwear or something else.

Nevertheless, they got through dinner without any unpleasantness. Cassie insisted on cleaning up so Eliot could make a fire. She poured from a new bottle of Chardonnay into her glass and took it to the living room couch. "Come sit by me," she said, patting the cushion immediately next to her.

He sat down but, after getting another good look at her crossed legs, remained at what he considered a healthy distance. "How are you feeling, Cassie? Any after effects from the auto accident?"

"I had a headache earlier but the Chardonnay chased it." She shifted her body, pulled her feet up behind her, and placed her hand on his neck. "You've been kind of distant, Eliot, like I'm some kind of Typhoid Mary. Don't you like me anymore?"

"Things are different now. You're a married woman and I respect that."

"Are we friends?"

"Sure, we're friends, but only that."

Eliot's cell phone came to life, making him grateful for the interruption. Without showing any emotion he answered, "Sheriff Waters." After listening for a few moments he handed the phone to Cassie. "It's your husband."

She sprang from the couch. "I'll take it in the guest room."

Eliot tended the fire while she was gone, adding several logs to the grate and pushing some glowing embers back from the screen. While she was still away, he went into the kitchen and finished putting things away. Fifteen minutes after her call had arrived, Cassie came back to the living room. "Sorry," she said, "but I had lots of explaining to do."

"Like Lucy *splained* to Desi?"

"Don't try to be cute, Eliot."

"What did he say?"

"He'll wire the money but he's not happy with me. It's all my fault, you see. None of this would have happened if I hadn't gone off to Colorado."

"He's got a point."

She slapped the cell phone into his hand with a smack. "You're full of crap, just like him." She turned away. "Excuse me, I'll be in the bathroom."

Eliot laughed when she was out of earshot. He was about to poke the fire when his cell phone rang. He recognized the caller ID and answered crisply, "Waters."

"Hello, sheriff," said Deputy Flint. "Sorry to bother you."

"No problem. What's going on?"

"A little disturbance downtown. Marcia at the Dew Drop says things are about to go ballistic. If you could meet me, I believe we could calm them down."

"I'll be there right away." He breathed a quiet sigh of relief.

"You're leaving?" Cassie had suddenly reappeared. "Where are you going?"

"Duty calls. One of my deputies has a situation and needs some help."

"Then I'll be all alone. What if that stalker is out there? What if he knows I'm here and you're not? He could break in and finish me off."

"You'll be OK and I won't be long. Lock up after I leave and don't answer the door if anybody comes, which I doubt will happen anyway. There's ice cream in the freezer in case you get hungry."

"I *do not* believe this," she grumbled as he walked out the door. "I'll stick with the wine, thank you very much."

There was actually no *situation* at the Dew Drop Inn. Deputy Flint's phone call was a prearranged tactic that would give Eliot some options. He could use the call as an excuse to get away from Cassie for a while or he could tell Flint to handle the *situation* himself in case he'd started some foolishness with Cassie. Eliot liked having options.

He found Flint at the bar having a ginger ale while chatting with a grizzled old ranch hand who had been enjoying multiple tequila shooters. Eliot slapped Flint on the back and took the stool next to him. "Thanks for the call. Worked out fine."

"Glad to help, sheriff. How's she doing?"

"Not too bad, all things considered." He paused to ask the bartender for a beer. "Her husband's wiring some money and she'll be leaving tomorrow."

They talked for a while about prospects for the Denver Broncos until Flint finished his ginger ale. "Time to get back to work."

"One thing before you go. Something's been bothering me about Mrs. Hume's purse and cell phone getting lost in the accident."

"Her car's still at the garage. I'll get over there and check it again."

"You're a good man, Flint. Keep me posted."

After Deputy Flint left, Eliot nursed his beer through four innings of a Rockies game being shown on the TV above the bar. He finished his beer, made a stop in the men's room and paused to greet several patrons on the way out. *Doesn't hurt to wave the flag before the next election rolls around.*

He paused at his front porch to look inside the cabin but couldn't see Cassie. He quietly unlocked the door and went inside, not wanting to wake her in case she was asleep. He went back toward the guest room, peeked inside and could tell that she was sleeping. He went into his own bedroom, placed his cell phone on the table next to his pillow and stripped to his shorts. But before slipping to bed, he picked up the phone and checked for messages. *Why hasn't her husband called back?* He set the bedside alarm to wake up early and have her call him again.

Eliot had a sexually graphic dream about Cassie, replaying one of his favorite memories of their long ago affair. It was Christmas Eve and she'd been able to get away from Dwight for a short period, telling him that she had some last minute shopping to do. Eliot was staying in a Phoenix motel and only in town for the explicit purpose of spending a few hours in bed with her.

His dream gradually changed to something more tangible when he was awakened by her touch and the familiar fragrance of her perfume. She cuddled up close, kissed him, and hummed a few random musical notes.

Fully awake and realizing that she was actually in his bed, his whole body jerked in a spasm. "What are you *doing,* Cassie? This isn't right and you need to get back in your own bed."

"I'm cold . . . need you to warm me up."

"I'll get an electric blanket and hook it up to your bed."

She hugged him tighter. "I heard noises outside. Could be that stalker and I just don't feel safe in there by myself."

"There's nobody out there. Now get back."

She rolled and climbed on top of him, smothering his face with kisses. "Am I too heavy for you?"

By now, both of his hands were exploring her naked body, touching the contours of her smooth back, and caressing the curves about her waist. She was attacking his willpower and he could feel himself relenting, becoming aroused and actually enjoying it. She raised the upper part of her body and teased him by lowering one breast to his mouth and then the other, letting him kiss one and then the other. He detected a faint cinnamon taste when he licked her nipples and wondered what kind of body oil she'd applied to her breasts.

He eased her off to the side. With a familiar move, he removed his shorts and quickly got on top of her. She spread her legs and pulled him inside with one hand, wrapping the other arm around his waist and moaning, "Oh yes."

Eliot moved quickly with strength and little finesse.

Cassie cried out, "Slow down, you're hurting me."

He only moved faster, pumping and grinding, squeezing her buttocks hard with both hands.

"Eliot, please, take it easy," she wailed.

He finished with a shuddering climax, rolled off and back to his side of the bed, breathing heavily while lying on his back.

"What the hell was *that?*" she said.

"Just the thing you came all the way to Colorado for."

She jumped out of bed and stood in the doorway, the glow of the hallway's night light silhouetting her shaking body. "Goddam you, that was sure as shit *not* what I wanted. What the hell's wrong with you?"

"Kind of thought you'd like it that way. You never complained before about some healthy sack action."

"Healthy? You call that healthy? It was damn close to rape."

"Then it must have warmed you up pretty nice."

She let loose a frustrated scream and went back to her bedroom, slamming the door hard. Eliot found his shorts and was sound asleep a few minutes later.

CHAPTER NINE

Eliot's alarm went off at 6:45 the next morning. It woke him but he stayed put for several minutes, thinking about what happened with Cassie last night and what he had to do about getting her out of Leadville today.

He pulled on a pair of jeans and a maroon sweatshirt and went out to the kitchen. "Damn it, I forgot to set up the coffee maker," he growled to an empty room. "Well I'll just make a big old pot right now and grind those beans as loud as I can." Which he did, provoking the result he hoped for.

Cassie came stumbling out to the kitchen with swollen eyes, wild hair, and wearing a Ralph Lauren dark blue sweat suit with white trim. "Think you could have made any more noise?" she grumbled.

Eliot lifted his coffee mug in a toast. "Morning, sunshine."

"Fuck you."

"You already did that. Have some coffee."

She made a noisy production of pouring a cup, finding a carton of milk in the fridge for a small splash, and banging around cabinets and drawers until she found several pink packets of artificial sweetener. Once the necessary ingredients were added and coffee stirred she took her cup into the living room and plopped on the couch. Eliot followed her and sat on a chair, ready for a serious face-to-face discussion.

"Here's the deal, Cassie. I don't know what's going on but your husband never called back." He handed her his cell phone. "Call him now and get that money wired to Leadville."

She looked down and away from his gaze, both hands cradling her cup. "It's too early. He's probably still sleeping."

Eliot dropped the phone in her lap. "Then wake him up."

He went back to the kitchen, filled his cup and stood in a spot where he could watch Cassie in the living room while she made the call, but giving her a small degree of privacy. The call was brief and Eliot returned to his chair.

"He's wiring the money," she said. "Are you happy now?"

"When's he going to do it?"

"Oh, whenever. Strangely enough, he doesn't seem to be all that eager for me to come back."

"I can't imagine why," said Eliot, a smug look on his face.

"Damn you, Eliot, you owe me an apology. I don't deserve that kind of treatment, not even from my worst enemies. You're supposed to be my friend. Friends don't treat friends like that."

"Look at it this way. Remember when you dumped me and went back to Dwight? That was ten times tougher on me than what happened to you last night. Just think of it as a small piece of payback."

"You're an idiot."

Eliot finished his coffee and got up. "It's another work day for me. I'll be in the bathroom getting ready. Plenty of food in the kitchen if you want some breakfast."

After he finished taking a shower and shaved, Eliot dressed in his working garb—slacks, western shirt, bolo tie—and went out to the living room. His spirits rose when he saw a smiling Cassie holding his cell phone close to her face and having an animated conversation. *Must be good news from her husband.*

He came closer and she handed him the phone. "It's for you," she said.

"Your husband wants to talk to me?"

"Nooo . . . It's Ms. Hardcastle. I'm going to take my shower now." She took several steps but turned back to face him with a mischievous grin. "I think you've got a lot of *splainin* to do, Mr. Waters."

"What? Hello, Sharon?" She'd hung up.

Eliot promptly left the cabin, climbed into his SUV and grumbled, "This is lookin' to be one crappy day."

Chance Cullen arrived at the western entrance of Mineral Palace Park at 6:35 A.M. The temperature was in the low 70s and had started its climb to the low 90s. He looked around the park, his hands shielding his eyes from the morning sun, and saw Stephanie to his right doing some kind of exercise. He jogged over and called out, "Nice morning for a workout."

"You're late." She'd been looking in his general direction while bending forward with her feet spread wide, her hands alternately touching the opposite shoe in a windmill motion. "Watch what I'm doing, Chance. Then try it yourself."

"What do you call that?"

"Getting warmed up."

"I'm already warm. Just hiking over here made me sweat."

"No arguments, please."

This lady was not about to feel sorry for him. "OK, teach."

He took a similar stance and was soon doing the same moves, mostly in synch with her.

A minute later she stopped. "That's a good start," she huffed.

He took a moment to look at her outfit, a white sweat suit and a red cotton band stretched around her forehead. She was checking him out as well and smiled. "You like my outfit?" he said.

"Is that character on your T-shirt a political statement?"

"Mickey Mouse? Naw, it was my size and the price was right."

"How do you feel this morning? Think you can run a bit with me?"

"I'll try anything once."

"Let's first do some leg exercises." She did five deep knee bends. "Try that."

He copied her moves but on the fourth one he lost his balance and toppled over. He got up and zipped through five more. "All right, I did it."

"I knew you could."

They did several more short exercises including leg stretches and jumping jacks. She led him toward the eastern edge of the park, bordered by a bustling I-25, where there was a large body of water. "This is Lake Clara," she said, "and it's a little over a quarter mile once around."

"This park is beautiful. Coming into the hospital from the western entrance, you would never know it even existed."

"Another one of Pueblo's hidden treasures."

She took off her sweat suit. Chance, who'd started with only running shorts and T-shirt, took advantage of the moment to watch her. He wasn't disappointed. She wore loose running shorts, a bright red T-shirt and a bra that hugged her chest for support but couldn't disguise her attractive figure. He rubbed a sweaty hand across his beard and said softly, "Nice legs, lady."

She smiled. "OK, here we go." She started jogging along the shore but slowed to look back at Cullen who was following. "Come up here beside me."

He picked up the pace. "I like the view from back there."

"Uh huh. No more talking now, save your breath."

They made it once around the lake and back to her pile of clothes. Chance had kept up but was breathing hard. "How about a break, Steph?"

"Right. Let's take five."

Chance fell to the grass and took a sitting position. Stephanie sat opposite him, her legs crossed while breathing almost normally. "Maybe another year of this and I'll be in pretty good shape," he said.

"Guess you didn't do much before you . . . "

"We got outside most every day. Fooling around with baseball in the summer and some football in the winter. Never running like we just did."

"How do you feel now?"

"Not bad." He noticed the faint glow of perspiration on her tan face and legs. "Actually, I feel great. First time in a long while I've smelled freshly mowed grass."

"Think you could do another quarter mile?"

"Um . . . I'd better pass. Have a full day of work ahead of me. Like you."

"Fair enough," she said.

"How about tomorrow? I'm game if you are."

"Very good, Chance. I've got another quarter mile loop for

you, around the swimming pool this time."

"Hey, wear a bikini and we can take a dip after the run."

She laughed. "What am I going to do with you?"

"We'll think of something."

She shook her head. "Got a question for you. Where do you see yourself a year from today?"

"My God, I didn't think there'd be a quiz on top of physical torture."

"C'mon now, fess up."

"Let me think about that for a sec." He looked into her shining blue eyes and saw a genuine interest in him instead of just passing curiosity. "OK, next summer I'll have a different job that pays 200,000 bucks a year, driving a brand new BMW convertible, living with you, running every morning and doing some special exercises in the evening." He winked and grinned.

She groaned. "Glad I asked."

"Hey, nothing wrong with setting some goals."

"*Realistic* goals are fine."

"Seriously, Steph, I don't know where I'll be then. Or even a week from now. Like you said last night, one day at a time." He took her hand. "That ten years spent in prison is gone forever, time I'll never get back. I'd like to make up for it somehow and try to get my life back. Can you understand that?"

"Yes, I think so and I see your frustration. But there's another way to look at it. You're ten years older now and probably more mature. Maybe you should consider that everyone else is not on the same schedule you are."

"Don't rush it. That's what you're saying."

She squeezed his hand and got up. "Another quarter mile for me before a shower and clocking in. See you in the wing later?"

"You bet, have a good one." He watched her jog back toward the lake and thought about their conversation. *Maybe those goals aren't so unrealistic after all.*

Eliot called Sharon immediately after he got to his office. It rolled over to her voice mail so he asked her to call him back as soon as possible. An hour went by without a call so he tried again but it went to her voice mail. He made two more calls later in the afternoon and she answered on the second one. "I'm pretty busy, Eliot."

"That woman you talked to. What did she tell you?"

"I don't have time for this right now. OK?"

"It's not like you think it is."

"Oh, really? So you're a mind reader now?"

"The woman's disturbed and she's been causing all kinds of trouble up here."

"*I'm disturbed.* Call me later and I *may* have time."

"What's a good time tonight?" he said, but she'd already hung up.

He was about to get himself some coffee when his phone rang. He hoped it was Sharon but the screen showed UNAVAILABLE as the caller. "Sheriff Waters," he said.

"Winston Hume here. I'm told you're the fellow who's been looking after my Cassandra."

"That's correct, Mr. Hume. I hope you're wiring some money for her."

"I've already taken care of it. Let's see, they said to pick it up at McKee's Drug Store. Does that make sense?"

"Yes, sir, it's just down the street from my office."

"Is my wife handy, sheriff? I'd like a word with her."

"Uh . . . no, she's at my place. I left her to have some breakfast and get cleaned up for the trip."

"Your place? That seems highly unusual. Do you do this sort of thing for all the unfortunates who have accidents and find themselves homeless?"

"I'm sure she'll tell you all about it when she gets home. I'll head over there right now and see that she collects her money and gets on that bus. Thanks for your cooperation, Mr. Hume." *Looks like Cassie gave her husband only part of the story. Maybe I should have mentioned us sharing a bed last night for a brief spell.*

After ending the call, Eliot drove to his cabin and found Cassie in the living room watching TV. She'd dressed, made herself look stunningly attractive again, and gave him a silent hand wave. "Let's go, Cassie," he ordered.

"What about my money?"

"Just talked to your husband and it's on the way."

Cassie pulled her cosmetic bag out to his SUV and he stored it in the back along with her suitcase. They drove into town and Eliot went with Cassie into McKee's Drug Store. When he explained Cassie's lack of identification due to her auto accident, the elderly agent merely waved his hand and accepted Eliot's explanation as good as the real thing. The agent counted out a thousand dollars in fifties and twenties and Cassie signed a receipt form.

Their next stop was the Silver King Inn on Poplar Street where the Greyhound Bus made an appearance twice daily. They unloaded her luggage from the SUV and took it inside to the lobby. Cassie took a seat but Eliot remained standing. "The bus to Denver should be along within the hour so you can wait here for it."

"Can you wait with me?"

He sat down next to her. "I can't stay too long."

"Guess I made of mess of it, didn't I."

"Why'd you go to all this trouble, Cassie? You not only screwed things up for yourself but got me in trouble with a woman I care deeply about."

"Desperate times call for desperate measures, Eliot."

He got up and turned to leave. "You're a sad case. Get some help when you get back to Scottsdale."

Deputy Flint came striding into the lobby and carrying a large plastic bag. "Glad I caught you before Mrs. Hume got on that bus." He handed her the bag and said, "Something pretty valuable you've been wanting to get back."

She reached into the bag and pulled out an expensive black leather purse and clutched it to her chest. She smiled at Deputy Flint but remained silent.

"Where did you find it?" asked Eliot.

"In the trunk of the rental and behind the spare tire. Must have got stuck there when the car rolled over."

"How come you missed it before?"

"It's pretty far back in there and the dark color made it blend in with the tire."

"Look inside, Cassie, and see if everything's there."

She rummaged through her purse and pulled out a cell phone and a wallet thick with cash and credit cards. She made a quick check and looked up at Eliot with a crooked smile. "Yep, looks like it's all here."

"Uh huh," said Eliot, turning to look at Flint. "Now I'm no expert on females and their personal belongings, deputy, but wouldn't a woman driver want to keep her cell phone and purse real handy in the front seat instead of locking them up in the trunk?"

"Makes sense to me, sheriff."

"I'm leaving now," said Eliot. "Deputy Flint, I'd like you to stick around and make sure Mrs. Hume gets on that bus."

He turned and pointed a finger at Cassie and said, "If you ever show your face around Lake County Colorado again, I'll put you in jail so fast it will make your head swim."

Chapter Ten

Sharon paced up and down her office cubicle, venting her anger, uncertainty and frustration. She'd just talked to Eliot, something she hadn't wanted to do but relented only because he'd left three voice mails. Foremost in her mind was his assertion that the woman she'd talked to earlier this morning—Cassie somebody?— was *disturbed.* She sure didn't sound disturbed. In fact, she sounded well in control of the situation, purring silkily about how she'd had this awful auto accident, oozing sincerity about how her sweet friend Eliot had brought her up to his cabin, and was now taking such good care of her. Cassie's emphasis on *such good care* made Sharon want to vomit.

Detective Wasserstein came around the corner and looked into Sharon's office. "You're wearing holes in the carpet, Hardtack. Having love troubles are you?"

Sharon stopped pacing and glared at her. "What's it to you?"

"Ooh, I see we're a bit touchy today. Couldn't help overhearing your conversation. Sounds like your buddy's got himself in a tub of hot water."

"You might say that."

"I did say that. Could there be another mountain mama in the picture? Maybe he gets a tad lonely during the week up there when he can't be with you."

"Don't you have any cases to work, *Deborah*?"

Wasserstein only laughed and went back to her own cubicle.

Sharon sat down at her desk, stared at the computer screen and tried to remember what she'd been doing before Eliot called. She pulled the threads together but was interrupted by Sgt. Hess barging into her office.

"Hardcastle, now."

He turned and marched away swiftly. Sharon scampered to catch up with him. "What's going on?" she said. He didn't answer.

She followed him straight into the section's conference room. The two men already sitting at the table looked up at Sharon but didn't get out of their chairs. Hess and Hardcastle sat down opposite them.

"This is Detective Ted Birdsall from CAP," said Hess, pointing to the man on the right. CAP stood for Crimes Against Persons, another Pueblo Police section which dealt with such things as assault, murder and kidnapping.

Birdsall, a short man in his late fifties, stuck out a meaty paw for a handshake. Sharon touched him lightly and cringed at the touch of his sweaty palm. Birdsall nodded but neither one said anything.

Hess glanced at the other man, a handsome fellow in his early forties. "This is Special Agent Dan Mahoney."

Mahoney extended a well-manicured hand, held hers a few seconds longer than necessary and said, "Pleasure to be working with you, detective."

Working with me?

"OK, now that we're all here," said Hess, "who wants to

go first?"

Birdsall began. "Last night we got a call from Gloria Streckfus, wife of City Councilman Frank Streckfus. I responded to the call and interviewed her at the Streckfus residence. She reported that her husband has not been home for the last two nights and was worried about him. She'd already checked with Parkview and called around to some friends but nobody had any clues about where he might be. Our people checked with the state police, people in the councilman's office, other law enforcement data bases, but his name never came up. When he was officially declared missing, that's when Mr. Mahoney here called me."

Hess asked Mahoney, "What's the FBI's interest in this?" Sharon relaxed slightly, mentally thanking her boss for the question she wanted to ask.

"The usual," replied Mahoney, "if it turns out to be a kidnapping."

"Why would you think that?" asked Sharon.

Mahoney smiled and focused his gaze on her. "As you know, detective, Streckfus is well off financially. Maybe a couple of hoods are out there hoping to score a big reward for a quick ransom." Sharon shuddered at Mahoney's implication of her knowledge. He continued, "I understand one of his best friends is Brian Mansfield. Has anyone checked with Mr. Mayor?"

An awkward silence followed until Birdsall cleared his throat. "I'll check with him right after we're done here."

Sharon said, "You seem to know a lot about Mr. Streckfus and the mayor, Agent Mahoney."

"Probably not as much as you, detective."

"Would you like to share? Like, show me yours and I'll show you mine?"

Mahoney smiled even wider. "I'd love to see yours, detective, but the answer is no. You and the others don't have security clearances."

"Then why don't you go back to your office and play silly damn games on your computer instead of stonewalling us here?"

Sgt. Hess turned to Sharon and made one of his exaggerated grins, his signal to her. *Let it go.*

The conversation meandered for ten minutes and touched on theories, what ifs, and several bizarre possibilities including a political conspiracy to embarrass the city's top officials. Finally, Mahoney said, "I guess that's it for now. Let's be sure to keep each other in the loop."

"Agreed," said Birdsall. He and Hess got up quickly and left the room.

"Have a minute, detective?" said Mahoney.

About halfway out of the room, Sharon turned and said, "Yes?"

"Have any plans for tonight? I'd like to buy you dinner."

"Are you serious?"

"Sure. We could talk about the case and ways to collaborate."

"As a matter of fact, I do have plans. A high colonic, which I think will be a lot more fun than having dinner with you."

She left quickly and didn't hear Mahoney laughing.

Sharon was at home that evening, frying bacon and well into her second glass of Chardonnay when her cell phone came alive. Might as well get this over with, she thought. "Hello, Eliot."

"Have time to talk?"

"Just a sec." She turned off the heat under the frying pan, sat at the kitchen table and grasped the wine glass with a free hand. "Ready to copy."

"I owe you an explanation about the woman you talked to this morning."

"I'm listening."

"Her name's Cassandra Maugham. I met her almost twenty years ago at the Scottsdale Rodeo. We had a fling for a couple of months, then she dumped me and went back to her husband. Haven't had any contact whatsoever with this woman for all these years until she showed up at my office last week. Just like that, right out of the blue with no advance notice."

"Trying to connect with you again."

"Yep, but I couldn't quite see it right then." Eliot went on to describe his dinner with her at Quincy's, getting her a room at the Silver King, the auto accident, seeing her at the hospital, and all his hard work getting her back to her third husband.

"Quite a story. Did you leave the door open for a return engagement?"

"Hardly. Told her I'd arrest her if she ever came back. Faking that accident and blaming it on a fictitious stalker is worthy of some jail time."

"Is she nuts?"

"Don't think so. Just desperate and emotionally screwed up."

The one thing Eliot hadn't volunteered was what happened last night at his cabin. Sharon had a pretty good idea of what *might have happened* but she held back, not wanting to ask that crucial question and hearing an answer that could destroy their relationship. "So that's it?" she asked.

"Everything worth talking about." He paused a few seconds, waiting for her to say something, but she was thinking about everything he'd told her. "You still coming up this weekend?"

"The damnedest thing happened, Eliot. Frank Streckfus is

missing. I sat in a meeting this afternoon with my boss, a homicide detective and an FBI agent. I'm involved somehow and will probably get hauled into it deeper. So no, I'd better stick close to home this weekend."

"The FBI, huh? Not a good sign. Well, I'm disappointed but I understand. We still good, Sharon?"

"We'll talk some more later."

After dinner and unable to get interested in a book or anything on TV, Sharon decided to take a drive. When she saw a light inside the Streckfus home, she parked at the curb and went up to the front porch.

Gloria Streckfus eventually opened the door and Sharon held up her badge. "Detective Hardcastle, Mrs. Streckfus. Do you have a few minutes?"

"Is this about Frank? Have you heard anything?"

"No, but we're still looking. I just have a few questions."

"Oh, all right. Come inside."

The immensity of the living room and the conspicuous luxury of its furnishings almost overwhelmed Sharon. *Clearly the home of big money.* The two women sat in facing chairs next to a huge fireplace which had been stocked with logs and ready to burn when autumn arrived.

"You have a beautiful home."

"A bit late in coming. Makes up for all the dumps when Frank was in the army."

"I didn't realize the city pays so well for a serving councilman." The change in Gloria's facial expression told Sharon her snarky comment was not appreciated.

"You mentioned having questions but I gave Detective Birdsall

all the information I have."

Sharon looked her over and thought she looked pretty good, considering the stress she must be under. "Where are you from originally, Mrs. Streckfus?"

"Believe it or not, I grew up right here in Pueblo. Went to C. U. up in Boulder, that's where I met Frank. After graduation and his being commissioned a second lieutenant, we got married and saw the world, as the recruiting posters say. My parents still live here, one of the reasons we moved back from Virginia. He didn't want to at first, but I wore him down. He enjoys being a big cheese in our city politics and believes it was the right thing to do."

"You have children?"

"Two teenagers, Kate and Joanna. They're upstairs doing homework. Or they should be."

"How are they taking their dad's disappearance?"

"No big deal. They're pretty used to him not being around. Deployments, business trips, meetings and political rallies. All kinds of reasons not to be at home."

"I get the picture." Sharon came to a quick opinion of their marriage; one that probably started off good but now had all the love squeezed out and replaced by comforts which only a lot of money could provide. "I understand your husband has been friends with Brian Mansfield for many years."

"They were in Iraq the same time doing Bush and Cheney's dirty work."

"Are they still close?"

"What's this got to do with Frank's disappearance?"

"Probably nothing. Just figuring the mayor may have some ideas on what might have happened."

"Maybe you should talk to his highness about that."

His highness?

"Frank told me about an argument he had with Brian last Friday. Don't know what it was about but Frank was in a blue funk all weekend. Storming around the house, cursing every little thing that didn't go his way. No way to please him. So I took the girls out for shopping, the movies, and dinner at *La Renaissance.*"

"Aren't you friends with the mayor and his wife? I saw a nice picture in the paper of the four of you at a library branch opening."

"We used to be but I've been getting the cold shoulder from them lately." Gloria paused. "Yes, you should definitely contact Brian. He may know something."

"Detective Birdsall is doing that right now." Sharon took a deep breath. "You and Mr. Streckfus travel a lot, correct?"

"Him more than me."

"Passports up to date?"

Gloria laughed faintly. "Always. Frank makes sure of stuff like that."

"Would you mind if I looked at them? I'd like to jot down the ID numbers and some other items."

Gloria gave her a strange look. "Sure, I can do that."

She excused herself and went to the rear of the house. After fifteen minutes passed, Sharon had become nervous. *What's taking her so long?* To Sharon's relief, Gloria finally returned with a puzzled look and handed her a single passport. "This is weird. Frank's passport is gone. I looked everywhere but I could only find mine."

Sharon quickly wrote a few things in her notebook and stood. "I'll be going now. Thanks for your help, Mrs. Streckfus and try not to worry. We'll be sure to call if anything turns up."

Once inside her car, Sharon phoned Detective Birdsall and

gave him a summary of her meeting with Gloria Streckfus. She concluded by saying, "Think I should have a talk with the mayor?"

"I've already tried that. Mrs. Mansfield told me he's gone somewhere and she doesn't know when he'll be back. How about you updating Mahoney with this?"

Sharon hesitated. "Sure, I'll do that." After hanging up she laughed. "When pigs fly."

Chapter Eleven

Chance was doing warmup exercises at Mineral Palace Park when Stephanie showed up early Friday morning. "Don't get ahead of me," she called out.

"You're late," he said. He stopped doing deep knee bends. "I'm feeling really good today, Steph. How about you?"

"I'll let you know when I wake up."

He started doing jumping jacks. "C'mon, join me. Better than coffee."

She matched him to the twenty-fifth repetition when they both quit. "What next, Captain Jock?"

"Whatever you like. Pick your poison."

She did some body stretches and deep knee bends while he amused himself with pushups, trying to impress her. "I'm ready now," she said.

They shed their sweat suits and he admired her running outfit. It was like the one she'd worn the previous two days except today's T-shirt was light green.

She laughed when she got a good look at him. Mickey Mouse had been replaced by two large blue letters, the logo of the New York Giants football team. "My God, Chance. Couldn't you get one with a better team?"

"The selection wasn't too great. It was this or the St. Louis Rams."

"Let's run. All set?"

"Lead the way."

"No, you run next to me. Like yesterday and the day before."

Off they went around Lake Clara. As they neared the quarter mile mark, Chance remarked, "Let's keep going. Wanna try for a half mile today."

"Don't push it. If you get sick, go back. I'll meet you there."

"I won't get sick." Her implied challenge only made him more determined to complete a second lap alongside her. "I will *not* get sick."

"OK, but I'll keep an eye on you."

They made it side-by-side back to their piles of clothes. Chance was breathing hard but Stephanie was just getting warmed up.

He paced in the shade of a huge oak tree, cooling off and trying to catch his breath. "Did you speed up the pace near the end?"

"Just a wee bit. I'm surprised you noticed."

"I'm finally getting you, Steph. Full of tricks and not to be trusted."

She laughed. "What took you so long?"

Chance wiped his head and neck with a small towel and sat in the grass close to her. "What about tomorrow?"

"What about it?"

"It's Saturday and you're not working."

"Yea, I get to sleep in."

"Guess I do too."

"I think you should work out anyway. I'll have one of my buds check up on you. Give me a status report."

"Hey, if you can sleep in, so can I." He paused. "Seriously, I need a favor. Something I'd like you to do for me."

"Will it be fun?"

He laughed. "Depends. I've been checking want ads and found some cars for sale by owners. I'd like to check them out but haven't made any appointments yet. Thought I'd see if you'd help me first."

"You want me to drive you around to look at these cars? Is that what you're *driving* at?"

He groaned at her pun. "Sure, and I'll buy you lunch. But my work shift starts at three."

She pondered for a moment. "That'll work. Make your calls this morning and leave me a note this afternoon in the wing before I leave."

He reached out for her wrist, leaned toward her and pulled her close enough to plant a kiss on her cheek. "Thanks, Steph."

She was mildly startled and made a face while sniffing. "Eww, *eau de sueur.*"

"What?"

"You. That was French for sweat."

He grinned and toweled his face again. "Guilty as charged."

She patted her head, arms and legs with her own towel. "Got a question for you, Chance, and it's personal."

"Sounds exciting."

"Maybe, maybe not. Something you said the other night at the Pass Key about getting up to Leadville. Knowing somebody up there who wasn't exactly a friend."

"Is there a question in there somewhere?"

"What's that all about?"

"Kind of a long story and not a very happy one."

"If you don't mind . . . I've got the time."

He made a grimace and rubbed his red-bearded chin with a fist. "Back about a dozen years or so, I was riding rodeo on the southwestern circuit. It was a pretty good life for a while, moving around to different towns, meeting some interesting people and making a few bucks."

"By interesting people, you mean women?"

"Yeah, but I hung out with two regular guys. Riders like me, Emilio Suarez and Muddy Waters. Eliot was his real name but we called him Muddy because he always wound up in a dirty wet hole when he got thrown. One day at Fort Collins we were talking about prize money and what we were getting for different rodeo events. We figured we were being cheated and decided to confront the guy in charge. It was late on Sunday, the last day of rodeo, when all three of us went to the guy's office. It got ugly real fast and Emilio, the stupid bastard, had a hot temper. Not only that, but he had a gun. Whipped it out and shot the guy dead."

Stephanie jerked and shifted her body slightly.

"Yeah, all hell broke loose. The police threw me in jail and the D.A. filed charges, conspiracy to commit murder."

"But you weren't the guy who shot him."

"Right, but the other two got away and made it to the border. Can you imagine, a Mexican sneaking back into his own country? Emilio stayed down there but Waters came back when the heat was off. He's the guy in Leadville I want to see."

"So you took the rap."

"Yeah, convicted of manslaughter instead of murder. They knew Emilio was the killer but didn't do a damn thing about it. I couldn't afford a lawyer and the public defender I got was so lazy and incompetent, he didn't even want to try extraditing Emilio out of Mexico. So I got fifteen years but released after ten because of good behavior. You already know about that."

"Why do you want to see this Waters guy?"

"I've got lots of questions. Like, why did you run out on me? Why didn't you stay and try to help me? He knew what the score was. We were only trying to get money that was due us. We weren't looking to commit any crime."

"Are you trying to get some kind of revenge?"

"I'll hear him out, see what he has to say. Let the chips fall where they may."

"How did you find him?"

"The magic of the internet, using the computer in the prison library."

"That easy, huh?"

"It helped that he's the Lake County Sheriff."

"*The sheriff?* I think you need to drop this, Chance, right now."

"It's damn hard."

She got up. "I'm doing a couple of more laps before taking a shower. Think about all this while I'm gone. Think *real* hard." She jogged away at a fast clip towards the swimming pool.

I've been thinking about it real hard for the last ten years.

That same morning in a different part of Pueblo, Sharon Hardcastle entered the mayor's outer office. Her plan was to interview the mayor's secretary, Mrs. Schrader, and try to get clues about the disappearances of Streckfus and Mansfield.

But before she could say anything, she spotted Special Agent

Dan Mahoney, sitting in the visitor's waiting area and writing something on a small memo pad. "What are you doing here?" she said.

He looked up at her and smiled. "Same thing as you, I suppose. How did your high colonic go last night?"

Sharon hesitated and was slightly embarrassed to see Mrs. Schrader staring at them over the top of her glasses. "I'm following up on yesterday's meeting. See if I can learn anything more about Mr. Streckfus."

"Have a seat," he said, "and we can both talk to his honor when he's free."

"What? You mean he's here?"

"Yep, meeting with the police commissioner, I believe." He gave her a cockeyed look. "Probably talking about you."

She sat down. "This is not making any sense. Ted Birdsall told me last night that nobody knew where the mayor was. We thought it could be related to Streckfus."

"Well, detective, all I know is that he's back again. Maybe he didn't want to be found. You think he might have a lady friend tucked away somewhere? Like the South Carolina governor with a South American soul mate?"

Sharon was spared having to answer that one when the mayor's office opened and the commissioner left quickly without glancing at either of them.

"Show time," said Mahoney.

Mansfield welcomed Mahoney with a handshake, a big smile, and a politically correct, "Glad to see you, Special Agent Mahoney." He lost the smile when glancing at Sharon and muttered simply, "Detective." The mayor motioned them to take seats in front of his desk and asked, "What's this about?"

Mahoney glanced at Sharon and then said, "It's about Councilman Streckfus. He's been missing for three days now."

Sharon interrupted, "I talked with Gloria Streckfus last night and she's worried about him, afraid something might have happened to him."

"And why does this concern me?" said Mansfield.

"We understand that you and Mr. Streckfus are close friends," said Mahoney. "Perhaps you can shed some light on the situation."

Mansfield grasped the knot of his necktie, loosened it and unbuttoned his shirt collar. "Frank Streckfus is not missing. I talked with him earlier this morning."

"You did?" said Sharon. "Where is he?"

"He's in Saudi. It's Friday evening over there and he's staying at The Four Seasons Hotel in Riyadh. Nothing but the best for good old Frank."

Mahoney and Sharon were stunned until he broke the silence. "I'm having a problem with this, Mr. Mayor. Why would Mr. Streckfus run off to the Middle East like that and not tell his family?"

"I knew about his travel plans, Agent Mahoney. As for not telling Gloria . . . well, you'll have to ask him about that when he comes back."

"Mrs. Streckfus also mentioned an argument you had with Mr. Streckfus last weekend," said Sharon. What was that about?"

"Why do you need that?" said Mansfield, his voice strained and his face red.

"Just asking. Wondering if it's related to his trip."

Mansfield stood. "You'll have to excuse me now, Agent Mahoney and Detective Hardcastle. Duties of my office are calling and I don't have any more time to spend on your fishing expedition. *Do not* bother me again with this nonsense."

Once in the mayor's outer office, Sharon stopped and turned to face Mahoney. "What the heck—"

He held up one hand. "Not here." He pointed to the door and she followed him outside. "Need to make a call," he said, turning away and touching his cell phone. Sharon took advantage of the break to make a call herself.

"Just calling the office," he said when they came back together. "Updating them on Streckfus. Asked them to check the hotel, make sure he's still there."

"I called Mrs. Streckfus and told her the news."

"Is she relieved?"

"She's royally pissed. He'll be in big trouble when he gets back."

"*If* he gets back," said Mahoney.

"What does that mean?"

"Hey, detective, it's about lunch time. Are you hungry?"

"I could eat. But if we do this, you'd better start calling me Sharon."

"Fine, I'm Dan. There's a good Tex-Mex place a couple of blocks from here."

The restaurant turned out to be the Cactus Flower Cantina where she and Eliot had their first date. She told Dan she'd been there before but didn't elaborate.

Once they were seated, had their orders taken and were sipping iced tea, Dan said, "How did you get mixed up with Streckfus and the mayor?"

"Mansfield called me into his office one day. Boom, right out of the blue. Wanted me to look into Streckfus's financials and make sure his good buddy wasn't getting himself into trouble."

"Any idea why he chose you for this job?"

"It's the kind of stuff I do every day. Fraud, embezzlement, ID theft."

"What did you find?"

Sharon smiled, pointed a finger at him and waved it from side to side. "No, no, no, I'm tired of playing games. I happened to know the FBI has been watching Streckfus for a long time and I want to know why. You were pretty damn cagey at yesterday's meeting, talking about a kidnapping and a ransom. You knew all along this deal was about something else."

"I think I underestimated you, Sharon. All right, I'll tell you what I can, given its sensitivity. This has to remain just between us. Agreed?"

"Got it."

"OK, it goes back to the early nineties when *Captain* Streckfus was serving in Iraq. He and his comm-elec outfit were involved in SIGINT—Signal Intelligence—and made many contacts with other people in country, some good guys and others not so good. Nothing wrong with that. It was all part of his job. He wrote up his contacts and made the documents official but classified. Later at Fort Meade, more of the same only on a global scale. Fast forward now to 2004 when he lands a high level position with Informatics International in Virginia."

"That's public knowledge," she said. "He traveled a lot to Europe and the Middle East while he worked for them."

"Correct. Back at Fort Meade, his position required special security clearances. The rules about travel overseas carried over to his civilian employment for several years and he was supposed to report any contacts with foreign nationals."

"Was he a good boy?" said Sharon.

"Yes and no. Very selective about documenting such meetings.

At first, we only sampled his reports but when a couple of *unusual* meetings went unreported, we began watching everything he did out of the U. S."

"Something's going on but you're not sure what it is."

"We've got a pretty good idea. Streckfus is basically a junk man, clever and sophisticated, but a specialist in reclamation and salvage. When the U. S. pulled out of Iraq, we donated or sold lots of our gear to the Iraqis rather than bring it home. He acted as a middleman for a number of big transactions, all for a fee, of course. But the situation in Afghanistan is different. We're destroying in-country gear so it doesn't fall into the wrong hands and that's got the Taliban, government crooks, and black marketeers very angry. We also know the mayor's hands are not clean either. He and Streckfus are partners in this venture and the argument they had is probably related to it. Could have been a disagreement on what to do next."

"Streckfus has been very careful so far. His financials are squeaky clean and I was able to verify that when I was checking on him for the mayor."

"But we know he's got money, lots of it. A big house and expensive cars. And you don't fly off to the Four Seasons in Riyadh on chump change."

"Looking at his travel profile, I'd say he's got it parked in a Swiss bank, the Caymans, or both."

"Maybe Streckfus isn't sharing the wealth with his good buddy."

"I've wondered about the same thing," she said. "So what do we have?"

"A pretty shrewd businessman. Wheeling and dealing with corrupt and greedy officials, surely something illegal but just out of our reach."

"Out of *your* reach. This isn't in my job description."

"Let me refresh your memory. Aren't you in the CAP Section, crimes against property?"

"Sure, but this is an international problem and more of a federal case."

"But you've come this far. Don't you want to see how it ends?"

"Send me an e-mail."

They continued with awkward small talk over lunch and split the bill. Once outside, Sharon extended her hand and said, "See you around, Dan. It's been a blast."

He took her hand and held on to it. "Fool that I am, let me try again. How about dinner tomorrow? No shop talk, just out for a pleasant evening, some laughs, and getting to know each other."

His touch, the look in his eyes, and the sudden absence of arrogance caused a sea change in her emotional ocean. She wasn't going to Leadville this weekend and didn't have plans for anything else. And, since Eliot had his little escapade with Cassie, why shouldn't she have some fun? "Yes, I'd like that."

Chapter Twelve

Chance paced up and down the sidewalk next to the Masonic cemetery on Saturday morning. He'd chosen the location on purpose, knowing Stephanie could easily find it. The unstated reason was his home; he wasn't proud of it and didn't think she'd be favorably impressed when she saw it.

She pulled up to the curb at nine o'clock as Chance waved her over. Once inside and sitting in the passenger seat he said, "Right on time." He looked her over and was pleased. She was dressed for a warm day, like him, except she was hatless and wore large sunglasses. "Looking good, Steph, like an Italian movie star."

"Not true, but it works for me."

He laughed. "Nice car, smells almost new. What make is it?"

"It's a Mitsubishi, almost nine years old."

"Didn't they make bombers in World War Two?"

"Yes, they did. And the air freshener hanging from the rear view mirror makes me think I'm driving something newer."

He held up a section of newspaper and a city map. "I've found a couple for sale. The people I talked to said I could come by any time this morning."

She examined his map and pointed to one of the marks he'd made. "Let's try this one first. It's not too far from here."

They arrived at a modest house where an elderly woman was trying to unload a 95 Camaro for $2,500. It was in poor condition and the woman was unwilling to negotiate a lower price. Chance told Stephanie in private that his financial situation forced him to consider older vehicles like the Camaro.

They drove on to a rural home west of Pueblo's city limits. A man about Chance's age introduced himself as Jeff, took them to his backyard and pointed at a red Ford F-150 truck. "There she is, my pride and joy. Got a few miles on 'er but she'll get you where you want to go."

Chance stepped into the cab and started the engine. It sounded healthy enough and he took note of the 175,258 mileage. He turned off the ignition, got out and commenced negotiating. Jeff's asking price of $4,300 came down but his bottom line was stuck firmly at $3,900.

Seeing they were rapidly getting nowhere, Stephanie took Chance aside. "If this truck is what you really want, use what money you have for a down payment and get a loan for the rest."

"I've already been down that alley and it's a dead end. I've got no credit history and have to establish myself all over again."

"What about me giving you a loan?"

He glared at her. "Heck no, I'm not letting you do that."

"Then you'd better come up with some more ideas."

"Let's keep looking. There's a few more places to go."

They said goodbye to Jeff and returned to her car. Instead of starting the engine, Stephanie stayed outside and made a call on her cell phone. When she got in Chance asked, "What was that about?"

"I just remembered something. A buddy from the hospital is getting a new car, a wedding gift from her husband. She's thinking of selling the one she has rather than trade it in. She'll show it to us if you're interested."

"Just like that, huh?"

"Yes or no?"

"OK, let's do it."

They drove east on U. S. 50, back through Pueblo, and entered a residential community next to Walking Stick Golf Course. Stephanie pulled into the driveway of a modest adobe-style home where a woman was mowing the front lawn. They got out and the woman shut off the mower.

Stephanie started the introductions. "Chance, this is my friend, Sarah."

She offered her hand accompanied by a beaming smile. "A pleasure to meet you, Chance. Steph tells me you also work at Parkview."

"In housekeeping on the third floor. And you are where?"

"The O. R. I'm a surgical nurse." She dabbed her face with a small towel. "I'll open the garage door from the inside so you can get a good look at the car. Take as long as you want. How about some iced tea? It's already made."

Chance said, "Sure, that'll be great."

He got into the driver's seat of a white four door sedan and Stephanie sat on the passenger's side. "This is a beautiful car," he said, turning on the ignition and smiling as the engine purred softly. "Just over 100,000 miles on the odometer. You happen to know what year it is?"

"An 03, I believe."

"You know what she wants for it?"

"I have no idea."

He turned off the engine and they walked completely around the car, checking the chassis and tires. "What do you think?" she said.

"This is another wild goose chase. Blue Book for a Toyota Camry like this one is probably around four thousand bucks. Let's chug-a-lug our tea and move on."

"You don't know that," she replied in a strained voice. "Give it a *chance*," she said, elbowing him in the ribs on the emphasized word.

"I should have changed my name before meeting you."

Sarah poked her head inside the garage. "C'mon inside where it's cooler."

They entered her living room and made themselves comfortable on a sofa next to a fireplace while Sarah served tall glasses of iced tea with lemon. Stephanie and Sarah talked hospital gossip while Chance looked around the room at the furnishings, artistic knickknacks and several paintings. "Beautiful home, Sarah."

"Thank you, Chance, we love it."

The conversation continued until Sarah asked, "Do you like the car?"

"It's nice," said Chance. "I can tell you've taken good care of it."

"I have a good mechanic and only drive it around town for work and shopping. And up to Leadville to see my folks every now and again."

Chance looked sharply at Stephanie for a moment. *Leadville again.* "Guess I have to ask. How much are you asking for it?"

Sarah looked at Chance, then at Stephanie, and back to Chance again with a worried expression. "Is $1,200 too much?"

Chance was momentarily speechless. "$1,200? Did I hear you right?"

"I can come down a little, but not much."

"No . . . no, $1,200 is fair. More than fair. I'll take it." He whipped out his checkbook from a pocket in his shorts.

"Great. Make it out to Sarah Dolan. I'll get the title and make out a receipt."

The transaction took less than fifteen minutes. Sarah took the check, gave him two sets of keys, the title, and a receipt. "Enjoy your car, Chance. And don't forget to take the paperwork to the DMV and have them put it in your name."

"Will do, Sarah, and thanks again." He glanced at Stephanie and said, "You'll need to back out of the driveway first."

"Give me a minute, Chance."

After he'd left, Stephanie and Sarah exchanged spirited but quietly restrained high fives. "You rate an Oscar for that one," said Stephanie.

Sarah giggled and made a bow. "Just one of my many talents."

They hugged and Stephanie said, "See you later, girlfriend."

When she got to the driveway, she called out to Chance, "Follow me to the restaurant for lunch. I'm buying."

Dan Mahoney made seven o'clock dinner reservations for Saturday at Rosario's, an Italian restaurant located downtown near the Historic Arkansas Riverwalk. He met Sharon at the entrance and admired her freshly coiffed blonde hair, a gauzy short summer dress in shades of pink, orange and lavender, and her shapely legs. "You look so different, I almost didn't recognize you."

"Is that a compliment or an excuse?"

"You look lovely, Sharon, not at all like a policewoman."

"Thank you, Dan, and you don't look anything like a fibbie." He wore tan slacks, an open collar light blue shirt and a light weight navy blue blazer. "I thought all you guys dressed and slept in suits."

"Ouch."

"All right, now that the mutual admiration society has been called to order, let's go inside and have dinner."

He opened the door for her. "Sharp sense of humor there, lady."

Once seated at their table, Dan ordered a bottle of *Montepulciano d'Abruzzo* and they began studying the elaborate menus.

"This is my first time here," she said. "I've heard their beef is excellent."

"It's true. I've had several lunches here and never been disappointed."

After placing their entree orders—filet mignon for her, New York steak for him—they touched wine glasses and Sharon said, "What shall we drink to?"

"Mom, apple pie and the American way?"

"How about a quick wrap on this case?"

He sipped the wine. "Are we talking shop now?"

"Do you only ask questions or can you make a simple declarative sentence once in a while?"

He laughed and she was soon laughing as well. "I'll drink to the quick wrap but I do have some news."

"Well heck, tell me so we can get it out of the way."

"All right, something I learned this morning. Our rep in Riyadh reported that Streckfus checked out of the Four Seasons. They tracked him to the airport where he left on a Saudia Airlines fight to Kabul."

"Kabul? Not your usual tourist destination."

"True. He took a room at the Inter-Con, a fairly nice hotel with a rather checkered history. In case you don't remember, it was assaulted by suicide bombers several years ago, twenty-one people killed, nine of them Taliban. Lots of U. S. military and Afghan Security Forces were staying there for meetings."

"Is it still dangerous?"

"Probably not, but no place in Afghanistan is safe these days."

"Streckfus must be on a mission, taking a risk like that."

"According to our sources, his royal partners in Saudi are not happy with his progress. They're putting the screws to him and want some results."

"So he's off to the big sand box for some arm wrestling."

"How long have you lived in Pueblo, Sharon?"

Sharon blinked hard. "Whoa, are we done talking business?"

"I hope so."

"You need to check your brake lights, Dan."

"Sorry, I'll make a smoother lane change next time."

"I've been here twelve years, a regular cop for seven and detective for five. Several years as a beat cop in Kansas City. Before that, paralegal work and schools in St. Louis, my home town." She went on to describe her Catholic elementary and high school education in Creve Couer but intentionally omitted any reference to her friend, Trish Guinn. Letting Mahoney know of Trish's position at FBI Headquarters would open up a can of worms and only make the situation worse. "Not a terribly exciting bit of history, but now you know everything."

"I doubt that. You've done very well, a nice upward career

path ending . . . where? Maybe Chief of Detectives here in Pueblo one day?"

"Not sure about that, Dan. Could be many years before even *thinking* about it." She sipped her wine. "So what about you?" Been with the FBI all your life?"

He laughed. "Yep, ever since graduating Fordham Law. I grew up in Boston, Charlestown actually, in a project called Mishawum. A tough neighborhood in those days but my parents kept me on the straight and narrow. They also made huge sacrifices so I could get into Boston College, Jesuits there like your Creve Couer high school. I could have studied law at B. C. but I was ready to get away from home."

"I understand completely, believe me. What about your family?"

"I'm the oldest of four, two brothers and a baby sister who works in the Red Sox head office."

"You a baseball fan?"

"Absolutely. Dad took family to Fenway many times and I sure miss the games. But I catch them on TV whenever I can."

"My dad's a baseball nut," she said, "a dyed-in-the-wool Cardinals fan. He worked as a kid in the old Sportsman's Park and got to watch the greats, like Musial, Kurowski and Schoendienst. Got in free, of course, and made money."

"Wouldn't it be a hoot if the Cards and Red Sox made it to the World Series?"

"Never gonna happen," she said. "The Cards are looking good but more beer and fried chicken in the locker room will sink the Red Sox before October."

The waiter brought their food and the conversation quieted, aside from comments on the excellence of the beef. Sharon asked about his FBI experiences and he replied, "Nothing terribly exciting. I've worked out of field offices in Boise, Flagstaff and now here in Pueblo. Frankly, it's been kind of boring lately. I was hoping the case we're working could lead to something bigger. If they offered me an assignment to the Middle East, for example, I'd be on the next flight."

"Be careful what you wish for, Daniel."

They finished eating and, after their plates were removed, the waiter came back with two smaller menus. "Would you like to try one of our delicious desserts?"

Dan and Sharon answered simultaneously; he voted *no* but she gave an enthusiastic *yes.* "Don't worry, Dan, I'll share." She turned to the waiter, "The cappuccino gelato, please."

Over coffee and gelato, they talked about personal subjects. Sharon told about a teacher she had in eighth grade, a nun who also chaperoned their graduation dance. The nun prowled the floor, telling each couple not to get too close. "Have to make some room in there for the Holy Ghost," she would tell them. Dan's only memory was an unpleasant one about being forced to change his handwriting style.

Dan also mentioned being married for a short time early in his FBI career but divorcing after three years. His wife, a native New Yorker he'd met at Fordham, couldn't stand living in Boise, a city so unlike The Big Apple. She also resented Dan being away from home on assignments as well as the extra hours he spent in the office. He admitted the marriage had been a mistake and hoped that next time, if there was a next time, he'd be fortunate enough to fall in love with a more compatible woman.

Sharon mentioned having relationships but was never married, citing the sad fact that Mr. Right had never made his appearance.

She brushed aside questions about her love life, saying only that she dated occasionally but police duties keep her too busy, adding that she wasn't in a good position to meet eligible and law abiding men.

After Dan paid the bill with a credit card he said, "How about a stroll along the riverwalk. There's still daylight left."

"Sounds nice."

The sun had disappeared behind western peaks and the temperature had come down. Sharon placed her arm around his and they passed boutique shops, pausing to admire small boats cruising the river's placid waters.

"I've enjoyed our evening," he said. "Hope we can get together again soon."

"I've had a nice time, too." *He's much less arrogant than the guy I met at the meeting in our section's conference room. And the total opposite of Eliot Waters.*

Dan was about to say something when his cell phone came alive. He pulled it from an inside blazer pocket and answered, "Mahoney." After a short pause he said, "I'll be right over."

She knew immediately their date was over. "Bad news?"

He slipped his phone back inside his blazer and gave her a crooked smile. "I think you're going to look stunningly beautiful in black."

"What are you talking about?"

"Streckfus is dead. Murdered."

"Good God, does his wife know?"

"They're sending a chaplain and some people to her home right now."

He took her hand and gave her a light kiss on the cheek. "I'll call you."

"Please do, and thanks for dinner."

Sharon sat on a bench next to the river and watched Mahoney stride briskly back to Rosario's parking lot. An emotional tsunami washed over her, leaving her sad, confused and lonely.

If only Eliot was here, right now, we could talk about this.

CHAPTER THIRTEEN

Sharon eventually returned to Rosario's parking lot but sat quietly inside her car before starting the engine. Such an early, abrupt and unexpected ending to her dinner date made her unsure about what to do for the rest of the evening. Oh well, she thought, I have a DVD and a book at home.

She drove from the parking lot and, without paying much attention to the route, soon found herself in front of the Streckfus home. The house was dark, the only one in the neighborhood with its lights out.

Sharon pulled over to the curb and shut off the engine. *That's funny. I expected all kinds of people to be there with Gloria and the kids, trying to help as much as possible.*

She waited for ten minutes, hoping that some movement, some evidence of life would make itself known. *It's not going to happen so I'm going home. Maybe I can pay a courtesy call tomorrow.* She was about to start the car when her cell phone rang. "Hello, Eliot, I was just thinking about you."

"That's *always* good news."

"That's the *only* good news."

"You don't sound right. What's going on?"

"You're not going to believe this. That councilman I've been investigating, Frank Streckfus? He's dead, a murder victim."

Eliot didn't respond.

"You there?"

"Yep, trying to take it all in. You OK? You sound kind of flustered."

"Just shaken up a bit. I'm all right."

"How'd it happen? Any details?"

Sharon took a deep breath. "When we talked the other night, I told you about meeting with an FBI guy and a homicide detective."

"I remember."

"About two hours ago, I was having dinner with Dan Mahoney and he told me a lot more about Streckfus."

"Wait a minute. Who's Mahoney?"

"A local FBI agent. He learned that Streckfus had flown off to Saudi Arabia and then went on to Kabul."

"You had dinner with this FBI fellow?"

"Something wrong with that?"

"Kind of hurts a bit. With you not coming up for the weekend . . . then having a date with another guy."

"Now you know how I felt when you were messing around with Cassie what's-her-face."

"That was different. I was forced into that situation by a clever woman."

"Yeah, I'll just bet you were pushing her away all the time. I never took you for a man without any willpower or backbone."

"Can we get back to the subject of Mr. Streckfus?"

"Mahoney had to get back to his office so I don't know how Streckfus was killed. Oh, and we had a meeting with the mayor yesterday and he practically threw us out of his office. Doesn't want us bothering him again."

"So you're done with this case?"

"Not quite. I'm in front of the Streckfus residence right now but all the house lights are out."

"How come you're there?"

"Sort of a follow-up to an earlier meeting with Mrs. Streckfus when I found out her husband was missing. I thought there'd be some friends with her and I could help out in some way."

"Maybe she went out for dinner and a movie."

"It's possible."

"You know, Sharon, this guy Streckfus and what he's been doing on the other side of the world seems way out of your bailiwick."

"Definitely, but I'm only involved because the mayor dragged me into it."

"So now you can forget about it since he told you to back off."

"I still want to find out exactly what happened to Streckfus and how the mayor is involved. I won't drop it. I can't drop it until I learn everything."

"Are you seeing this FBI dude again?"

"I might," she said with a teasing lilt in her voice.

"Maybe I should come down to Pueblo and work with you on this. Two heads are better than one, don't ya think?"

"I'm going to be too busy, Eliot. Let's talk again soon." She ended the call and drove home. She changed into pajamas, brushed her teeth and settled comfortably in bed with a Jack Reacher paperback. Her cell phone's silence, for which she was hugely grateful, allowed her to get well into the story. Until eleven o'clock, that is, when she finished a chapter and was ready to turn out the lights.

"Hi Dan," she answered, "what's up?"

"Hope I didn't wake you but I thought you'd want to hear more about councilman Streckfus."

"You think well. What did you find out?"

"It's a very messy situation, an Afghan version of a mob hit. A hotel maid found him in his hotel room, stabbed many times and blood all over the place. Couple of things were left behind, the murder weapon and a type of charm or talisman. We think it's a message."

"Oh my God. Any chance of finding out who did it? Fingerprints, eye witnesses, hotel security cameras?"

"Nada. Our people are checking everything but it was a professional job. They won't find anything."

"This is terrible. I feel so bad for his wife. I stopped by their house on the way home but all the lights were out. The place looked deserted and it was too early for everybody to be in bed on a Saturday night."

"The chaplain and one of our agents were there before you and they found the same thing."

"What arrangements are being made for returning the body?"

"That's another sensitive issue. Our man in Kabul and a State Department rep are talking with the Kabul police and the Afghan government. They're balking about releasing the body, making all kinds of noise about him being a secret agent. The goons are wanting *baksheesh* to look the other way. You know what *baksheesh* is?"

"Under-the-table payola, I'd guess."

"Right. So it will take some *negotiating* but we'll get him home for a military funeral and the appropriate ceremonies."

"I can hardly wait."

"Like I said before, you'll look gorgeous in black."

"Seems like a poor choice of words . . . under the circumstances."

"Sorry, I was being too casual. One of my defense mechanisms for avoiding the after effects of a traumatic event. What do you do for things like that?"

"Go to Mass, maybe. Seek comfort and guidance from a merciful God. In fact, I've been thinking of going tomorrow. Christ The King has a 10:45."

"I know that church. It's high time I make an appearance myself."

"Don't be doing this on my account."

"Actually, you've inspired me. Can't neglect the spiritual part of my life."

"Are you for real, Mahoney?"

He laughed. "I'll meet you there. How about brunch after Mass.

"OK, but I'm warning you. We may be too holy afterwards to have any fun."

Sharon met Dan at the church's front door about ten minutes before Mass started. They went inside and found seats near the front. Both were introspective during the service, attentive to the readings, and quietly recited prayers along with the congregation. That is, until late in the mass when the priest asked everyone to share the gift of peace with each other. Sharon extended her hand to Mahoney but he slipped his arm around her waist, pulled her close and kissed her full on the lips.

A startled Sharon broke loose and whispered, "What did you

do that for?"

He laughed softly. "Opportunities like that don't come along very often."

Sharon knelt and pretended to pray while her thoughts strayed elsewhere. *That wasn't too bad, actually. Except he could have picked a better time and place.*

After Mass they drove their respective cars to the IHOP restaurant next to I-25 and ordered large breakfasts.

"Nice service," she ventured. "Are you feeling spiritually refreshed?"

"Very much. How about yourself?"

"I liked the St. Paul reading but could have done without all that eternal damnation in the sermon."

"Wish there was a way for the faithful departed to communicate with us. Tell us what it's like on the other side."

She gave him a cockeyed look. "I'd rather wait and be surprised."

After finishing their meals he asked, "What are your plans for today?"

"Catch up on my case load. I've gotten way behind, thanks to you and our two political leaders."

"Too bad, but I understand."

"And I don't care to have Sgt. Hess on my tail." He grinned and was about to speak when she added, "Don't even think of saying it."

He cleared his throat. "What I was going to say . . . . all that work and no play makes Jill a dull girl."

"Some other time, Dan, I promise." *I need to get this Eliot thing settled soon, one way or another, before I can think about a relationship with this guy.*

"Then I'll hold you to it."

"I'm also thinking of trying one more time to see Mrs. Streckfus. She must have come home by now."

"She has. The chaplain met with her this morning before our Mass started."

"And you're just now telling me this? Seems like a continuing problem with you, Dan. Extracting information is like pulling an impacted wisdom tooth."

"Sorry, old habits die hard. Guess I was preoccupied with the excitement of seeing you again."

She slipped out of the booth and shook his hand. "And with that bit of Irish malarkey, I'll take my leave, Special Agent Mahoney. Call me."

He laughed and kissed her hand. "That I will."

Sharon's next stop was her office. She updated the status of three cases and, close to five o'clock, shut off her computer and drove to the Streckfus home. Three cars in the driveway prompted her to have second thoughts.

What the heck, I'm already here. Might as well go through with it.

She rang the doorbell and a teenage girl opened the door. "I'm Detective Hardcastle and was here the other evening. Can I speak to your mom?"

"Sure," the girl said, pointing to the living room. "She's in there."

Sharon stopped at the living room's entrance when she saw people with Gloria Streckfus. An older woman sat on the couch next to Gloria, holding her hand, and Mayor Mansfield sat opposite them. Sensing Sharon's sudden presence, he jerked his head around and stared at her. He got up, murmured a few words to

Gloria, and came up to Sharon. What are *you* doing here?" he said.

"Good afternoon, Mayor Mansfield. Just paying my respects to Mrs. Streckfus. I heard the bad news and wanted to offer my condolences."

"How did you know? It's not even in the newspapers yet."

"Special Agent Mahoney told me. You remember him, don't you? We were in your office together."

"I think you should turn around and leave. *Now.* She's very upset and your presence isn't going to make this any better."

Sharon's anger was rising but this was not the right moment for a belligerent confrontation. "With all due respect, sir, I believe I'm a better judge of that. It's been my experience with similar cases."

"Is that so?" He turned, took several paces toward the front door, and called out over his shoulder, "You'll regret this, Detective Hardcastle."

Sharon made a mental note of his threat, went over to the couch and took Gloria's hand. "I'm so sorry, Mrs. Streckfus. My condolences on your loss."

"Thank you, detective." She turned to face the woman on her left. "This is Madeline, my friend and counselor."

Madeline said, "Nice to meet you, detective." She turned to Gloria and added, "I'll call you tonight and see how you're doing."

After she left, Gloria patted the seat cushion next to her and Sharon sat down. "Bad news travels fast."

"Unfortunately, it's true."

Gloria grabbed a tissue and dabbed her reddish eyes. "I'm still trying to put all the pieces together but I'm having a hard time. It doesn't make any sense, Frank off to some godforsaken third world country on the other side of the world. What could have caused this? The chaplain was comforting but he didn't know anything and the FBI guy wasn't much help either. What am I going to do?"

"Sorry, I don't know any of the details but it will all come out in time. How are your girls holding up?"

"They're confused and worried. Much like me, they just don't get it."

"How about your folks? Have you talked to them?"

"Oh God, no. I haven't called them. Mom will be devastated."

"I wish I could be more helpful."

Gloria squeezed her hand. "Just your being here helps a lot." She dabbed her eyes again. "I need a drink. Do you have time for a glass of wine?"

"Absolutely."

Gloria went out to the kitchen and returned with two large glasses filled almost to the top with white wine. She sat down and they touched glasses without vocalizing any of the usual toasts.

During the ensuing conversation, Gloria reminisced about her college days and Frank's aggressive courtship. She skipped around to various points in their life together, moving every couple of years when change of duty station orders appeared. When he retired from the Army and later moved to Pueblo, she looked forward to finally settling down in her girlhood community. She was proud of his civic activities and his accomplishments as a city councilman. Lately, however, she'd noticed a change in his personality. He was more irritable, impatient, quick to anger, and had an almost psychopathic obsession with money. "We've got enough," she said. "More than enough, actually. Why was he so . . . preoccupied with making more and more?"

Sharon had no answer so she took a large sip of wine.

"And what's with Brian, anyhow? He's been Frank's friend for years and now he's acting weird."

Sharon's detective enzymes perked up. "In what way?" she said.

"I saw him talking to you as he was leaving. What did he say?"

Sharon hesitated. "He thought my being here would upset you and suggested I leave." *I sure can't tell her about Mansfield having me investigate Frank's finances.*

"Interesting. He should be taking his own advice."

"What do you mean?"

"He wasn't very helpful. Wanted to know if Frank left any papers or sealed envelopes behind when he left the country. How in the hell would I know that?"

"How did the mayor learn of your husband's death? Did he mention that?"

She pondered for a moment. "I don't recall. Is it important?"

"Probably not, just wondering." Sharon finished her wine and got up. "I need to be going now." *Should I call Mahoney and tell him about this? Eliot?*

Gloria walked her to the front door. "Thanks again for coming."

"You have my number. I want you to call me if you need any kind of police help. OK?"

Gloria gave Sharon a hug. "I'll remember that. I have a feeling that I'll probably need some before all this is over."

CHAPTER FOURTEEN

Chance worked out alone on Sunday morning. Stephanie had declared a *chore day* with the necessity of doing laundry, cleaning house, and grocery shopping. She pledged to do her usual routines at a school track near her home and asked Chance to do his exercises without her. After sleeping late that morning, he honored her request with several laps around Lake Clara.

He worked the afternoon shift at the hospital and thought hard about having a drink or two downtown late that night. Now that he had wheels, he felt mobile and could patronize most any place he wanted. He also had a strong desire for some intimate female companionship.

As he left the hospital, he had second thoughts. *All I need is to get stopped by some cop and have him smell booze on my breath. Then it's bye-bye and a one way ticket back to Canon City. Besides, I've got an early date with Steph at Oh-Dark-Thirty tomorrow. Guess I'll just have a drink at home and get some sleep.*

Chance and Stephanie came to the park about the same time on Monday. "Get all your housework done?" he said.

"Just about. Had to give the last bit a lick and a promise."

She took off her warmups. "How's the new car working out?"

"Fine. Did a little sightseeing around town yesterday, explored a supermarket and treated myself to a big breakfast at IHOP."

"You worked yesterday, right?"

"Sure, the usual shift. Pretty quiet in the wings last night."

"What did you do after work?"

He gave her a curious look. "Why do you care?"

"I don't, really. Just curious."

Chance began loosening up. "The usual stuff. Couple of drinks downtown at a gentlemen's club, did a little dance, loaded up my system with all those poisons you like to sweat out of me."

"Then I'll do just that, smarty pants."

"Hey Steph, just kidding."

"Let's get moving, jokester."

Off they went, this time with three brisk laps around the pool. Back at their piles of clothes, Chance collapsed on the grass under a shade tree while Stephanie kept in motion with a slow circular pace around him. After several minutes of cooling off and normal breathing was restored, she sat next to him, her legs crossed in front. "Got all that nasty poison out?" she said.

He rolled to his side, their knees touching, and looked up into her eyes. "Why are you doing this?"

"Running around the park?"

"Spending all this time with me. There must be dozens of guys in this town who'd be better for you. Why not some other guy?"

"You don't think you're worth it?"

"Well . . . yes and no. Hey, don't get me wrong. I'm grateful for your help, taking me around yesterday and meeting Sarah for that great car deal."

"You're welcome, but I think you're being too hard on yourself."

"Maybe so, but I'd hate to think you're on some charity kick. Like a Rehab-The-Con Project."

She frowned. "I'm not like that, Chance. I enjoy our morning exercises and had a fun time Saturday. So relax and don't over think this. And if some knight in shining armor rides over the Rockies on his white horse, you'll be the first to know."

"Hope I have my Excalibur with me when Sir Lunch-a-lot shows up."

Stephanie laughed out loud. "There you go."

Chance got up. "I'm hitting the shower now. Have to swing by the DMV and get the car registered in my name."

"Before you go . . . you're off tomorrow, right?"

He smiled. "Yep. What time should I pick you up?"

"Got a better idea. How about dinner at my place? You're probably ready for a home cooked meal by now."

"Heck yes, that sounds great. What can I bring?"

"Just a good appetite. Find me this afternoon and I'll give you directions."

Chance passed his landlord outside as he was leaving on Tuesday afternoon. "My, my," said Maynard, "you must have a hot date tonight."

"Yeah, a pretty special lady."

"Where ya takin' her?"

"Nowhere. She's cooking dinner for us." He stopped for a moment. "She said not to bring anything but that doesn't seem right."

"You're kinda rusty at this dating stuff, aren't you?"

"What would *you* do?"

"Take her some flowers. You can't miss with a dozen or so nice blooms."

"Good idea, Maynard."

"I'll expect an after action report tomorrow morning."

"Ha, in your dreams."

Chance drove to a King Sooper and looked over the selection of flowers on sale. He picked a dozen roses of soft reds, pinks and yellows from a refrigerated glass case and drove to Pueblo West's Purcell Boulevard entrance.

Stephanie had given him a hand drawn map yesterday and he easily found her small adobe style house around seven o'clock. When she came to the door and saw the roses in front of his face, she put a hand to her mouth and said something like, "Oh my, they're beautiful."

Chance beamed and made a mental note to thank Maynard.

She took the flowers and held the blooms up to her nose, her eyes half closed while she moaned softly.

"You approve?"

"I love them, come inside. You didn't need to do this but it was so thoughtful. I'll put them in some water."

He followed her into the kitchen, watching her closely. She was barefoot, wore snug white shorts and a light blue top that allowed her tan midriff to show. While she cut the flowers' stems and filled a vase with water, he looked around her small kitchen; white cabinets and walls papered with blue check print and sunflowers. A table near the window had been set with a yellow tablecloth and two places for dinner "Nice place, Steph." He went to the back door and looked outside. "Plenty of privacy with enough space so your neighbors aren't hearing every noise you make."

"It's very quiet out here and I do have neighbors that look out for me. Have any trouble finding it?"

"None at all, your map was perfect."

She placed the filled vase on a counter and backed away to admire her arrangement. "Beautiful, huh?"

"I'll have to do this more often."

She turned and moved closer so that he could feel the soft contours of her breasts touching his chest. She kissed him softly and he responded, his arms pulling her tighter, his hands under her top and caressing the silky smoothness of her back.

"Wow," she said.

"Wow for sure."

Without relaxing his hold, Chance kissed both sides of her neck, alternating back and forth until Stephanie broke free and took his hands in hers. "That was nice, but I'd better be looking after our dinner."

He grinned. "I don't mind waiting."

"I know it's been awhile and you've been so patient and understanding. I appreciate that more than you'll ever know."

He let go of her hands and pulled her into a hug. "I've often thought about what it would be like again, when and if I met the right woman. I knew I lucked out when I saw you working on that paratrooper guy at the hospital. You have a lot of compassion for people, something in pretty short supply these days." He relaxed his arms and she stepped back. "So . . . what's for dinner?"

"We'll talk some more later about that. Do you like fish?"

"Never had a chance to eat much but sure, I like it."

"We're having baked salmon, rice and a big garden salad. It's almost ready and I've got a bottle of Chardonnay in the fridge if you'll do the honors. Or you can have beer if you don't care for wine."

"Wine is fine." He found the bottle and filled the two glasses on the table about half way. Stephanie set a platter of salmon and a bowl of steaming brown rice on the table while Chance brought the salad from the fridge.

After they sat down, he raised his glass. "To the beautiful chef."

She touched her glass with his. "Hope you enjoy it."

He took several bites. "Absolutely delicious. Did you work today? I'm wondering how you managed to put all this together?"

"Did a lot of prepping before I drove in this morning."

"And your usual exercises at the park?" He said with a teasing tone.

"As a matter of fact, no. Only so much time in the day, you know."

He raised his glass again. "Another toast to good planning."

The conversation subsided and became unfocused, dealing with generalities about Parkview and his visit yesterday to the DMV. Chance felt a small degree of nervousness and he could tell Stephanie was not her usual in-control self. With the passionate kisses and exciting embraces, they had taken a first step, a rather big one, to a new level in their relationship. He felt even more confident they'd travel a much greater emotional distance together before tomorrow's sunrise.

The bottle of Chardonnay was empty, their plates clean, and they looked across the table at each other in silence for several moments. He pushed his chair back from the table and announced, "Let me help you with the clean up."

"Stay right there." She came around, sat on his lap and gave him a wet kiss.

"You taste like salad dressing."

"Am I too heavy for you?"

He stood, one arm under her leg and the other around her waist. "Not a bit."

"Aren't you happy now with my exercise program?"

"Before meeting you, I probably couldn't have done this."

"Think you can make it to my bed?"

"Give me directions and we'll be there before you can say Jumping Jack Flash."

On their way down the hallway, he started to lose his grip and bumped her against the wall. "Hold tight, Steph, almost there."

She giggled. "Maybe you should let me walk the rest of the way, Hercules."

"No way, have to transport you safely to paradise."

"It won't be a Garden of Eden if you drop me."

"Not to worry." He huffed and puffed, found her bedroom at the end of the hall and tried to place her gently on top of the bed. But he lost his balance, fell on top of her, and they rolled around in a jangle of arms and legs while laughing and kissing.

The fading sunlight shone through the double windows. "Do you want it dark?" she said. "I can close the blinds."

"No, I want to look at every beautiful inch of you."

She kissed him. "Works for me."

He still had a hand under her top and brought it around to cup her breast. "I see you're not wearing a bra."

"Which means I'm already two steps ahead of you."

He rolled off and stood at the bed's side. "Then I'd better get moving." Before removing all his clothes he pulled a foil packet from his wallet. *Better safe than sorry, especially after that first-night-of-freedom orgy.*

Stephanie had already shed everything, was lying under a light blue sheet which she'd pulled up to her chin, and eagerly awaited him with arms extended.

Their bodies melded together and they communicated perfectly without a spoken word, lips hungrily kissing and hands exploring. Chance was aroused but was taking it slowly, gratified and excited just to witness her pleasure.

Apparently things weren't going fast enough. "I'm so hot, so ready, and I want you now."

He slipped inside and she pulled him closer, moved her pelvis back and forth, stronger and faster. She approached her climax with high pitched squeals and reached a frenzied orgasm punctuated with loud screams of "Yes . . . yes . . . yes, *oh yes.*"

After a long moment he said, "I'm sure the neighbors heard *that* one."

"My God . . . if they didn't, I hope they saw the fireworks."

Still entwined with each other, they rolled over so that Stephanie was now lying on top of him. Chance said, "And I thought I was the horny one."

"You have no idea. Sorry I was so quick on the trigger. You OK?"

"Never better. I not only enjoyed it a lot but got an even bigger thrill watching you and being a part of your pleasure."

She teased him with her tongue. "I think you're on to something there, lover."

He caressed her back with sweeping motions from top to bottom. "I love your skin, touching you everywhere."

She jerked up and back. "We haven't finished our dinner."

"What are you talking about?"

"I made us dessert." She jumped out of bed and slipped on a short white kimono with black Japanese figures. "I'll bring it back here."

Chance made a bathroom visit while she was away. He came back to the bedroom, turned on a bedside lamp, and propped up the pillows on both sides. He was sitting up, a sheet covering the lower half of his body, when she came back with two large white bowls. "What's this?"

She handed him a bowl and sat up on her side against the pillows. "Brownies, vanilla ice cream and a river of hot fudge."

"Meaning a gazillion laps around the lake tomorrow?"

She licked a smudge of chocolate from her lips and smiled. "There are other ways we can burn off the extra calories."

He devoured several bites. "Mmmm, death by chocolate."

Stephanie took their empty bowls back to the kitchen. When she came back to the bedroom, she removed her kimono and slipped into bed. Chance turned out the lamp and each moved into the other.

"What are you doing tomorrow?" she said.

"I have to check in with my parole officer in the morning."

"Let's have lunch. Can you meet me in the cafeteria about noon?"

"Yeah, sounds good. And if we eat fast enough we can duck into a linen closet for a quickie afterward."

"Ooh, that would be interesting. But it might cost us our jobs."

After several quiet minutes, Chance said, "I've been thinking . . . you know more about me than I know about you."

"What do you want to know?"

"Any serious relationships in your dark and dangerous past? Any skeletons in the closet I should know about?"

She gave him a brief kiss. "Pretend I'm an onion and peel back one layer at a time. One surprise after another."

"You're a mysterious woman, Miss White. But that's not totally fair."

"OK, one thing, and then we'll talk about something else. There was a guy I dated before I came down to Pueblo. He had a bad temper but managed to control it most of the time. Our relationship was going sour; I knew it but he was clueless. When I got the job offer from Parkview, I decided to break it off."

"And he wasn't too happy about that."

"That's putting it mildly. It got violent and he was physical with me."

"*Son of a bitch.* Who is this guy?"

"Let me finish. Went back to my parents for a couple of days, long enough to clear out of my apartment. Then I left Denver for Pueblo."

"Did you file charges against this maggot?"

"I thought about it but decided against it. I just wanted to get far away and not have to deal with him anymore."

"Has he tried to contact you?"

"No, thank God."

He pondered this for a moment. "Now that I have wheels, maybe we can drive up to Denver and pay this guy a visit."

"Are you crazy? Now I'm sorry I told you."

"When did all this happen?"

"About two years ago. You're the first guy I've been with since then."

"That explains a lot. But I want you to know that I'd never, never, do you any physical harm. I was brought up to treat women with respect. It's different with guys and Lord knows I had my share of fights in prison. Won some, lost some."

"You still have lots of anger inside, Chance, like me, but even more so. I feel safe with you and could see a gentleness in you when we first met. The physical exercises will be good for both of us, get that anger out of our systems. And the TLC we just had can't hurt either."

"I don't know what to say."

"Then just kiss me goodnight. I'll try not to wake you when I leave."

"We'll see about that."

He gave her a long passionate kiss and felt her fading to sleep as their embrace became more relaxed. Though he was himself sleepy, he wasn't ready to surrender just yet. This feeling, a sublime mix of love, peace, security and well being might disappear during the night and never be captured again.

CHAPTER FIFTEEN

Sharon stayed late in her office after spending most of the day with an embezzlement case. A city employee was suspected of creating fake invoices for work performed by an asphalt paving contractor and getting kickbacks from him.

At home she fixed herself a quick meal, cleaned up the kitchen and rambled about the house wondering what to do next. She wasn't sleepy and wasn't interested in talking to Eliot. She'd said everything to him Sunday evening that needed to be said and there was nothing new on the Streckfus case to talk with Dan Mahoney about. She was at loose ends and felt in the middle of something like the doldrums, a dead calm before a violent storm. Nothing on TV interested her and she didn't have the mental energy to start reading a new book.

When her cell phone rang and she recognized the caller's ID, she was happy for a welcome surprise from her Washington FBI buddy, Patricia Guinn. "Hi Trish. I should be the one calling you and not the other way around."

"It's been awhile. You sound a little down, like you're working too hard."

"You will *not* believe what's going on here."

"Did you spend the weekend with your mountain man?"

"No, something came up so I stayed in Pueblo."

"What happened? A lover's quarrel?"

They talked for a while about Eliot's experience with Cassie Maugham. Sharon repeated his telling of the story, her own suspicions about what really happened and Eliot didn't own up to, and the uncertain impact on their relationship. Trish kept silent but at the end she said, "Is this a deal breaker for you two?"

"I don't know. Been too busy with something else to give it much thought."

"So you're just letting it slide?"

"For now. Oh, we'll probably get back together again and hash it out. But in the meantime, we need to do some heavy duty thinking about where we go from here." After a pause she said, "Is this why you called, to get an update on my love life?"

"No, but I always like to hear about love's fickle ways."

"Then why *did* you call?"

"OK, now for the real deal. I assume you've heard about Frank Streckfus being found dead in Kabul."

"Yes, Dan Mahoney told me."

"Ah, so you've made the acquaintance of Dapper Dan."

Sharon summarized her meetings with Mahoney: the conference room when Streckfus went missing, seeing Dan again in the mayor's office, their dinner date at Rosario's, and going to Mass the next day. "My boss pulled me into this deal and I didn't have much say in the matter."

"Wow, you two are moving pretty fast. Kind of nice, isn't it, having a local boyfriend on the side. Puts the pressure on Eliot since Mahoney has the geographical advantage."

"It's been all business, Trish. And what's this Dapper

Dan thing?"

"Let's just say he has a large fan base among the ladies here at Headquarters. Sort of like the fishing boat skipper with a huge net, pulling in the big catches."

"Oh for God's sake. You think I care?"

"Just giving you a heads up. I don't know what he's sharing with you about Streckfus but I've seen some message traffic and heard some talk."

"What's your take?"

"I can only say this incident has generated a slew of theories about what *really* happened with no official conclusions reached."

"Mahoney told me that Streckfus was found dead in his hotel room, many stab wounds and lots of blood. They also found the murder weapon and some kind of charm, like a message from the Afghan mafia."

"That much is true. Did he mention the room had been tossed?"

"No, he didn't"

"Another thing. The Kabul police are no dummies. They checked the knife for fingerprints and tracked them to a souk merchant. The guy sells dozens of these knives to our military so it's only natural for his prints to be on it."

"Damn. Sounds like a set up."

"Yep, and a pretty amateurish one at that. The charm is also from the souk."

"Is this a dead end?"

"Not quite. Our people are still checking out a few leads but the chances of catching the guy who did it are pretty slim."

"Mahoney said there were complications about releasing the body."

"No longer a problem. The ambassador flexed a few muscles

and they're flying him home tomorrow."

"Glad to hear that. Mrs. Streckfus needs to have closure on this."

After a pause Trish said, "That's about it, girlfriend. Be careful now."

"Hey, let's talk about *your* love life. You dating anyone these days?"

No answer. She'd already ended the call.

At one point during the night Chance began thrashing and moaning so loudly that he woke Stephanie. She turned on her bedside lamp and said, "What's wrong, Chance? Are you ill?"

He sat up, opened his eyes and looked around the room as if he didn't know where he was. He flopped back on his pillow. "Oh God, having a bad dream."

She placed her hands on his forehead and bare chest. "You're soaked."

"I need some water."

"Stay there, I'll get you some. She went off to the kitchen and returned with a plastic bottle of cold water.

He guzzled nearly half of it. "That tastes so good."

She sat on his side of the bed. "Do you often have these nightmares?"

"Every once in a while. Still having trouble getting some prison experiences out of my head."

"Maybe you can get help," she said.

"What kind of help?"

"Counseling. Talking to a pro about those times."

"A shrink, you mean."

"Why don't you ask your parole officer about that?"

He gave her a sullen look, thought about it, and finally said, "OK. I'll ask her."

"Good." She turned out the light and got back into bed.

He cuddled up to her, his chest against her back, fitting together like two spoons. One arm was draped across the top of her head while he cupped her breast with the other hand. He kissed her neck and whispered softly in her ear. "Being right here with you is pretty nice therapy."

She twisted her head around and kissed him. "We're both damaged goods, Chance. It's going to take more than this."

They drifted off and slept peacefully until Stephanie's alarm clock buzzed. She took a shower, got dressed, and started making breakfast. Her absence soon awakened him. He collected his scattered clothes and ambled out to the bright sunlit kitchen. "I smell coffee," he said.

She was standing next to the coffee maker and poured him a cup. "You didn't need to get up."

"Sure I did. Wanted to catch you before you left, see what you look like in the dawn's early light."

"Nothing special. You've seen me in this outfit many times at the hospital."

"I'm not talking about clothes. It's your face, the glow of your skin and the look in your eyes."

She grinned. "Must have been the dessert."

"More like the treat before dessert."

She had an English muffin and orange juice. He had more coffee while looking over the front page of *The Pueblo Chieftain.* "See anything newsworthy?" she said.

"Big article about one of our local politicians. A city councilman was found dead in his hotel room. In Kabul, Afghanistan, under very suspicious circumstances."

"What the heck was he doing there?"

"Doesn't say. Only that it wasn't city business. There's a quote by the mayor saying he'd been a good friend since their Army days together. Praised him for all the good work he'd done on behalf of Pueblo."

Stephanie went off to the bathroom to apply some finishing touches while Chance continued sipping coffee and reading the paper. She came back and said, "I'm leaving now. Come kiss me goodbye."

He wrapped her in his arms and kissed her. "I'm missing you already."

"We'll see each other again for lunch, right?"

He slipped both hands inside her panties, grasped her cheeks, and pulled her closer. "Why don't you call in sick? Then we can go back to bed for a while."

She broke free of his hug. "I think you need a cold shower, Mr. Cullen."

"I'll do that and get myself spruced up for our lunch date."

She turned and called out, "Be sure to lock up when you leave. And it wouldn't hurt you to run around the block several times."

Chance came to the hospital cafeteria about noon and saw Stephanie standing next to the salad bar. She recognized him and he moved up close to her, expecting some kind of welcoming kiss.

"Uh, uh," she said, "no PDA."

"What?"

"No public display of affection."

He stuck his hands into his pockets. "Well, OK then. But I'll get you later."

She smiled. "I certainly hope so."

They made themselves salads, hers larger than his, and Chance added a slice of sausage pizza to his tray. They paid for their meals and found an unoccupied table.

Stephanie asked, "How was your meeting with Ms. Acosta?"

"Pretty good, but I can't be traveling outside the city just yet."

"Are you saying Pueblo West is out of bounds?"

"No, we're OK on that."

"How about counseling? Did you check with her on that?"

"I did. Turns out my situation isn't all that unusual. She gave me a list of names and most of them take Medicaid."

"Wonderful. I did some checking this morning. Several psychiatrists are right here in the hospital. Your employee health benefits might cover you completely and appointments could be arranged to fit your work schedule. I made some notes and I'll give them to you later."

He reached across the table and squeezed her hand. "Thanks, Steph."

She puckered up her lips and gave him a quiet air kiss. It made him chuckle which in turn made her giggle.

"How was your morning?" he said.

"Kind of rough. I have a new patient, a young woman banged up pretty bad in an auto accident."

"Somebody hit her?"

"No, she'd been drinking and wasn't wearing a seat belt."

"Aw, that's terrible. Any of her passengers get hurt?"

"She was alone and did it all to herself. Think I'll be seeing her for a while."

As they were finishing lunch, Chance spoke up. "I've got an idea. How about me fixing us dinner tonight?"

"You?"

"Sure, I'm off this afternoon and I can pick up some things. Head over to your place and have it almost ready when you get home. What do you think?"

"I think I'd like to kiss you right now."

He wagged his finger. "No, no. PDA not allowed."

"Then we'll have some PDA tonight. Private display of affection. *Very* private and lots of it."

CHAPTER SIXTEEN

Sharon was in her office late Wednesday when she received a call from Eliot. "Hold on for a second," she answered, standing up and peering into a nearby cubicle for signs of Detective Wasserstein. She was out. "OK, Eliot, I'm here."

"Just checking in, Sharon, see how things are going."

"A mile a minute."

"Any more on the councilman? When we talked on Saturday the situation was kind of sketchy."

Sharon gave him a long story about Streckfus' numerous stab wounds, the left-behind murder weapon and talisman, the upset condition of the hotel room, and the difficult negotiations with the local police and Afghan government for release of the body. She didn't say where all this information came from and it prompted Eliot to ask about its source. "FBI," she answered.

"From your Mahoney fellow?"

"Some of it from him, some from my pal Trish in D. C. The interesting thing is that I get more from her than Dan tells me."

"Not your typical trustworthy lawman, I'd say."

Not wanting to dwell on trusting lawmen in general, Sharon said, "How was your weekend?"

"Getting kind of busy. The Leadville Trail Marathon is next Saturday and all the flatlanders are starting to show up, getting themselves acclimatized to our elevation. Should have a pretty good turnout this year."

"Are you expecting any trouble?" she said.

"Naw, they knock themselves out running around the mountains."

"I'll bet all the restaurants appreciate the extra business."

"Getting back to the deceased councilman, you mentioned his room being searched. Someone pulling a robbery on a rich American tourist?"

"Not according to Trish. None of Streckfus' personal stuff was taken. Money, credit cards, watch, cell phone. All of it still there."

"And the guy who sells knives like the murder weapon . . . he's in the clear?"

"So far, anyway." She made a heavy sigh. "This case has more holes in it than a kitchen colander. But it's not my problem."

"Who's case is it?"

"The FBI's, I guess. Whoever has jurisdiction in Kabul. Kind of a circle-jerk between the U. S. and Afghan governments."

"I'll bet you'll be glad when all this is over."

"I suppose, but there's something going on right now here in Pueblo that isn't kosher. I went over to the Streckfus home on Sunday evening and spent some time with his widow, Gloria."

"How's she holding up?"

"Pretty good, all things considered. But the mayor was there and we had an unpleasant conversation. Told me I shouldn't have intruded and I'd better stay away from her. Gave me the willies."

"Did Mrs. Streckfus hear this?"

"No, but I told her about it. She said Mansfield has been acting weird and I should pretty much ignore him. She was happy for my presence and grateful for any police-type support I might give her."

"You told me once the mayor and Streckfus were long time friends since their army days. Why wouldn't he want you to help his buddy's widow?"

"Exactly."

"Well, it's a damn shame he has to flex his political muscle in a situation like this. Doesn't help people get over the trauma of losing a loved one."

"I'm going to steer clear of him from now on," she said, "and let Sergeant Hess field any more requests coming from the mayor's office."

"Any progress at all getting the body released?"

"Yes, good news there. They did release it and it arrived early this afternoon at The Springs airport. The Kapoulis Brothers Funeral Home took charge and will have public viewings starting tomorrow."

"And the funeral?"

"On Saturday, a big deal military thing at Fort Logan National Cemetery. Kind of a long ride up to Denver and back."

"Nothing closer than that?"

"There's a move to get one in The Springs but Fort Logan is it for now."

"You plan on attending?"

"Not sure. Depends."

"I can come down for it . . . if you'd like the company."

"Thanks, but you'd better stay put. Keep those runners on

the right trail."

"I understand what you're going through, Sharon, but we need to talk. Kicking the can ahead isn't helping our relationship. If we still have one, that is."

Another deep sigh. "You're right, Eliot. We need to talk and it should be face-to-face. And sooner than later. How about the weekend after next? I'll commit to it right now. No more delays."

"Sounds good, I'll count on it."

In the after midnight darkness of Stephanie's bedroom on Wednesday evening, she and Chance were locked in a close embrace and breathing hard. They had just finished making love and were cooling off, kissing each other and murmuring words of endearment. "You are so sweet," he said, "and that was awesome."

"Best you ever had?"

"No question about it. I could get mighty used to you, honey girl."

"That *was* wonderful, Chance, and very considerate of you for being so patient, taking your time like that."

"Just wanted you to enjoy it as much as I did." After several moments of cherished silence he said, "You ready for some dessert now?"

"Not me, brownie boy. But you go ahead."

"You going on a diet all of a sudden?"

"Nope, just getting back to my training program. Have to be in good shape for Saturday's *enduro*."

"What's happening on Saturday?"

"The Trail Marathon in Leadville. I told you about that."

"Damn, I must have forgot."

"I'm driving up in the morning to do a couple of runs. Get myself acclimatized before the race."

"So you're gonna be gone for . . . how long?"

"I'll be back Sunday afternoon. Can you do that math?"

He made sequential taps on her ribs with his forefinger. "Yep, I counted up four days and that's too long."

"Three and a half, actually."

"What will I do with myself while you're gone?"

"Oh you poor thing. You'll be working every night and exercising every morning. Can I trust you to work out while I'm gone?"

"Sure, I'll do that." He gave her a quick kiss. "But I'll miss your whiplashes across my back." He paused. "Where will you be staying up there?"

"In a motel with two of my buddies."

"Male or female?"

"Erica and Alexis, physical therapists like me from Colorado Acute. I think you can figure out their sex."

"Oh boy, three wild girls on the town."

She laughed. "Yeah, right. Not much in the way of trouble spots in that neck of the woods. Besides, they're both married and aren't big on partying all hours of the night. They're buff like me and want to keep themselves in great shape."

"For bedroom calisthenics, I should think."

She punched him in the ribs. "You need to get your mind off sex."

"I admire your self-discipline, Steph, but I can't imagine you any way but buff."

"Wait right there." She turned on the bedside light, threw on her kimono, went over to a dresser and opened the bottom drawer.

She brought back a large brown scrapbook and said, "Scoot over, I want to show you some pictures." She turned on his bedside lamp, sat on the bed and opened the photo album to the first page. "I don't show these to just anybody."

"Is that really you? You're adorable but a wee bit chubby there."

"Yeah, major fat. Me, when I graduated from kindergarten." She turned the page. "Here I am at a sixth grade Halloween party. Then over here is when I was a high school freshman, going to a dance where no boy ever asked me to get off my butt and trip the light fantastic. Are you seeing a trend here?"

"Unfortunately, yes. You've put on a few pounds."

"A few? I'll spare you further torture. Bottom line, I have a weight problem, probably something I inherited, but I work hard to keep it off and not come back."

"That's quite a story. But something must have happened along the way because you're much lighter now. How'd you do it?"

"Peer pressure. High school girls can be pretty cruel sometimes but they did me a big favor. Sent me into a tailspin for a while but I got help from an A-1 counselor. By the time I was a senior, those same girls were singing a different tune. I was more popular than ever and I believe they regretted creating such a beautiful monster."

"Their loss is my gain."

She put away the album, they turned out the lights and she came back to bed.

"Thanks for sharing those pictures with me, Steph."

"I think we're good for each other, don't you?"

He gave her a long goodnight kiss. "Good, better, best."

Late Thursday afternoon Sharon was still in her office, pacing in and out of her cubicle, when Detective Debbie appeared. After watching for several minutes Wasserstein said, "What's going on, Hardtack?"

"Trying to reach a decision. Should I go now or later? Maybe not go at all."

"Go where?"

"Kapoulis Funeral Home. Streckfus' body was returned from Afghanistan yesterday."

"Oh yeah, I heard about that. Why are you still involved in this?"

"Good question," said Sharon. "Probably give his widow some support." The major reason for not going was her dislike of looking at dead bodies. However, she was not about to admit this to another police officer, and Wasserstein in particular.

Debbie made a leering grin. "Along with the handsome special agent maybe? I heard you two are getting pretty cozy, running down leads, digging for clues, out and about with romantic dinners."

"Wrong, wrong, wrong. It's all strictly professional. And I have the feeling this case is not over yet. I won't be satisfied until I find out what's really going on."

"Spoken like a true detective. Go for it."

Sharon left quickly and drove straight to the funeral home. When she entered the building she noticed an immediate change in temperature; it felt about twenty degrees cooler. A tall thin man about sixty, wearing thick glasses and a beautifully tailored dark blue suit and vest, greeted her. "May I help you?" His voice was low and the tone somber.

"The viewing for Mr. Streckfus."

"This way, please." He escorted her down a long carpeted

hall to a large room where they stopped at a double door entry. "Would you care to sign the guest log?" he said, pointing to an open book resting on a small table.

He left quietly as she signed her name. She took a few moments to look at the names before hers. Brian Mansfield was one of the first who came but she didn't see Dan Mahoney's name on any of the earlier pages.

She entered the room but stopped after several steps to get her bearings and see if Gloria Streckfus was there. Sharon spotted her in a simple black dress while talking to a small group of people. *I'll say hello when she's free.*

Sharon saw a casket of dark maple at the far center of the room, an American flag draped across the lower half, and the top half raised to allow visitors to see Frank's upper torso. A shiver ran through her body and she hoped she wouldn't have to get close enough to look inside.

There were about two dozen visitors in the room, many of whom looked like his associates in government or business. She noted many beautiful floral arrangements placed on metal stands on both sides of the casket. Two flags on stanchions were also present, holding the stars and stripes on one side and a dark blue flag edged in gold braid on the other. She took a moment to view a framed color photo of Frank in his early army years wearing medals on a full dress uniform.

"There you are," said Gloria, touching Sharon's arm which caused her to jump. "Sorry, didn't mean to startle you."

Sharon took both of Gloria's hands. "Again, my sincerest condolences."

"Thanks, I'm so glad you came." She kept one of Sharon's hands and pulled her toward the casket. "Come see my husband."

Sharon started to resist but finally said, "OK."

She wasn't sure what to expect but was immensely relieved to look down on the peaceful face of Frank Streckfus, almost exactly the way he looked in the newspaper picture taken at the new library branch opening. He was dressed in a blue suit, a white shirt, and a dark maroon tie.

Gloria dabbed her eyes with a handkerchief and said, "They did a beautiful job, didn't they. I was afraid I wouldn't get to see him again before they buried him."

Sharon was at a loss for words but got down on a kneeler and Gloria did the same. After a short prayer, they got up and Gloria said, "Let's go sit down."

They found comfortable seats at the back of the room. "How are your girls holding up?" said Sharon.

"Not well. My parents took them out for an early dinner."

"Have you had anything to eat?"

"A bit. I've been too busy with arrangements here at the funeral home. And two officers from Fort Carson came down to talk about services at the cemetery. Caisson, honor guard and bugler. They wanted to talk about survivor's benefits but I told them to save it for another time. I'll get something to eat later."

"Maybe we can go out for a quick bite."

She grabbed Sharon's hand. "Yeah, let's do that." She paused and continued, "What I'm not hearing about is progress, how they're catching the guy who killed Frank. Can you tell me anything about that?"

Sharon hesitated, thinking of what she'd heard from Trish Guinn and Dan Mahoney. She didn't want to divulge any of that in case the information turned out later to be false. "Not really," she said. "You mentioned talking to an FBI agent on

Sunday afternoon."

"Yes, a fellow named Maloney . . . or Mahoney. I forget which."

"It's Dan Mahoney and I know him. I'll give him a call and arrange a meeting at your earliest convenience."

CHAPTER SEVENTEEN

"Where the hell have you been, Mahoney?" Sharon was calling from the privacy of her kitchen after having a meal with Gloria Streckfus.

"Obviously none of the right places. Is something wrong?"

"Many things are wrong. I just got back from the funeral home after spending time with Mrs. Streckfus. You remember her, don't you, Dan?"

"Of course. What's your point?"

"My point? She's wondering why nobody's telling her about her husband, keeping her informed about the search for his murderer. And me too, for that matter. Last time you talked to me was our after-Mass IHOP brunch."

"You need to calm down so we can discuss it like professionals."

"Damn you."

"Or maybe we should have this conversation in the morning. Clear heads, a good night's sleep, maybe a nice breakfast together."

"OK, OK, I'm calming down." She made a few exaggerated huffs and puffs into the phone for his benefit. "I'm only saying that she needs to be kept in the loop, what steps are being taken to nail the guy who killed him. I can't do it because I don't have the communication channels to your people over there. You're the one who has to talk to her and copy me in the process."

"You know, I hate to be the bearer of bad news but there is no news."

"Nothing?"

"Nada. Bupkis. Zero. No new leads and the trail is as cold as the Norwegian winter olympics. Somehow, I don't think Mrs. Streckfus would enjoy hearing about our complete lack of success in finding the killer. Not to mention my own embarrassment, on behalf of the Bureau, in not finding the guy."

"So that's it? You're giving up?"

"I didn't say that."

"Can't you at least talk to her? Tell her how sorry you are, how you guys are turning over every grain of sand looking for clues? I could come to a meeting, just the three of us. It might go better with me present."

"All right, I'll call her. See what we can set up."

"I've been thinking a lot about this and I always thought there was something fishy about it. The missing link could be right here in Pueblo if only we could find it. We might even be looking at it and not recognize it."

"Like the proverbial needle in a haystack."

"I do have an idea. Gloria told me once that Mayor Mansfield had been asking about Frank's papers."

"When was this?"

"After he'd gone missing but before he turned up dead."

"What's your idea?"

"Maybe Gloria would let me spend some time in Frank's office, going through all his personal effects. Computer, file cabinets, desk, secret hiding places."

"That might be considered an invasion of privacy in some legal circles."

"Do you have a better idea?"

"You're thinking of doing this without a search warrant?"

"Just two police officers looking for clues about her husband's demise. This is the kind of detective work I do every day, something I'm pretty good at."

"Let me think about it," he said. "But we should hold off mentioning it until our meeting. Make sure she's in the right mood."

"I'm fine with that."

"Before I call her, what are you doing this weekend?"

"The funeral on Saturday. Gloria insisted on me coming. She's reserved me a seat in the funeral cortege to Fort Logan and back."

"And Sunday?"

"Haven't decided yet."

"A good decision would mean spending it with me."

"Goodbye, Mahoney. Leave me a voice mail when you have a time and date for the meeting."

Stephanie finished her lunch at the Cloud City Coffee House and walked down Harrison Street to the office of Lake County's Sheriff. She entered the building and the receptionist asked if she could help her.

"I'd like to speak to Sheriff Waters. If he's available."

"Is this a police matter?"

"No, it's personal."

"And your name is . . . ?"

"Stephanie White. I'm up from Pueblo to run the marathon

on Saturday. I can come back later if he's busy."

The receptionist picked up the handset on her phone, had a brief conversation, and told Stephanie to go through the door on her right. "He'll see you now."

After she went inside the sheriff got up from his desk and walked around to meet her, his right hand extended. "Afternoon, Ms. White. Welcome to Leadville."

"Thanks for seeing me, sheriff." He was tall with a muscular build, a black handlebar mustache with gray tips, and piercing blue eyes holding promise of patient consideration or fierce combat, depending on which side of the law you stood. A western shirt with bolo tie, khaki trousers with a silver concha belt, and shiny mahogany cowboy boots completed his colorful outfit. Overall, he was not what she expected but, on reflection, she realized that she really didn't know what to expect.

He pointed to a chair next to his desk. "Tell me what's on your mind."

His down-home aw-shucks manner could be disarming, she thought, so I'd better be careful. After sitting down she said, "I came up early for the marathon to get in a practice run before Saturday."

"And you're from Pueblo?"

"That's right. I'm a physical therapist at Parkview Medical Center."

"I've been to your hospital a couple of times. Last January on some police business, a woman wrecked her car after burning down her husband's cabin here in Leadville. Only she escaped from Parkview before we could arrest her."

"I remember hearing about that."

Eliot placed his hands on top of the desk, joined together and forming a steeple, but he said nothing.

"Um . . . the reason I'm here . . . well, it's kind of awkward. I have this friend, he works at Parkview too, and he tells me he knows you . . . used to be good friends a long time ago."

"Really? What's his name?"

"Chance Cullen."

Eliot rubbed his chin and pondered this news for a moment. "I'll be damned. Old Chance alive and well in Pueblo. You say he works there with you?"

"That's right, in housekeeping."

He pushed his chair back and crossed his legs. "Why are you here, Ms. White? Did he send you?"

"Not at all. He has no idea I'm even talking to you."

"So?"

"So I thought I'd take advantage of being in Leadville to meet you."

"Mission accomplished."

"He's pretty angry with you, sheriff."

"What did he say about me?"

"He just got released from the state penitentiary and now he's on parole. If he wasn't on parole, he'd probably be sitting here right now, asking why you ran out on him when Suarez killed your rodeo boss."

"He was in the pen?"

"For ten horrible years, sentenced to fifteen but out early because of good behavior. He was convicted of manslaughter, took the rap because nobody was left to testify on his behalf. He blames you for not being there when he needed you."

"So he's your friend, huh?"

"Yes, a close one and I want to help him. We have a pretty

good relationship and it could grow into something even more meaningful."

"Well, Ms. White, your *close friend* is an idiot. Or he was back then when Suarez flew off the handle. I tried to pull Chance away from the crime scene and high tail it out of there with me, cross the border and lay low until the whole thing blew over. He had no more to do with that shooting than me. But some jail-happy cop needing a collar or a district attorney trying to add another notch to his prosecution gun belt wasn't going to buy it. I'm sorry he wound up doing time but it was his own fault. He's got no beef with me. If he'd done what I told him, he'd never have been locked up."

"He doesn't see it that way, sheriff. Not that way at all."

"Then maybe you can explain it to him. Get him to see the light, enjoy the good relationship you two have, and start a new life."

She looked downward at her clenched hands for a moment. "He said they used to call you Muddy."

"Muddy?" He chuckled. "That they did. Always seemed to find a bit of wet sod when a bronco told me my time was up. Did he tell you what we called him?"

"No."

"Last Chance Cullen. Toward the end of the day, telling him that some bronco or Brahma bull was his last chance for a big payday. Or maybe some over-the-hill filly in a cantina was his last chance to get lucky."

She glared at him. "I don't consider myself in *that* category."

Eliot came around and sat on the corner of his desk. "Maybe I'm being too hard. He's basically a good man, Chance, and I think he's pretty lucky finding someone like you who believes in him and wants to help him get back on his feet."

"Thanks, sheriff, I appreciate that."

"I'm planning on coming down to Pueblo next weekend myself. I've got some fence mending to do with a pretty close friend."

She smiled. "Anyone I might know?"

"I doubt it. She's a detective in your city's police department."

"Really? That's an interesting situation."

"Now, you'll have to excuse me, Ms. White, I have some patrolling to do. Hope everything works out for the best."

Sharon breathed a sigh of relief when she left the Fort Logan cemetery and got into the air conditioned limousine from the Kapoulis funeral home. The graveside service had been brief but the summer heat had made it unpleasant for everyone even though most had been seated under a large tent-like canopy.

The limousine driver, no longer required to be part of a cortege caravan, headed south. The other four passengers, who had been rather talkative on the way up from Pueblo, were quiet. Sharon thought they had learned she was a police detective and didn't want to share any sensitive information. *Just as well, gives me time to think.*

And think she did as the car turned into C-470, the beltway which partially circles the south side of Denver. The last time she'd been on this stretch of highway was last January when she and Eliot were chasing a deranged Leslie Krag in a blinding snowstorm. It had ended badly for Leslie, now paralyzed for life and a prisoner in her own home. Strangely enough, it had brought Sharon and Eliot much closer. But now their relationship was strained because of Cassie Maugham's sudden return.

Sharon put Eliot out of her mind as the limousine sped south on I-25 and passed Castle Rock. She recalled the graveside burial ceremony, the first military funeral she'd ever witnessed. The caisson carrying the flag-draped casket, the chaplain's simple but comforting remarks with glistening snowcapped peaks of the Rockies' front range behind him, and how everyone flinched when the honor guard fired a volley of shots with their rifles. The bugler played the slow and mournful Taps, and it brought tears to her eyes, but she wasn't crying for Frank Streckfus, a man she'd never met. The tears were for Gloria, Kate, Joanna, and all the veterans who died in Afghanistan, Iraq and Viet Nam. She recalled the two soldiers in dress blue uniforms folding the casket's flag so precisely in half, then in short snappy motions, back and forth, until the final shape was a triangle with three white stars prominent on the blue field. Finally, an officer with eagle insignia on his shoulders knelt in front of Gloria, presented her the flag and said, "On behalf of the President of the United States, the United States Army, and a grateful nation, please accept this flag as a symbol of our appreciation for your husband's honorable and faithful service." Sharon dabbed her eyes with a tissue while the other passengers only stared in uncomfortable silence.

They arrived at the funeral home shortly after five o'clock. She desperately wanted to get home and have a stiff drink but saw Gloria standing at the funeral home's front door, waving and wanting Sharon to join her.

"I had a call from the FBI agent," said Gloria, "suggesting the three of us get together. I assume you know about that."

"I do. He owes you a status report on their investigation and I've got some ideas of my own about our next step."

"He mentioned you two searching Frank's office for clues."

Sharon became angry but Gloria continued, "Don't be mad, detective. I pressured him into telling me what you were thinking."

Sharon said, "We thought it would be better to explain it *after* the funeral."

"I understand, but I'm just as anxious as you are to find the killer."

"Then you're all right with us digging through his personal effects?"

"My attorney advised against it but I'll allow it. With certain limitations."

"What are they?" *This could mean a lot of work with little or nothing to show for it.*

"I want to be there in his office when you're doing it, even though it may take several days. You can make notes but nothing leaves the room. Is that understood?"

"I think we can live with that but what happens if we find evidence?"

"Evidence?"

"Right, information or clues pointing to the commission of a crime."

"The only crime I care about is Frank's murder. I want that bastard found, convicted and executed. End of story."

"We want that too, Gloria. But there's the possibility, however remote, that something may happen, some piece of information we may find that points to the potential for another crime having been committed. As officers of the law, neither Special Agent Mahoney nor I can ignore that."

"I won't have Frank's reputation tarnished or his legacy destroyed."

Sharon feared they were about to reach an impasse. "Let me

give Mahoney a call and see if he's OK with your restrictions."

"Fine. I'd like to start this process tomorrow."

"Um . . . can I get back to you on that?"

"Do it."

Gloria left and Sharon went to her car which she'd left in the funeral home's parking lot. She sat for a minute before starting the engine. *Think I'm going to need more than one stiff drink.*

CHAPTER EIGHTEEN

Sharon poured herself a healthy shot of Cutty Sark over two ice cubes as soon as she got home. She took the tumbler into the bathroom, had a shower and changed into a T-shirt and shorts. Back in the kitchen, she put a frozen lasagna into the oven and looked over her mail: couple of bills, an ad for a credit card, and a Land's End catalogue. She finished her drink and poured another, not quite as large as the first, and called Dan Mahoney. "You ready for some business?" she said.

"Sure. How was the funeral?"

"A beautiful service and very impressive with all the military pageantry but terribly hot. They had a canopy but it wasn't big enough to give everybody some shade."

"How's Mrs. Streckfus?"

"That's why I'm calling. I talked with her at the funeral home when we got back. She said you already mentioned the three of us having a meeting and going through Frank's office. I'm not very happy about that, *Special Agent.*"

"The woman forced me into it, Sharon. She seems different somehow, on a crusade or something. She's taking charge, more in control, aggressive, even abrasive. Not sure what I'm talking about here."

"Well said, Mahoney. I agree with you. She's changed and wants to find her husband's killer, even letting us rummage through his office. Her lawyer doesn't like the idea but she's going ahead with it anyway."

"Score one for our team."

"Don't pop the champagne cork just yet." She described Gloria's conditions for the search. Mahoney didn't respond after she'd finished. "Dan?"

"Sorry, just thinking. If we start our *excavations* tomorrow, what's to stop Mrs. Streckfus from cleaning out her husband's office now? Taking anything that looks remotely suspicious and running it through the shredder or erasing his computer?"

"Nothing at all."

"She's had plenty of time to do this. Days and nights."

"Right, I get it."

"So the likelihood of us finding any *evidence* is about nil."

"Probably so, but I still think we should do it. Even for show. Two dedicated law officers doing their duty. And, who knows? We may get lucky."

"Speaking of getting lucky, when are we having our next date?"

His sudden subject change along with the sexual innuendo caused her to splutter the scotch and ice cube she had in her mouth. "Tomorrow afternoon at the Streckfus residence?"

"How about Mass again tomorrow morning? And brunch afterwards?"

Sharon hesitated. "OK, I'll meet you at the church, same time as before."

"Great. I'll call Mrs. Streckfus and let her know we'll be coming about two-ish."

Later that evening, as Sharon was at her computer, Eliot called. "Just thinking about you," she said. "How's the marathon going?"

"Finished for this year. I think most of the runners have cleaned themselves up and tucking into a big meal right about now."

"Are you expecting any trouble tonight?"

"No, but we're ready, just in case. Did you attend the funeral?"

She gave him a report, almost identical to the one she told Dan Mahoney, including a brief mention of her planned activity on Sunday afternoon at the Streckfus home. "We may not find anything but we have to go through the motions, I guess."

"So if you find something that smells like evidence she won't let you have it."

"Correct."

"But you can make notes, take them to the D. A. and maybe get him to convene a grand jury. Or something else along those lines if it looks serious."

"That's a possibility."

"Any others?"

"Appeal to Gloria's sense of justice, fair play, civic responsibility."

"Somehow that doesn't seem too promising." He paused. "Wonder if the mayor knows about your little fishing expedition."

"Mansfield?"

"You told me once that he asked Mrs. Streckfus about some papers the Mr. might have left behind. I recall this happened when he went missing but before he was found murdered."

"You've got a good memory. And having him involved in this is another complication that we don't need."

"Those two fellows were good friends so it seems logical that the mayor would be a mite concerned about two police officers rooting around his buddy's office."

"I'm getting a headache, Eliot, thinking about all this crap. It's still Mahoney's case and I'm just along for the ride."

"Well then. On a more pleasant note, I had an interesting experience Thursday when a woman came into my office with a fascinating story."

"Not that damn Cassie woman again."

"Whoa, Nellie. Her name is Stephanie White and she's a physical therapist at Parkview Medical."

Sharon calmed down. "Was she in some kind of trouble?"

"No, she was up for the marathon. But she's in a relationship with a guy I knew back in my rodeo days. He works at the hospital too, that's where they met."

"And he asked her to look you up?"

"Not quite. She told me he didn't know she'd be talking to me."

Sharon hesitated. "Think I'm missing something here."

"It's kind of a long story but me and this guy, Cullen's his name, parted on bad terms many years ago. He's on parole after finishing a stretch at the state pen in Canon City. I'll tell you everything when I come down next weekend."

"Yes, I'd like to hear more. What about Cullen? Are you going to contact him?"

"I don't know. Maybe, maybe not. He may not want to see me again. I'd like to get your opinion on it before I decide."

"I can hardly wait," she said. "We'll have plenty to talk about. I can give you input on the Cullen business and you can help me with the Streckfus case. How does that sound?"

"A win-win all around. Let's do it."

After the call Sharon took two aspirin and watched the end of an old movie on TV. She got ready for bed but remembered she hadn't turned off her computer. As she started the shutdown sequence, she noticed a new e-mail in her INBOX and opened it. There were no words in the subject block and the red letters of text startled her.

**BITCH. YOUR IN WAY OVER YOUR HEAD.
I KNOW WHERE YOU LIVE.
BACK OFF NOW BEFORE ITS TOO LATE.**

Sharon had a restless night, tossing and turning. Though she had the ceiling fan going and the overnight temperature had cooled, she awoke at 2:15 A.M. soaked in perspiration. She went to the kitchen, took two aspirin with half a bottle of cold water from the refrigerator and went back to bed.

She lay still in the darkness and thought about the threatening e-mail, making a mental list of possible senders: Brian Mansfield and various felons she'd arrested who were now serving time in prison, although anyone in the latter category would probably be a long shot. Letting her mind ramble, she reluctantly admitted that even Gloria Streckfus or Leslie Krag, the deranged woman she and Eliot had chased last January, could have done it.

The sender's e-mail address was also puzzling; n4L7k2c9a@axtel.net.mx. *How could anyone on my suspect list send it from Mexico?* She'd never be able to remember that string of characters if it were her own address but, under present circumstances, she'd never forget it. There were ways to backtrack and find the identity of the sender but that particular talent was above her pay grade. Ironically, she might have persuaded Frank Streckfus to have one of his buddies at NSA perform a bit of detective work on her behalf. Or maybe Dan

Mahoney has a contact at *No Such Agency,* as Washington politicos sometimes called it.

She gave up the ghost about four o'clock and slept soundly, waking up to bright sunshine about eight o'clock with a panicky feeling that she'd overslept.

Her headache was gone. She read *The Pueblo Chieftain* over coffee and a toasted English muffin, scanning the front page coverage of councilman Frank Streckfus' funeral. The paper's photographer got a beautiful and poignant picture of the kneeling officer presenting the flag to Gloria. She put the paper aside without finishing the article, ate the last of her muffin and went to the bathroom for a shower.

Sharon was seriously introspective during Mass, her thoughts hopping around to the Streckfus case, to the mysterious e-mail, and to her relationship with Eliot coming in a distant third. Dan Mahoney must have suspected something was amiss because he didn't try any close encounters this time when the celebrant priest urged everyone to extend the Sign of Peace to their neighbor.

They went to IHOP again for brunch. After the waitress took their orders Dan said, "All right, what's going on with you?"

"Huh? Or, sorry. Have a lot on my mind right now."

"One of your cases or the Streckfus business?"

She pulled out a folded paper from her purse and slid it over to him. "Probably more of a personal thing."

Dan unfolded it and read over the entire e-mail which she'd printed. "Hope this is not some kind of joke. Any idea who sent it?"

"Could be any number of suspects. At this point, the one most likely would be the mayor. I'm pretty sure he knows what we're doing and doesn't want us poking around in

Streckfus' office."

"But this e-mail came from Mexico. Or at least through an ISP down there. You know anyone south of the border?"

"Not a soul." She paused to sip her orange juice. "Any chance of you checking it out for me?"

He folded up the paper and gave her a bright smile. "For you? Of course, I'll give it the highest priority."

Sharon was tempted to say something equally as snarky but kept silent.

Their omelets arrived and the conversation was muted for several minutes. "How do we handle the digging this afternoon?" she asked.

"Completely professional, of course. I've got an idea I want to bounce off you."

"Then bounce away."

"Because of Mrs. Streckfus' ground rules, we can take notes but that's it. Not a big deal because, as I said before, she's probably removed stuff already. Since she's giving us no advantage at all, we should give her the same in return. We make our own set of notes but we say *nothing* to each other while we're in his office. We'll be like Sphinxes, steal away to huddle later and figure out what we have."

"What's the advantage for us not talking while we're searching?"

"It puts her on the defensive. Maybe she'll feel sorry for herself and spill some dirty secrets."

She gave him a jaundiced look. "I think you've been reading too many comics."

"Heck, I don't know what's best. Never done this kind of thing before. But I do believe we have to protect ourselves and the integrity of this case, assuming there's anything here at all. It's the longest of shots, Sharon, looking for something crucial in Pueblo for a murder that happened in Kabul."

"Then we play it by ear."

"Right. With our eyes wide open."

"Then we'd better have some more coffee."

They both laughed as Dan poured some more into their cups.

Gloria Streckfus greeted them cooly at the front door and led them directly to Frank's office. Sharon and Dan looked around the room, taking visual inventory of two bookcases, a single file cabinet, and a large oak desk whose top had just seen a coat of furniture polish. A desktop computer rested on a table in back of the desk, connected to a printer, and could be operated by a person sitting in the brown leather chair by turning 180 degrees. Sharon thought his office was probably the cleanest in Pueblo, much cleaner than her home office or her cubicle at the police department.

"How about a soft drink?" said Gloria. "I've made some ice tea if you'd rather have that." Dan and Sharon opted for the iced tea. "Please go ahead and start, I'll be right back."

Dan walked over to the computer. "How are you with Macs?" he said.

"I love Macs. Have a laptop at home and a desk machine at work."

"Why don't you have a go at it and I'll start with the file cabinet."

Sharon sat in the swivel chair and turned on the computer. Dan pulled a load of files from the cabinet and took them to a love seat along a side wall. Sharon breathed a sigh of relief when the first display came up and didn't request a password. She began by methodically checking file folders with ordinary names: Army, Council, BusLtrs, PersLtrs, Finances, RealEstate, etc.

Gloria returned with their ice tea. She took a comfortable seat in a far corner of the room, opened a hard cover novel and began reading.

Sharon made only a few innocuous notes on her tablet during the first hour, more for show than content, and felt her attention span and level of interest starting to wane. She occasionally glanced at Dan, exchanging weak smiles without saying anything, and thought he was getting to the same uncomfortable situation.

Sharon stood. "I need a potty break, Gloria. May I use your bathroom?"

"Sure, turn left when you go out the door."

When she came back, Dan took a similar break.

Close to the three-hour mark, Sharon felt totally saturated. She was looking at Frank's e-mail files when Dan stood, looking as tired as she felt.

Before either Dan or Sharon could speak, Mayor Mansfield entered the room and stared at all three startled people. "What the hell's going on here?"

Gloria stood and faced him. "They're looking for clues, Brian, anything that might be related to Frank's murder."

"And you have a bona fide search warrant for this, Detective Hardcastle?"

"No sir, we don't. But Mrs. Streckfus gave us permission."

Mansfield turned back to Gloria. "Are you out of your mind? This is highly illegal what these two are doing whether you allowed it or not. Did you bother to ask your attorney about this? No, you probably didn't. I want them out of here immediately."

"Now just a minute," said Gloria. "I did consult with my attorney and asked these people to come here today. And you've got a lot of nerve, Brian, barging in here like this. It's my home and I'll do what I damn please."

Dan went over and stood next to Gloria and Mansfield. "We're here to help, Mr. Mayor. I know that sounds like a cliché but it's true."

"I'm going to call your station chief, Mahoney, and the police chief, Hardcastle. You'll both be lucky having jobs before the sun sets."

Sharon shut down the computer, grabbed her tablet and went to the doorway. "Let's go, Agent Mahoney. We're wasting our time here."

Dan gathered up his notes and said to Gloria as he was leaving, "Sorry it turned out this way. I'll be in touch."

Sharon was sitting in her car behind the steering wheel when Dan came out the front door. She waved him over and he got into the passenger seat. "Damn it all," said Dan, "that Mansfield is some piece of work. Looking more like a crook every time I see him. Maybe I should have asked him about having friends in Mexico." Getting no response to his tirade, he glanced over at her. "What are you smiling about?"

"Would you believe Frank Streckfus made a tiny error? Seems he moved some e-mails to the trash can before he left the country."

"How do you know that? And why is that a mistake?"

"They're still on his computer. He forgot to empty the trash before shutting it down."

"My God, did you get a look at them?"

"Better than that. I forwarded them to my personal account."

He lunged at her and, both hands clasping the sides of her

head, gave her a long warm kiss. "You are fantastic."

"Why thank you, Special Agent. Now why don't you get in your car and follow me. I'll fire up my beloved Mac, print some e-mails, pour us a drink, and we can talk to each other."

CHAPTER NINETEEN

Dan Mahoney parked along the curb in front of Sharon's house and watched her pull into the garage. She opened the front door and he went inside, at once feeling comfortable in the coolness, the welcome feeling of the off-white walls, the tasteful furniture and minimal display of pictures and knick knacks. The home of a professional, he thought, but still on the feminine side, a person who navigates the human jungle but enjoys coming back to her refuge for comfort and security.

"How about a drink, Dan?"

"We're not going to see those e-mails first?"

"No hurry, they're not going anywhere. And we don't have any artificial limitations like the last place."

He slipped an arm around her waist. "No limitations? I like that."

She pulled his arm away and went out to the kitchen. "I'm having a vodka tonic. I've got beer or Pepsi if you'd rather."

He joined her. "Vodka tonic is fine with me." He watched her make the drinks, carefully slicing a fresh lime and squeezing it over the glass. "You've obviously tended bar at one time in your life."

"Dad was the mixologist. Taught me how to fix a few potent potables. You'll have to try my Singapore sling sometime."

He took a sip of his drink. "Nice. I would definitely like to sample your sling, bling, and any other *goodies* you might care to dispense."

"You have a one track mind, Mahoney."

"Wherever that particular train takes me."

"Well, my dad also had some advice for me, freely given whenever he was mixing. Such as, 'Run for the roundhouse, Nellie, he can't corner you there.'"

Dan laughed. "Sounds like a cue to start looking at some e-mails."

Sharon lead the way back to one of her bedrooms, which doubled as an office, and turned on her computer. Dan pulled up a chair and watched as she clicked on her e-mail icon and the INBOX began to fill.

When the process stopped Dan said, "Looks like we hit the jackpot."

"Some of them looked plain vanilla but several may be important."

Sharon started printing each e-mail, two copies at a time. "What about Frank's computer?" he asked. "You didn't delete the ones in the trash can, did you?"

"Not at all. I left them, but each one will have a little arrow, showing it's been forwarded somewhere."

"Not a problem, I hope."

"Shouldn't be."

"I've been thinking about the councilman," he said. "A fairly distinguished military career, successful in business, and a trusted political leader here in Pubelo. So the question comes to mind . . . why did he get mixed up with all this crap in Iraq and Afghanistan? Was it the money? I mean, how much does a guy need?"

"It's been bothering me too, Dan. All through the funeral I kept having the same thoughts. And now he's left a widow to clean up the mess and whatever else we uncover as well. Gloria talked about his legacy. I wonder what kind of legacy helps her daughters become adults without their father around?"

"I don't know, Sharon. Don't have a clue."

She collected the printer's output and separated the pages into two piles. "I've put them into chronological order, Dan, the oldest on top so we can follow the sequence of events."

They picked up the first e-mail from their respective stack and started reading.

From: strikeronezero@comcast.net
To: retloc81005@gmail.cm
Subject: My trip
You are really a horse's ass, you know that? OK, I'm leaving for a few days, against my better judgement, and will meet Younis in R town. Will try to get this unscrewed. You'd better get Hagerty in line or this venture's heading south.

"R town is Riyadh," said Dan, "and Younis is probably Prince Abdullah Faisal Mohammed, the one I told you about."

"And I'm pretty sure that number in the 'To' line is the ZIP code for City Hall. So 'retloc' must be his honor the mayor. Who's Hagerty?"

"Don't know," he said.

Sharon picked up the next e-mail, giggled a bit and crumpled it up into a ball.

"What was that?"

"A joke. Chris Christie's top ten tips for losing weight."

The next e-mail was more serious.

From: strikeronezero@comcast.net
To: younis@sahara.com.sa
Subject: Heading your way
Arriving RUH 10:00 PM Tuesday on Saudia 208 via Rome. Request reservation at 4 S. Will stay as long as necessary to iron out money flows to Z town. Expect your full cooperation. Have no desire to see Hagerty in the big sand pile any time soon.

"Ah, Mr. Hagerty again," said Dan. "I have a feeling he's the contact in Kabul for the operation and probably not a nice guy."

"And Z town?"

"Zurich, most likely. Swiss banks with one or more numbered accounts for hiding all the salvage revenues."

They continued reading e-mails. Only one more was relevant, confirmation of Streckfus' reservation at Four Seasons. The rest were jokes or items related to city council business.

"So, what do you think, Special Agent?"

"We did some excellent work today, Detective." He leaned forward and managed to give her a side-of-the-mouth kiss. "You and I make a great team and I think we should have another drink."

Sharon took a moment to shut off her computer. "I'm really tired, Dan. I've been putting in a lot of extra hours on this case and haven't had a day off in a while. What I'd like to do is have a bowl of soup, take a shower and hit the sack."

"I understand."

She took his hand. "We are a good team, no question about it. Can I give you a rain check on that drink?"

"Sure. I need to head back to my office anyway and contact our man in Kabul. See if he can get a line on this Hagerty guy."

She walked him to the front door. "Let me know what you find out."

"Of course. But I don't want to wake you if you're sleeping."

"Send me an e-mail. I'll check my computer when I get up." She gave him a direct kiss this time and he pulled her into a warm hug.

"You sure I can't fix up my own brand of soup for you? I serve it with lots of TLC along with the crackers."

"So long, Dan. And don't forget to check out the e-mail I got from Mexico."

"Hasta La Vista, Baby," he said, walking down the sidewalk and singing, "South of the border, down Mexico way."

She watched him drive away. *If I wasn't so tired, I would have had another drink which could have lead to something else. And that might not have been so bad at all.*

Sharon woke to her alarm clock at 6:00 A.M. on Monday and felt fully refreshed after a solid nine hours of sleep. While having her first cup of coffee, she turned on her computer and found an e-mail from Dan Mahoney.

Hi Partner, I got lucky. A Bureau Buddy tracked your crazy e-mail to a shop in Nogales, just over the AZ border at I-19. The sender was listed as Clarke Layton with a Phoenix address. Who is this guy? Looking forward to more hugs, kisses and your Singapore sling, Dan.

Clarke Layton? What the hell?

She called Eliot immediately and woke him from a sound sleep. "Sorry, but I just got some disturbing news."

"About the Streckfus murder?"

"Not at all, but I'll tell you about that later." She read him the threatening e-mail which she'd received yesterday. "This is bullshit, Eliot."

"All right, calm down now. Any idea who sent it?"

"I sure do. My FBI pal has a buddy who traced it. Clarke Layton sent it, Leslie Krag's stupid private eye. He sent it from Nogales through a Mexican ISP. That woman needs to be institutionalized."

Silence.

"Are you there?"

"It wasn't Leslie Krag."

"How do you know that?"

"Are you sitting down? Promise you won't go into orbit when I tell you."

"I'm sitting, I'm sitting. Tell me."

"It goes back to Cassie Maugham."

"Her?"

"When she showed up in Leadville, I asked her how she found me. Turns out Layton set up shop in Phoenix and she hired him. A crazy coincidence but I didn't give it much thought at the time."

"Well you'd better think real hard about it now. That woman has gone too far and that e-mail really upset me. She needs to be locked up, having her private eye send me threats like that. He could lose his license."

Eliot chuckled. "As you'll recall, he has a nasty habit of doing stupid things like that. One of the reasons he's not living in Colorado anymore."

"If Layton lives in Phoenix he shouldn't be too hard to find."

"Leave it with me, Sharon. I'll give the Maricopa County Sheriff a call and ask him for a favor, a little professional courtesy to settle it."

Sharon made a nervous laugh. "Good idea. Get Sheriff Joe to put Mr. Layton in a pink suit. Think your Cassie friend would look good in pink?"

"Those two can't hurt you, Sharon. They're just trying to scare you." He paused and continued, "How did your meeting go with Mrs. Streckfus?"

"It was a lot of work, but I'm pressed for time this morning. Can I call you about noon? It's quite a long story."

"Noon is fine. Maybe I'll have some good news for you by then."

Chance was doing warm-up exercises at Mineral Palace Park early Monday morning when Stephanie arrived. Instead of walking from her car, she jogged straight into him, knocked him on the ground and showered him with kisses as they rolled around together in the cool damp grass.

When they came up for air he said, "Guess you're glad to see me."

"Can't believe how much I missed you." She kissed him three times, once on the lips and on each cheek. "Mm, mm, mm."

He laughed. "And you're not concerned about PDA?"

"What public? It's just that old fellow by the lake walking his dog and he doesn't care two hoots about us."

He slid his hands inside the back of her shorts and began gyrating his pelvis.

She broke free and jumped up. "Guess you missed me too."

Chance got up. "Wasn't sure you'd be here today. How'd the marathon go?"

"Not bad at all. Had to get back here and make sure you were following our exercise program."

"*Your* exercise program. Did you win it?"

'Came in 34th and that's better than last time. Even beat Erica and Alexis."

"I want to hear what you three did when you weren't running?"

"Oh no, that's very secret, hush hush and confidential. What happens in Leadville stays in Leadville."

"Glad I asked. Ready for twenty laps around the pool?"

"Let me warm up first and then we'll see how far *you* can go."

Together they did a series of jumping jacks, windmills, deep knee bends and pushups. They jogged side-by-side without conversation and did four solid laps before returning to their clothing stacks and sitting down together under the shade of a large oak tree. Chance unfolded two small towels he'd brought from home, gave her one and dried himself off with the other.

"What did you do while I was away?" she said.

"Nothing like your adventure. A workout every morning followed by cleaning up everyone's mess at good old Snarkview."

"And after work?"

"Home to bed and sleeping alone in a cold bed."

"You poor thing."

"I did get a few things done. That list you gave me? I have an appointment with a doctor in Adult Outpatient Services on Wednesday morning."

She leaned closer and put a hand on his. "Good for you. I know he'll be able to help with those nightmares."

"I've also been thinking about my job and the schedule they have me on. Kind of hard adjusting to the sleep routine working those kinds of hours."

"Are you thinking of leaving Parkview?"

"Not really. But when I first talked to Julian, I could have taken a job in the kitchen and worked the same hours you do."

"Why didn't you?"

"Thought I'd be partying after work and sleeping in the next day."

"And then Snow White came along and screwed up your plans."

"But I wouldn't have met you if I'd been in a back room scrubbing pots."

"See? Some things work out for the best after all. But if you want to change jobs, be sure to check all the openings. The cafeteria isn't your last chance, Chance."

"What?"

Stephanie trembled slightly. *I almost blew it.* "I'm just saying there are plenty of opportunities at the hospital."

He patted his face and neck with the towel. "Haven't heard *that* in a long time. That's what they called me back in my rodeo days. Last Chance Cullen. Always trying to win a big payday on the last bronc or bull. Did it sometimes just to get back at those smart asses."

Stephanie relaxed again. "I'm heading for the shower. You can stay and run a few more laps."

"Afraid not. Have to clean up and check in with Ms. Acosta."

They both stood. "Why don't you come out to the house after work?" she said. "If you're not too tired."

He grinned. "Thought you'd never ask."

Chapter Twenty

Eliot called a meeting with his deputies on Monday morning to review their active cases. Afterwards, he sat quietly at his desk making a to-do list on a yellow tablet. So far, he had five tasks for himself: the first three related to current cases in Lake County, number four was Clarke Layton, and number five was Chance Cullen.

He decided county business could wait and called the Maricopa County Sheriff's office. He got a short runaround but was finally connected with Deputy Sylvester "Sly" Starnes. After a bit of sheriff chit chat, Starnes said, "What can I do for you today, Sheriff Waters?"

Eliot told him about Sharon's e-mail from Clarke Layton. "Had some trouble with Mr. Layton up here on another case and I've reason to believe he's living in Phoenix somewhere."

"How does Detective Hardcastle figure into this?"

"She's a good friend and we worked a case against Layton and his client."

"And Ms. Maugham?"

"She lives in Scottsdale and was here in Leadville recently stirring up trouble. She wrecked her rental car on purpose but I couldn't prove it so I let her go. She's also a long ago personal acquaintance but I wouldn't call her a friend anymore."

Deputy Starnes seemed amused with Eliot's discomfort, sensing that there were some personal problems between Eliot and Sharon. "OK, they're both in Maricopa County. What would you like me to do about this, sheriff?"

"Put the fear of God into these people and get them to stop badgering Detective Hardcastle. Not sure there's enough hard evidence for an arrest of either one but Layton should be put out of business. Permanently."

"How about sending me that e-mail and whatever else you got on Layton?"

"I'll be happy to do that. By the way, Cassie's now married to a fellow named Winston Hume."

"Can't make any promises, Sheriff Waters. Got lots of other things on my plate at the moment but I'll try to help you."

"Much obliged, Sly. I'll get that info off to you in an e-mail this morning."

After the call, Eliot went off to the coffee stand and poured himself a cup. Back at his desk again, he thought about Chance and Stephanie White's recent visit. *Seemed like a nice woman with no ulterior motives other than acting as a peacemaker between Chance and me. Wonder if what she said was on the level?*

He called the prison at Canon City and reached Assistant Warden Travis Wilcox. "Sheriff Waters from Lake County, warden. I'm calling about a convict who was recently paroled by the name of Chance Cullen."

"What do you want to know, sheriff?"

"Whatever you can tell me."

"Is he in trouble already? Damn it, he's only been out a couple of weeks. I told him to keep his nose clean or he'd wind up in a cell block here again."

"Hold on, warden, it's nothing like that. I knew Chance a number of years ago and I just found out he'd served time in your institution."

"Oh, well. He was paroled his first time up and he's in Pueblo for all I know. You'll have to check with the parole office there."

"I'll do that. What's his prison record look like?"

"You'll have to send an official request through channels if you want that kind of information. Otherwise, I can tell you he was a pretty good inmate, one of the better ones actually. Couple of minor infractions along the way but he straightened himself out well enough to chop five years off a fifteen year sentence. Too bad more of our inmates are not like him."

"I appreciate the information, warden, and I don't have any more questions. Many thanks for taking time to talk with me."

Eliot went back to the coffee stand, filled his cup and returned to his desk. One more call, he thought, and I can get back to my real job.

He called the Parole Board office in Pueblo, reached Ms. Acosta after being shuttled around briefly and had a conversation with her similar to the one with Wilcox. He ended the call by asking her not to mention it to Cullen and she agreed.

Eliot forwarded Sharon's e-mail to Starnes and sent a longer one documenting Clarke Layton's activities six months ago. He grabbed his hat, left the building and got into his SUV. He sat behind the wheel for a moment feeling pleased with himself. He was sure that Chance was on the road to recovery and he'd done a good thing for Sharon. *And if Deputy Sly comes through with*

some good news it just might earn me some affectionate
forgiveness when we get together on Saturday.

Sharon was startled by Dan Mahoney's entrance into her office cubicle. "What are you doing here?"

"Thought I'd stroll down from my office on such a nice day. I've got some news and hoped to interest you in lunch."

She glanced at her watch. "A bit early but I could eat."

She was about to shut down her computer when Detective Debbie came around to the cubicle's entrance. "Isn't this nice," she said, holding out her hand directly to Mahoney. "Don't believe we've met. I'm Detective Wasserstein."

Sharon preempted her. "This is Special Agent Mahoney."

"You certainly *look* special. Call me Debbie."

Dan was slightly flustered but took her hand and mumbled, "My pleasure."

"You two working on a case . . . or something?"

"Yes, I'm helping Agent Mahoney . . . on something," said Sharon.

"About the Streckfus murder I should imagine."

Sharon gave Dan a sharp look which essentially said *Get Me Out Of Here.*

He took her by the arm and guided her from the building as Wasserstein called out, "Don't forget where you live, Hardtack."

Neither one said anything until they reached a diner about one block away. Once they were seated Dan said, "Must be fun working with her every day."

Sharon sighed. "The bane of my existence."

After each ordered iced tea and a club sandwich Dan asked, "Have you gotten any flack this morning over our visit yesterday with Mrs. Streckfus?"

"Strangely enough, no."

"Me neither. The mayor was pretty angry and I fully expected a royal reaming from the boss this morning."

"Maybe Mansfield is waiting for the right moment. Timing is everything with politicians, you know."

"Either that or creating a big firestorm right now would reveal too much of his out-of-country partnership with the late Mr. Streckfus."

They stopped talking while the waitress delivered their food. After she left, Sharon said, "You said you had some news for me."

"We know a lot more about Edward Hagerty. He left Kabul the day after Streckfus was murdered on a flight to Zurich, stayed there a day, and flew to New York. After that, we don't know where he went."

"Who is this guy Hagerty?"

"He's Army, like Streckfus. A supply sergeant who left the service under less than honorable conditions. He landed a job in Kabul with a company that has a government contract. Have you ever read Catch-22?"

"A long time ago."

"You might remember a character named Milo Minderbinder, a lieutenant in Yossarian's squadron who was the mess officer. But Milo's real claim to fame was his ability to profit from the war. That's Hagerty, a modern Minderbinder. The Army's strategy in Afghanistan is to recover everything and bring it back, no matter what the condition, so it doesn't fall into the hands of Al Queda or the Taliban. With some clever inventory management techniques, equipment can slide out the back door while money comes into his pockets. That's the essence of his scam."

"*That's treason.* Helping the enemy and getting rich while he does it."

"Yeah, add that to a murder charge and he'll spend the rest of his life in prison."

Sharon dropped a chunk of her sandwich on her plate. "It's been a week since Hagerty got to New York. He could be anywhere now."

"True."

"Even in Pueblo."

"Bingo."

"You think he's here now?"

"I wouldn't be surprised. Think back to those e-mails we swiped from Streckfus' computer. Hagerty has a connection with both Streckfus and Mansfield, some kind of problem that required Streckfus to get back to Kabul and get it ironed out."

"And he gets a knife in the belly for his troubles."

"The hotel room is searched and Hagerty probably comes away with nothing so he flies to Zurich, claims some money, and then heads to New York."

"Then he's coming to see the mayor and get everything straightened out. You think Mansfield knows about this? Should we give him a heads up?"

"He'd be a fool if he didn't have suspicions. Our best bet is to keep an eye on him, his home, and all the other places he frequents. We don't want to tip our hand and give anything away on this case unless it's absolutely necessary."

Sharon's cell phone, lying on the table next to her ice tea, made some music. She glanced at the screen and continued to let it ring.

"You going to answer that?" said Dan.

"It's not urgent, I'll call him back later."

He looked at the screen, trying to read the caller ID even though it was upside down. "Maybe some news about that e-mail you got from Mexico."

"Later, Dan."

"Sorry, I wasn't trying to pressure you."

The phone went silent. "It was my friend, Eliot Waters. He's the Lake County sheriff and we have sort of a relationship."

"Professional or personal?"

"Little bit of both." She paused to take a deep breath. "You traced that e-mail back to a guy named Clarke Layton, a private eye who used to live in Denver. He had a client who burned down her husband's cabin in Leadville, crashed her car on U. S 50 and wound up in Parkview Medical. Eliot and I worked that case and Layton left Colorado. His detective practices were unethical and bordered on being illegal"

"So Layton's trying to get revenge?"

"Not Layton. His client."

"I don't get it. The woman arsonist is just *now* trying to get revenge?"

"No, another client. An old girlfriend of Eliot, lives in the Phoenix area."

"Ah, I'm beginning to see the light. If she can't have him, then no other woman gets him either."

Sharon made a crooked smile. "Good thinking, Agent Mahoney."

"Hmm." He reached across the table and took her hand. "This spot of trouble could actually turn out well for me . . . and us."

"Us?"

"Sure, why not?"

She pulled back her hand and grasped her glass of iced tea. "Give me some time to think about that."

Sharon and Dan returned to their respective offices after lunch. She found a note on her chair; Gloria Streckfus had called and asked her to drop by any time after work for a chat about an important matter. Good timing, she thought. I can give her an update on this Hagerty guy.

She retrieved her cell phone's voice mail and heard a petulant message from Eliot, wondering why she hadn't called him as promised. She first checked the adjoining cubicle and made sure that Debbie Wassertein was absent. She called Eliot and apologized when he answered, saying that urgent police matters had taken up her free time. "Stuff about the councilman's murder?" he wondered.

"Right. I learned about the FBI's work in Afghanistan." She went on to give the details about Edward Hagerty which Mahoney had related at lunch, ending with a somber statement about the mayor's dirty hands and the jeopardy he's in.

"Are you or the FBI talking to the mayor?"

"We're pretty sure he knows *something* about this but for now the FBI is only watching him closely."

"Be careful, Sharon, and don't get yourself hurt by this case."

"I hear you loud and clear, Eliot."

"On another subject, I talked with a deputy sheriff over in Maricopa County this morning and he's going to have a talk with Mr. Layton and then Ms. Maugham. He's pretty busy right now and made no promises, but I have a hunch he'll follow through with something soon."

"Thanks. Please keep me posted."

"Will do, and keep cool."

"Easy for you to say with those low temperatures at 11,000 feet."

Sharon disconnected and turned on her computer. But before she could call up one of her case files, Debbie Wassertein appeared at the cubicle's entry. "Oh good, you're back from lunch. You got something going with that gorgeous man?"

"Sorry to disappoint you, Deborah, but no. We're only collaborating."

"Ooh, collaborating, coordinating . . . and soon to be cohabitating. *Hoo Ha*."

Sharon pointedly ignored her and opened her case file. Wasserstein went back to her own cubicle, humming a tune sounding suspiciously like the wedding march from *Lohengrin*.

CHAPTER TWENTY-ONE

Sharon pulled into the Streckfus driveway about six o'clock. She felt nervous arriving close to the dinner hour but it was the best she could do. There was a city-wide crime epidemic of rent checks being stolen from apartment lock boxes and Sgt. Hess had called a late afternoon meeting to review the problem.

Her fears were allayed when Gloria answered the front door. "Come inside, Sharon. Let's go back to the sun porch where it's cooler."

Sharon sat in an overstuffed white chair liberally decorated with printed yellow daisies and sunflowers. The view of a neighbor's back yard wasn't too interesting but the room was cool and comfortable. "How about some wine?" said Gloria.

"Sure, I'm off duty now."

She poured two generous glasses of Chardonnay, handed one to Sharon and sat across from her. "To happier times," said Gloria, lifting her glass in a toast.

"That's for sure," said Sharon, taking a big sip. "You wanted to talk about something."

"You read my mind, just like a true detective. After you and your FBI colleague left yesterday, I had a good talk with his honor,

The Lord Mayor of Pueblo."

Sharon tried to stifle a soft laugh but Gloria noticed.

"Oh, don't be shocked. He's so full of himself and I can't take him seriously after all these years. But he had an interesting proposition. Wants me to take Frank's seat on the city council."

"Really?"

"That's right. If the seat remains open, there's the possibility of a tie when issues come up for a vote during council meetings. He figures if I take the seat, he'll have an ally on the council and I'll rubber stamp every one of his pet projects."

"Can he do that?"

"He has the authority to fill it with a person of his choice. The political thing to do is get somebody he can count on, although I'm not sure that I'd care to be his duty stooge. Of course, this person has to live in Pueblo, be a registered voter and obviously one without a prison record. It also makes sense. In the Federal government, governors have appointed widows to fill the seats of representatives or senators who've passed away while in office."

"Are you going to do it?"

"Not sure. Told him I'd think about it."

Sharon touched her glass against Gloria's. "You'll do a great job, I'm sure of it."

"Thanks, Sharon. And if I do, I'll need all the support I can get." She pointed at her, adding, "And that means *you*."

She went back to the refrigerator, brought the bottle of wine out to the sun porch and refilled their glasses. "By the way, I guess you noticed I wasn't too happy with Brian when he showed up yesterday."

"I did. Thanks for coming to our defense."

"I got him calmed down and he finally agreed not to call your boss today. Ditto for the Special Agent."

"I was wondering about that. Kept expecting to be hauled on the carpet by the chief and have my butt chewed out."

"Don't think you're totally off the hook, Sharon. You'd better keep a low profile for a while and not get him agitated."

"Thanks, much appreciated." She took a full sip of wine.

A loud commotion in the hallway interrupted their conversation, followed by the entry of Kate and Joanna, Gloria's teenage daughters, into the sun porch. The girls paused momentarily when they noticed Sharon but Kate, the older sister asked, "Dinner almost ready, Mom?"

"Later. Look in the fridge and help yourselves to some carrots or celery stalks."

Joanna pulled the side of her mouth open with a finger and made an exaggerated retching sound.

"*Later, girls*," said Gloria frostily.

They did a prompt turnaround and left in a cloud of giggles.

"Have to admire their youthful spirit," said Gloria, "even if it does get on my nerves sometimes." She paused for a moment. "What are your people telling you about finding my husband's murderer?"

Sharon almost choked on her wine and, during a coughing spasm, tried to come up with an answer.

"You know something. What is it?"

"Has Agent Mahoney talked with you at all today?"

"No, he hasn't. *What's going on?*"

"Look, I shouldn't be talking about this. It's the FBI's case, not mine."

"I'm his widow and I have a right to know."

"OK, I have some news. Have you ever heard of a man

named Hagerty?"

The relaxed look on Gloria's face changed to one of puzzled concern. "The name rings a bell . . . I don't know . . . maybe one of Frank's old business associates. What about him?"

"I had lunch today with Agent Mahoney. The FBI in Kabul believes Hagerty is the number one murder suspect."

"He's in Kabul, this Hagerty man?"

"Unfortunately, no. He left the country the day after the murder."

"Who is he? And why do they think he's the killer?"

"They don't know for sure if he's the one or not. He's only a suspect at this point. They want to find him and question him."

Gloria wrung her hands nervously and took a deep breath. "Where did he go, do they know?"

"They tracked him to Zurich. He was there for a day and then flew to New York. But they lost his trail and not sure where he is now."

"Good God, that was . . . over a week ago. He could be anywhere."

"Sad, but true."

Gloria went over to the tall glass panels at the edge of the room, stood quietly for several moments while staring into the distance, and turned around. "Frank had a saying when crazy things were happening and beyond his control. 'This is way above my pay grade.' That's the way I feel right now. I don't get it."

"Do you feel the need for police protection? Are you concerned about safety for yourself and the girls?"

"Should I be?"

"Just thought I'd ask. With this guy Hagerty on the loose, he might turn up here in Pueblo. He might have some hidden agenda for all we know. Keep in mind the police department is responsible for your safety."

She came back to her chair and sat down. "Maybe the girls and I should take a vacation until you people find this Hagerty guy. We haven't had our trip to the Caymans this year."

"Isn't it pretty hot there at this time of the year?"

"Yes, and being there without Frank . . . not sure I could handle that."

Sharon finished her wine and stood. "Think I'll be on my way now."

Gloria walked her to the front door. "I'm glad you could come. And please call me when you get any more news about this Hagerty person."

"Thanks for the wine. I'll be in touch."

After getting home and fixing herself a light dinner, Sharon decided she couldn't put it off any longer and called Dan Mahoney.

"What were you doing with Mrs. Streckfus?" were his first words.

"Thanks, Dan, good to hear from you too." She paused for dramatic effect. "Gloria wanted to talk so I stopped by her house after work. Is that too difficult to understand or should I spell it out for you?"

"Sorry, Sharon. Bad day in the neighborhood. How did it go?"

"I've got good news and bad news. Which would you like first?"

He groaned. "Whatever."

"Gloria was able to get the mayor calmed down yesterday after we left. Which is why our bosses never got the angry call today."

"That's nice."

"And Mansfield wants to appoint her to the city council, taking the seat that her late husband had."

"A politically smart move on his part. Did she agree to take it?"

"Not yet, she's going to think about it."

He was quiet for a second. "You think those two have something going on?"

"What? You mean having an affair? Why would you even think that?"

"Just wondering out loud. Thinking of different angles to this case."

"I think that angle is obtuse, like you sometimes."

"OK, what's the bad news?"

"I told her about Hagerty."

"Um . . . I think you should have left that to me."

"She pressured me, Dan, had me in a box. Remember when she did that to you? You told me she's a very persuasive person and you're absolutely right. She hit me with questions right out of the blue so I told her everything you told me at lunch today."

"OK, the cat's out of the bag. What was her reaction? Does she know Hagerty?"

"She's pretty upset and wants to be kept in the loop. As for Hagerty, she only said the name was faintly familiar. I asked if she was worried about her personal safety and her response was sort of vague. She mentioned getting out of town for a while, taking a vacation in the Cayman Islands where they've gone every year on vacations. Of course it's pretty warm down there right now."

"The Caymans, huh? I'd be heading to a cooler place myself,

like Breckenridge or Estes Park."

"Me too. Any word on what's happening with the mayor?"

"Nothing unusual. Staying close to home or the office."

"So we just sit tight and wait?"

"Unless we make something happen. When we first met, you mentioned looking at Mansfield's and Streckfus' financials and how clean they were."

"Correct."

"What about Mrs. Streckfus? Does she have any financial track record?"

"She will now, assuming she's inherited all the couple's assets."

"That's not what I'm driving at. Did you run a check on her . . . credit cards, checking accounts, investment income, things like that?"

"No, I didn't. I was only looking at Frank's stuff because that's what the mayor asked me to do in the first place. You think she's involved in this?"

"She could be. Don't you want to know for sure?"

"Guess I've got some spare time to dig into this." *Not sure where to start but I'm not telling him that.*

"You're the one," said Dan, "something you do every day in your regular job. I recall you telling me that once. Just remember to save some social time for your best FBI buddy."

"Is five minutes a day too much for you?"

"How about five hours? Is that too little for you?"

"Good night, Dan. Call me when you get some hard news."

Most of Sharon's daylight working hours on Tuesday and Wednesday were spent on Pueblo police matters and it made the time pass quickly. She took advantage of brief opportunities to get a line on Gloria Streckfus' finances. The local bank that held Frank's accounts turned out to be unhelpful; they had nothing on Gloria.

Late Wednesday afternoon she happened to be near Kapoulis Funeral Home. On a whim, she went inside and found their business manager, a young woman named Annette, who was eager to help. Sharon identified herself, told Annette that she was working on an unusual identity theft case, and would like to get any available information about recent payments to the funeral home made by survivors of the deceased. Annette's records showed seven payments made during the last two weeks: four by check, two with credit cards, and one, by Gloria Streckfus, was all cash. She agreed with Annette's pronouncement, "Paying with cash is certainly unusual." Sharon made some notes, thanked Annette and went back to her office.

That evening, Sharon got out the records from her earlier Streckfus investigation and added today's notes to the pile. Gloria had paid just over $12,000 for Frank's funeral. *Who keeps that kind of money laying around the house?*

Her cell phone rang with a call from Eliot.

"Hello, Sharon. Hope I didn't wake you."

"Not at all. Just trying to make sense of the latest from the Streckfus case."

"I'd like to hear more about that but first I want to tell you about a call I just had from Deputy Starnes."

"I could use some good news about now."

"Well, some of it is. He located our private eye friend and the idiot tried to get away. Starnes collared him and took him downtown. Layton's denying everything, says they can't prove it was him and that internet shop in Nogales has no legal standing in

Maricopa County, regardless of who sent the e-mail. He's got a point but Starnes says the whole thing would be too much trouble to prosecute so they'll let him go in the morning. Starnes promised that Layton will be strongly *encouraged* to leave the great state of Arizona permanently."

"That's all well and good but what about his client?"

"That's the not-well-and-good part."

"What happened?"

"Starnes went out to Scottsdale and talked with Cassie's husband, Winston Hume. Turns out she doesn't live there anymore. According to Starnes, Mr. Hume said she loaded up her silver BMW with clothes and other personal gear and moved out about a week ago. Probably not something she wanted to do."

"You mean he kicked her out?"

"That was the impression he got."

"So she's out there, on the loose, and she knows where I live. That's what she said in that damned e-mail. I'm not liking this, Eliot, and you'd better do something. Find that woman and lock her up."

"She won't be coming back to Leadville. I made it pretty clear that she'd wind up in my jail if she did."

"This is all your fault, dammit. Letting her stay overnight with you."

"It's nobody's fault, Sharon, just the way things shook out. So here's my plan. I'm coming back to Pueblo on Friday. Should be at your house in late afternoon."

"That's really not necessary, Eliot."

"I think it is and I want to see you again. Besides, you don't know what Cassie looks like."

She said, "Wonderful," but it didn't sound wonderful at all.

"And keep your weapon handy," he said.

"My gun? Are you serious?"

"The woman's desperate, Sharon, and there's no telling what she's got in mind."

Chapter Twenty-Two

Chance Cullen took a shower after Stephanie left for Parkview on Thursday morning. They'd gotten up early and ran a quarter mile on a school track in Pueblo West as daylight was struggling to make its appearance. He felt good, happy with the way his life was going with Stephanie. He sang in the shower, a loud baritone just a bit off key, but not that it mattered.

He shaved, dressed for his afternoon work shift and went to the bright sunlit kitchen for a bowl of raisin and nut bran flakes with blueberries. It promised to be another hot day in Pueblo.

He thought about his meeting yesterday with Dr. Phillip Stark, one of the resident psychiatrists at Parkview. The session was basically a getting-to-know-you encounter with Chance doing most of the talking. Dr. Stark's basic message was that Chance's rehabilitation, like after other stressful life experiences, would take time. Stark was encouraged by Chance's activities since his release from prison. He had a steady job, was engaged in regular physical exercise, and had a promising relationship with Stephanie, a well regarded therapist at the hospital. In the latter category, Stark urged Chance to make many new friends because he shouldn't place such a large responsibility on Stephanie's shoulders for help.

Chance spent considerable time talking about his experiences in prison but didn't divulge details of how he got there in the first place. The injustice of his incarceration and the feeling of being betrayed by Eliot Waters would come later.

He cleaned up the kitchen and drove to Parkview to meet Stephanie at the cafeteria for what had become their standing lunch date. After their meal, he went back to his house and did a load of laundry. Back at the hospital that afternoon, he made his way to the office of Dorothy Dawson, his white-haired supervisor.

She waved him into her office and greeted him, "What's on your mind today, Mr. Cullen? Are you getting enough work to keep happy?"

This was a typical example of her expansive sense of humor, often joking with her staff to make their working conditions more bearable. Underneath it all, she felt everyone working at the hospital had a role to play in healing the sick, no matter how small or routine their job was. Even men like Chance performed a valuable service keeping the rooms and corridors clean.

"About my work schedule, Ms. D. The three-to-eleven shift is not working out so well for me."

"Why is that?"

"Well, I have a friend who works *normal* hours and it's pretty tough trying to have some time together."

"Would that be Stephanie White by chance?"

Chance brushed a palm across his mouth to hide the grin. "Yep, that's her."

"She's a nice person and you should consider yourself a lucky fellow. So you'd like to change your work schedule, huh?"

"Yes, I would. When I first interviewed with Mr. Julian he said I could have a job down in the kitchen working the usual daylight hours. What I'm doing now seemed like a better deal."

"And now you want to try the scullery work?"

"Not really, but I thought I'd talk it over with you first."

"A wise choice. You're a good worker, Chance, and I'd like to keep you. But I can't put you on a different schedule just like that." She snapped her fingers to emphasize her point. "So here's an idea to think about. Keep your present schedule for the next five days and give me time to work something out. I may be able to juggle a few things around for you. Is that fair?"

"Thanks, Ms. D, that's more than fair."

He left her office and started whistling a tune. *I'll keep this a secret until I get a definite schedule change. Should be a nice surprise for Steph.*

Sharon brought an egg salad sandwich to her office on Friday morning, hoping to spend a quiet lunch hour reviewing the Streckfus couple's financials. When noon rolled around the situation was encouraging since a major distraction, Debbie Wasserstein, was out for the day working on her own case.

While nibbling at her sandwich and occasionally sipping a diet cola, Sharon examined all her notes plus the printouts she'd collected on Frank and Gloria. This is pretty discouraging, she thought, not being able to find any clear evidence of monetary skullduggery when I know it's being done. Focusing on Gloria for a moment, she didn't see anything unusual. In fact, the only unique item was Gloria's social security number on the record of their home purchase and the relatively small mortgage they took out on the property.

Sharon continued tracking Gloria's financial trail on her computer. She learned that Gloria had only two credit cards, an unusual instance of spending discipline in today's plastic money climate: a Visa card she used for gasoline, restaurants, and online purchases from Amazon, and the other card from Nordstrom. Sharon found records for each card used over the last three months: three charges at Nordstrom's Denver store two months ago and only a handful of charges each month on the Visa card.

Sharon pushed back her chair, got up and went to the women's bathroom where she splashed some cold water on her face. *This is not making sense. There's nothing going on in Gloria's financials but she's got plenty of cash to spend and it's not coming through any traceable paper or electronic accounts. How does she get it and where is it coming from? The Caymans? Zurich? Or directly from Afghanistan? Pretty smart. Any cash over ten thousand deposited in a U. S. bank gets reported to the Feds, a sure way to attract attention.*

She returned to her cubicle and found two sheets of paper on her chair. The top sheet was a fax cover sent by Dan Mahoney with a note. "See attached photo of Mr. Hagerty taken under more honorable circumstances. What do you think?"

The black and white photograph of a man about forty showed him from the waist up, wearing a camouflaged field uniform without a hat. He had a rugged face, a jutting square chin, and a grin that couldn't disguise the contempt inside. Topping it off were Hagerty's eyes, dark and reflecting zero emotion. *Are these the eyes of a killer or am I assuming too much?* She picked up the phone and called Dan.

He answered immediately. "Guess you've seen Hagerty's photo."

"I have and he's guilty until proven innocent. Where did you get it?"

"From one of his buddies in Kabul. Took some arm twisting because the guy thought we might haul him in as an accomplice."

"So now we know what he looks like, although I doubt he'll be wearing a desert outfit if he shows up here."

"True, but not much he can do with that face."

"I've got something for you, Dan. I've been checking Mrs. Streckfus. On a hunch, I went by the funeral home yesterday afternoon. Get this, she paid cash for all her husband's funeral expenses."

"Cash? That had to be a bundle."

"Just over twelve grand." She heard him whistle but went on, "Ran a bunch of checks on her financials today and she's pretty clean, almost like she's not here. Has only two credit cards and doesn't use them very often."

"That twelve thousand . . . was it in hundreds or small bills? Did the funeral home make sure it wasn't counterfeit?"

"Listen, Mr. Special Agent. I was way out on a limb going into that place with a shaky story. If that accountant had been more savvy, I'd probably be standing in front of Internal Affairs right now while they investigated me."

"Sorry. Have you been able to find out where she's getting the cash?"

"Nope. It has to be coming from out of the country. You know as well as I do what the source is."

"All right, let me think about it. I'll talk to a few experts."

"Any other news on this subject?"

"No, but I want to see you. How about dinner tonight?"

"Um . . . that would be nice but I'm pretty busy."

"Guess I should plan ahead. Can't let the competition get ahead of me."

Sharon paused for a moment. *This has gone far enough.*
"Eliot's his name and we've had a relationship for some time now."

"Why haven't you told me? Who is this guy?"

"I told you before, he's the Lake County Sheriff. He's coming down to help with a problem related to that nasty e-mail you checked for me."

"He's behind that e-mail? I don't understand."

"Kind of a long story but I'll make it short. The e-mail came from Eliot's long lost girlfriend who just came back into his life after many years. She found out that Eliot and I have a relationship and she's hot to break us up. Even hired some stupid private eye to cross the border and send me that e-mail from Nogales."

"Can't you just ignore it, like some crank telephone call?"

"It's not that easy. The woman's left her husband and is probably heading this way. She's more than a little crazy and could be dangerous."

"Wish I could help you, Sharon."

"Thanks, but this is something Eliot and I have to work out together."

"Good luck. And if things don't work out, I'm a lot closer than Leadville."

Sharon sat quietly for a while, thinking about their conversation. It had added to her discomfort because she realized that she couldn't dismiss Dan's feelings out of hand. She continued working at her office as long as possible, updating notes on her cases and searching the internet for any kind of relevant information about them. But when six o'clock rolled around and Detective Wasserstein left with a parting shot about not having any handsome FBI agents panting at her doorstep, she headed for home and the unavoidable confrontation.

As expected, Eliot's SUV was sitting in the driveway. Eliot himself was parked on the living room couch, watching the news on TV with an open bottle of beer sitting nearby. He got up and gave her a hug but, when he tried to kiss her, his smooch landed on a deflected cheek instead of her lips. "Glad to see you, too," he said.

"Been here long?"

"Couple of hours. Stopped at King Sooper and bought some rib eyes and baking potatoes. I'll do the cooking honors if you'll build the salad."

"Thanks, Eliot."

"How about a drink? Can I fix you one?"

"Sure, a vodka tonic would be good."

He made the drink and brought it back where she was sitting on a chair facing the couch. He touched the beer bottle to her glass and said, "To happier days."

She drank freely. "We could sure use them."

Sensing she was waiting for him to make the first move, Eliot said, "Had an interesting conversation with Winston Hume this morning."

"I don't recognize that name."

"He's Cassie's husband."

"Lucky guy."

"He's thinking that way but only because she's gone. He also has some mixed emotions about me. Knowing that she was carrying a torch for me after all these years but glad I was able to see through it and have the courage to send her back with her tail tucked between her legs. So to speak. Anyway, his big regret is not finding out about her before they got married. He's a sadder but wiser man now."

"Does he know what happened in Leadville with you two?"

"Not all of it, but enough. I was pretty open with him, didn't see any reason to hold back now, and gave him all the details about her deception, the lies, and the stunt she pulled wrecking her car to land in the hospital."

"So he knows she stayed overnight in your cabin."

"He already knew because I talked to him the morning she left."

"Did you tell him what you two did that night?"

"No need, he's done with her."

"Well, we're not done and I'd like to hear about it. And I mean everything."

Eliot took a long pull on his beer. "You know the layout of my cabin. I put Cassie in the guest bedroom and I slept in my own bed, the same one you sleep in when you come up on the weekends. Sometime during the night while I was asleep, Cassie crawled into bed with me, complaining she was cold. I tried to get her to go back into her own bed but she wouldn't go. She was all over me like a wet blanket, wanting to have sex, but . . . I never thought a man could be raped by a woman."

Sharon glared at him. "Are you serious? She raped you?"

"Well, not quite. Guess she wore me down and I gave her what she wanted. Quick and pretty rough."

"So you had sex with her."

"Yeah, I did. Just what she came all that way for but she didn't like it much. Had plenty of nasty words after it was over."

"So you raped *her*?"

"Not at all. Like I said, it was pretty rough. I was angry and had to get it out of my system once and for all."

"Just because she interrupted your sleep?"

"Ha. Goes back many years ago to the time she dumped me. She didn't see us with any future together so she said *Adios* and went back to her husband. Not Winston, but a guy named Dwight."

"Winston is her second husband?"

"Third, actually. Lots of money and much older than her."

Sharon sighed. "Does Winston have any idea where she is now?"

"He's pretty sure she's not in Scottsdale. She left in her own vehicle, a silver BMW SUV packed to the ceiling with her clothes and all kinds of paraphernalia."

"She could be here in Pueblo."

"Yep, we'll have to keep a sharp eye."

"That makes two," she said.

"I'm not following you."

"Last time we talked I told you about Hagerty, still the number one suspect in Councilman Streckfus' murder. The've traced him to New York but that was over a week ago." She pulled Dan Mahoney's FAX out of her briefcase and handed it to Eliot. "Got his picture from the FBI this afternoon."

Eliot took several moments to stare at the photo. "We could be in for an interesting weekend. He's not looking for you, I hope"

"Heck no. The mayor is the most likely target and the FBI is watching him."

As the conversation withered, Eliot said, "Maybe I should get the grill started."

"Good idea, I'm getting pretty hungry."

Both enjoyed the food and neither felt the need to say much during dinner. The dual topics of their relationship and the Streckfus murder had been picked clean so they talked about other matters, mostly police-related incidents in their respective communities. As they were clearing the table and loading the dishwasher, Sharon was also thinking about what the sleeping arrangements would be that night. She felt a welcome reprieve when her telephone rang.

Dan Mahoney was calling. "Sorry to interrupt but I thought you should know."

"No problem, what's up?"

"Gloria Streckfus has been shot. She's in the ER at Parkview and I'm heading over there now."

Sharon looked straight at Eliot who sensed that something was wrong and stood ready to help. "We'll be right over," she said.

CHAPTER TWENTY-THREE

Eliot and Sharon drove to Parkview Medical Center in his SUV and found a parking spot close to the emergency room's front entrance. Sharon was first out of the vehicle and practically sprinted through the building's sliding glass doors as Eliot followed in brisk pursuit. She flashed her badge at the receptionist and said snappily, "Gloria Streckfus, brought in earlier, gunshot wounds. What do you have?"

The woman tapped her keyboard and stared at her computer screen for several seconds. "That's correct, detective. Dr. Bartlett is the attending physician. I'll send him a paging alert so he can make contact as soon as he's available. You can wait in the reception area." She looked up and added, "Another detective is down there now."

They walked down a hallway until Sharon spotted a familiar figure standing in the waiting area with a paper cup in his hand. Detective Ted Birdsall came over and said, "Hey, Hardcastle, guess you heard."

"Special Agent Mahoney called me and we came right over. Where the heck is he, have you seen him?"

"Haven't seen or heard from that guy since our last meeting."

She turned toward Eliot and said to Birdsall, "This is my friend, Eliot Waters, Lake County Sheriff."

The men shook hands. "Detective," said Eliot. *I'll let Sharon do all the talking.*

"What do you know about Mrs. Streckfus?" Sharon asked Birdsall.

"Details are pretty sketchy right now. The call came in about an hour ago and one of our squad cars responded. She'd been having dinner with friends at a downtown restaurant when she was attacked in the parking lot. No eyewitnesses but a guy heard shots fired and came out from the kitchen. Saw her body on the ground next to her car, called 911, and the ambulance brought her directly to the ER. We've got forensics checking her car and everything around it. They'll have it impounded later. Looks like a mugging."

"She has two daughters. What about them?"

"She was alone so I guess they're at home. I'll touch base with the responding officers, have them swing by the house and bring the girls down here ASAP."

"Good idea. Mrs. Streckfus has parents here in Pueblo somewhere and we need to get the word to them."

"Anyway," said Birdsall, "I've talked with the ER doc. She took three slugs, two grazing her arm and leg but one in her chest. She's in the OR now."

"How about the responders? Did she tell them anything?"

"Nothing that made sense. Guess she was in shock."

"Have you talked with her?"

"Not yet. Maybe when she comes out of the OR."

An awkward silence followed until Eliot said, "Maybe we should all have a seat and wait for Dr. Bartlett."

Sharon raised both hands in resignation. "Might as well."

They found chairs in a quiet corner and Birdsall tried to make small talk with Eliot about his being a Rocky Mountain lawman. After a few glittering generalities, Birdsall gave up and tried to read a six month old *Sports Illustrated* magazine.

About twenty minutes later, Kate and Joanna Streckfus came into the waiting area, accompanied by a uniformed policewoman. Sharon got up quickly to meet them. Kate, the older girl, ran up and grabbed her hands. "What's happening to Mom? Can we see her?"

"She's in the operating room right now."

"Is she going to die?" said Joanna.

Sharon reached out and hugged both girls. "Not if they can help it. We're all waiting to hear more from the doctor."

"Are you going to catch the man who shot her?" asked Joanna.

"That's another reason we're here, trying to find out just what happened. And yes, we'll track him down no matter how long it takes."

Kate and Joanna followed Sharon and took seats close to her. Time passed slowly over the next two hours as the three officers read magazines or talked and the girls played with their cell phones. Their boredom was interrupted when Dan Mahoney showed up. "What's the word?" he called out, not bothering to apologize for his late arrival.

"Well, well," said Sharon in a loud voice, "the Feds have arrived so we can all go home now."

Mahoney focused on Detective Birdsall who gave him essentially the same briefing he'd given Eliot and Sharon. "So she's still in OR?" said Dan.

"As far as we know."

Dan turned to Sharon. "Sorry I'm late. The boss trapped me in the office, wanting to know all about this latest development."

"You didn't miss much," said Sharon. "Of course, if you had bothered to call my cell phone, I could have saved you a trip. But then all of us would've been deprived of your infinite wisdom and scintillating company."

Dan ignored her gibe and shifted his attention to Eliot while extending his right hand. "Special Agent Mahoney. You must be the high country sheriff."

He gave Dan a firm grip. "Eliot Waters, Lake County. Pleasure to finally meet up with you, Special Agent."

"Guess Detective Hardcastle told you we've been working a case together. Probably nothing as exciting as the action around Leadville, right?"

Eliot caught Sharon's eyes rolling but kept focused enough to say, "We do have some *interesting* things most every day. Keeps us sharp so we earn our pay."

"Well then," said Dan. "Guess there's not much for us to do except to wait for the doctor to show up."

"Got a question," said Sharon to Dan. "Have you touched base with the mayor? He'd probably want to know what happened to Mrs. Streckfus."

"We've tried," said Dan, "but nobody's home at his place."

"The mayor has a habit of not being available when stuff hits the fan." Sharon started to add more, something about Hagerty being a likely suspect which would put Mansfield in jeopardy, but had second thoughts. *Birdsall surely doesn't know about this aspect of Frank Streckfus' overseas business enterprise and his murder in Kabul. Mahoney should be the one to tell Birdsall, if he needs to know.*

"I'll try to reach the mayor later," said Dan, "after we know more."

Conversation ceased when a man wearing surgical garb approached the group. The man seemed to know instinctively that the foursome now standing close to each other were in law enforcement. "I'm Dr. Bartlett," he said, "and you all are here about Gloria Streckfus, I assume."

"Yes, we are," they said as a harmonious quartet. Kate and Joanna got up and came closer.

"OK, then. It was touch and go for a while but she was very lucky. The bullet in the chest just missed her heart but tore up a few other things inside. She's in recovery right now."

"Will she make it?" asked Sharon.

"We'll know more in the morning but I'd say her chances are good."

"Can we talk to her," said Mahoney, "get some clues on who did this?"

Dr. Bartlett removed his cap and revealed a gray crewcut. "Look, she's been through a traumatic experience and doesn't need any additional stress. But I understand the urgency on your part. I have to warn you that she's heavily sedated and may not be lucid. I'll allow five minutes but *no more than that.*"

All four shifted position like they were ready to follow him to the recovery room. "Oh no," he said, "just one of you."

Kate spoke up. "We're her daughters, we want to see her too."

"All right, but you can't stay with her very long."

Detective Birdsall, a good ten years older than the other three officers, spoke up. "Aggravated assault is my job so I'll do the talking. Lead the way, doc."

The remaining threesome decided to wait and took their same seats.

Dan said to Sharon, "I'm putting my money on you-know-who as the shooter."

"You don't have to speak in code, Dan. Eliot knows about Hagerty and what Frank Streckfus was doing in Iraq and Afghanistan."

Mahoney glanced at Eliot and gave Sharon a startled look. His mouth was open but no words came out.

"Don't give me that, Mahoney. You know how I operate. Sharing information to get the job done, no matter who gets the credit. Taking advantage of expertise whenever and wherever I find it."

Eliot was chuckling to himself, eyes raised to the ceiling as he twisted the ends of his mustache.

Detective Birdsall returned and stood in front of the group. "No luck, she's pretty much out of it. Calling for Frank and a few other things that didn't make sense. I'll come back first thing in the morning and try again, go by the station on my way home and see if the responders filed a report. Maybe they found something."

Dan Mahoney got up. "We've done about all we can do. Let's call it a night and be sure to keep each other in the loop with any new information."

Sharon and Eliot remained seated and watched Birdsall and Mahoney walk away. "Can you believe that guy? He thinks he's in charge and wants us to give *him* stuff but keeps whatever he finds to himself."

"Texas people have a saying," offered Eliot. "The man is all hat and no cattle."

Sharon made a whimpering laugh. "Let's go home. I'm tired

and we've had enough excitement for one night."

They made their way to the hospital's front entrance. Eliot was complimenting Sharon on how nicely she treated Kate and Joanna when, just before reaching the doors, a strong male voice called out from behind, "Wait right there."

Eliot and Sharon stopped, turned around and stared at a man marching directly toward Eliot. He stopped about six feet away, hands on his hips. "You're Eliot Waters. I'd know that walk anywhere."

Eliot stared at him for a moment and broke into a half smile. "I'll be damned, Last Chance Cullen."

"Yeah, it's me all right and I've waited twelve lousy years for this." He charged, throwing left and right punches at Eliot's head, as a loud deep-throated growl came out of his mouth. Eliot ducked to one side but Chance's fist connected with his chin.

Sharon was temporarily paralyzed but, seeing Eliot brutally attacked, soon jumped into action. She tried inserting a fist between them and grabbed Chance's shirt collar with the other hand, trying to pull him away.

Eliot fought back, deflecting another punch, and landed a solid blow to Chance's stomach, knocking him off balance. Chance fell to the floor but held onto Eliot with one hand around his neck, dragging him down where the two wrestled in close combat, each striking mostly ineffective blows.

When the two rolled into a position with Chance on top, Sharon saw an opportunity. She got down, pressed a knee into Chance's back, and pulled one arm back and behind his shoulder. The result was immediate and he cried out in pain.

She shouted, "Stop it right now or I'll break it."

Chance went limp. Eliot pushed him away, rolled him over

and sat up.

"You OK, Eliot?" said Sharon.

He huffed and puffed, trying to catch his breath. "Haven't had this much fun since my rodeo days."

"You know this guy?" she said.

"Yep, he's the one I told you about. We rode together on the rodeo circuit years ago." Eliot felt his chin. "Still got a bit of the stupid streak in him though."

Chance moaned. "At least I don't have a yellow one down my back."

"What are you doing here, Chance?" asked Eliot.

"I work here."

"I know that. Kind of late to be hanging around, isn't it?"

Chance turned slightly to get a better look. "How did you know that?"

"Never mind. Something else I know, you're on parole. What just happened here could land you back at Canon City."

"So you're gonna arrest me? Ha. You're out of your territory, sheriff."

"But my friend who almost broke your arm could do the job. Chance, say hello to Sharon Hardcastle, Pueblo Police Department."

"Aw shit."

"Yeah, you're in a deep pile of it," said Eliot.

"So you're gonna screw me over again, huh? Like letting me rot for ten years in the pen?"

"Listen here, Chance. You should have gone south with me and Suarez, I told you that. But you hung back and let them railroad you."

"Why the hell didn't you come back? Testify at my trial and

tell them it was Suarez who killed that guy. Why didn't you do that?'

"Because I was laying low across the border and never knew anything until I did come back. By then it was too late. You'd already been tried, convicted and put away."

"Bullshit. *Twenty-four carat bullshit.*"

"I don't lie, Chance. No point to it now."

Two nurses going off duty paused to stare at the two men sitting on the lobby floor. One nurse asked Sharon if the men were hurt. She replied that it was a misunderstanding and they didn't need any medical attention. The nurses seemed satisfied with her explanation and left through the front doors.

"What's it going to be, sheriff," said Sharon. "Want to press charges?"

Eliot picked up his hat, which was knocked off during the fracas, and plopped it back onto his head. "What do *you* say, Mr. Cullen? One last chance to call it square between us?"

Chance looked up at Sharon and then back to Eliot. "All right."

The men got up, shook hands, and the trio walked outside together. Before parting Eliot said, "You've made a good start, Chance. A steady job and someone who cares an awful lot for you. Stay out of trouble and you should enjoy a pretty nice life."

"She told you about me, didn't she. When she was up in Leadville for that race."

Eliot laughed and patted him on the back. "Have her bring you up next time she runs one of those mountain races and I'll show you around."

Sharon added, "Yeah, and when you go, don't miss the big fish hatchery. It's one of Leadville's main attractions."

CHAPTER TWENTY-FOUR

While Eliot and Sharon were driving to her home from Parkview
Medical Center, Brian Mansfield was having a drink in the Bar
del Lago at the Colorado Springs Broadmoor Hotel. He had put
his wife on a plane at the nearby airport earlier in the day. She
was meeting friends in Cary, North Carolina and they would be
spending a week on the beach near Cape Hatteras. They had
parted on sour terms; she was sick and tired of his grouchy and
sometimes psychotic behavior during the past several weeks.
Secretly, he was glad to have the respite her absence offered.

Edward Hagerty had called him two days ago and demanded
a meeting to get their current problems settled once and for all.
Brian had suggested the Broadmoor for its upscale ambience but,
more importantly, because it was relatively remote and was a place
he wouldn't be recognized. He didn't want any of his
acquaintances seeing him with Hagerty in case legal issues arose
later.

Mansfield was sitting at a small corner table when Hagerty
arrived. No pleasantries were exchanged; they got right down to
business. "What the hell happened over there?" said Brian.

"What do you think? Our customers were starting to panic

because the troops were about to start the big *sayonara*. And our contacts in their government were making noises, worried about their *baksheesh*. The word was out that all the junk gear would be destroyed so the Taliban couldn't use it and the high value stuff would be shipped stateside. I was ready to cash out, get the hell out of country and retire to some tropical resort with a nice payout from your buddy. But no, he was putting the screws to me, wanting our customers to cough up more dough."

"A little squeeze shouldn't have hurt that much."

"There was nothing little about it. It was a big scam. He was bugging out and leaving me holding the bag while you guys are getting rich."

"Did you try to negotiate with him?"

"Yeah, and you know how that turned out. A failure to communicate."

"Why did you come here, Ed?"

"To get my share, what I deserve."

"We had a deal," said Brian. "Frank paid you out of his share. You're barking up the wrong tree, talking to me about getting more money. Maybe you should be talking to his widow. I think you have some clues about how they moved money around the world to different places."

"I had a *meeting* with her earlier tonight, kind of like the one with Frank. This one didn't go so well either."

"You saw Gloria? That wasn't a smart move."

"No matter. What's done is done. She won't be telling anybody about us so it's just you and me, Brian."

Mansfield paused for a moment as the realization of Gloria's possible demise sunk in. "So you're looking for money, from me. Do I understand you correctly?"

"Did I stutter or wasn't I clear enough for you? Hell yes I want money, everything that's coming to me. Plus interest."

"Interest."

"Yeah, and I'm thinking round numbers here. A million bucks would make me suddenly invisible and all those zeroes after the one would look pretty sexy on my bank statement."

"You know something, Hagerty? You're an idiot. Gloria has control of the money, that's the way Frank set it up. Accounts in Zurich and the Caymans, all out of the country so the Feds couldn't track it to him, me, or even you. So thanks to you, neither one of us will get a dime. How does that strike you?"

"I don't believe you. You're lying, just like Mr. and Mrs. Shitface."

"I think this conversation is over," said Brian, pushing back his chair and starting to get up.

Hagerty grinned and pulled open his sport jacket, revealing a small pistol in a holster attached to his belt. "You haven't heard what my little *friend* has to say."

Mansfield sat back in his chair. "You're even dumber than I thought."

"Not so dumb to swallow all the bullshit you're giving me."

Mansfield leaned forward. "Then let me give you some hot scoop. You know what happened after Frank left for Riyadh? Nobody in Pueblo knew where he was and everybody thought something had happened to him. I even had a detective and an FBI agent come to my office and ask a lot of questions about him." Brian suddenly remembered starting the whole thing by e-mailing Sharon, inviting her to his office, and asking her to review Frank's financials. In retrospect, he realized this had been a colossal mistake but he wasn't going to share this with

Edward Hagerty.

"I don't like the sound of that," said Hagerty.

"It gets worse. After Frank's funeral, I went over to Gloria's house on a Sunday afternoon. And who do I find, sitting in Frank's office big as you please, rooting around his files and going through his computer? The same damn two cops."

"How the hell did that happen? Did they have a warrant?"

"It was Gloria. She was sitting there watching them do it. I tried kicking them out but she wouldn't let me. She'd invited them to come and look for clues, anything that might lead to the capture of the guy who killed her husband."

"*Dammit to hell.*" His outburst attracted the attention of others sitting nearby.

"Exactly. I think you're starting to get the big picture, Ed." Brian paused to finish his glass of Johnnie Walker Black. "You want to be suddenly invisible, huh? Well, good luck with that. Once the local cops and the FBI pick up the stink, hiding places for us are going to be pretty scarce."

Neither man spoke. Finally, Hagerty said, "What are we going to do now?"

"I don't know about you, but I'm going home and try to get a good night's sleep."

Hagerty rubbed his palm across his forehead. "I have to get out of Colorado."

That night, Eliot and Sharon slept poorly but for different reasons. Gloria's shooting carried over into Sharon's dreams; she relived the experience but, when allowed to enter the recovery room, it was her friend Trish Guinn who'd been shot. Eliot's problem was being close to Sharon and not allowed to demonstrate any affection. She'd allowed him to share her bed but nothing more. Too exhausted, she claimed, but Eliot knew deep inside the invisible specter of Cassie Maugham was hovering over the couple as they tossed and turned.

Both were awake around seven o'clock. Eliot slid out of bed, pulled on a pair of jeans and said, "I give up. How about some coffee."

"Fine. Give me a couple of minutes."

He started the coffee machine and a full pot was ready when Sharon came out to the kitchen. He poured two cups and handed her one. "Morning, sunshine."

"Ugh," was all she could muster.

They took their coffee outside and relaxed on cushioned garden chairs under a large beach umbrella. Content to enjoy the fresh air, morning quiet and each other's company, little was said. Sharon placed a hand on his and said, "Thanks for last night."

"You're welcome. For going with you to Parkview or in bed."

"Both, but especially the latter. Very much appreciated."

"It wasn't because I wanted it that way. You know, Sharon, you have a . . . what do I call it? Something that sends out waves whenever I get close to you."

She laughed softly. "Good to know I haven't lost my touch."

Sounds from the kitchen broke the spell. "I think it's your phone," he said.

"Should've turned it off."

"Better answer it, detective."

She got up and soon returned to the patio, pacing around with the phone against her ear. She disconnected and said to Eliot, "That was Ted Birdsall. He's at Parkview and Gloria's awake. She wants to see *me* of all people."

"Want me to go with you?"

"Absolutely. And be in the room with us so we can compare notes afterward."

On arriving at Parkview, they learned Gloria had been transferred to the intensive care unit. "A good sign," said Eliot, "meaning she's going to make it."

Detective Birdsall met them at the ICU's entrance. "Any new information?" asked Sharon.

"Precious little," he replied. "Looks like a mugging at first blush. Purse on the front seat, license and credit cards strewn all over and no cash in her wallet."

"But?"

"Nothing at the car or the way the responders found her showed signs of a struggle. So why would a mugger shoot her if she was cooperating?"

"Good question. Did they get any prints?"

"A few. They're running checks on them today."

"Have you talked with her?"

"I did, but it was mostly a one-way conversation. Hope you have better luck. I'll hang around for a while in case."

Sharon and Eliot went inside the ICU, a large room with a half dozen smaller private rooms along the far wall and a long nurse's station on the opposite wall. They found Gloria sitting up slightly, her eyes half-closed, an IV drip plugged into one arm, and a number of wires leading from various body parts to several wall-mounted electronic devices above her head. "I'm awake," she said.

They took two chairs close to the bed and Sharon held Gloria's hand. "We came last night but the doctor wouldn't let us see you."

Gloria opened her eyes and looked at Eliot. "Who are you?"

"Eliot Waters, ma'am. Sharon's friend."

"He's also a sheriff," said Sharon. "Kind of a consultant on police matters." Sharon instantly regretted the last comment when Gloria scowled.

"Where's that Mahoney guy you've been palling around with? Why didn't you bring him?"

"I'm sure he'll show up soon. I was told you wanted to speak with me."

Gloria moaned and shifted her body. "Yes, I do. I want you to tell me why you and the FBI haven't caught that son of a bitch Hagerty. He's the one who did this to me and now he's on the loose, still out there and probably stalking Brian. He'll probably shoot him too if he doesn't get what he wants."

Sharon was speechless and turned to Eliot who only gave her a blank stare. She looked back to Gloria and said, "Um . . . I'm not following you. You say Hagerty shot you? And the mayor's in jeopardy now?"

Gloria made a guttural half laugh. "Don't pull that innocent act with me. You and Mahoney screwed this up big time. You know all about Hagerty and what he was doing over there. I made it so easy for you two but you didn't follow through. What kind of detective are you anyway?"

Sharon suddenly realized where this was going. "Those e-mails. The ones in the computer's trash can. You left them there on purpose . . . for us to find."

"Brilliant deduction, Miss Sherlock."

"Why did this Hagerty fellow almost kill you?" said Eliot.

"I have no idea and I'm through talking about this." She pointed a finger at Sharon. "Now you get out of here and catch

Hagerty before he does any more damage. Maybe your sheriff here can round up his posse and head for the hills."

Sharon said to Eliot, "I think we've overstayed our welcome. Let's go."

They left the ICU and came into the waiting room where they saw Detective Birdsall chatting with Special Agent Mahoney. Birdsall waved them over saying, "Dan's got something you ought to hear." Eliot and Sharon exchanged cool businesslike greetings with Mahoney and sat down.

"I talked with the deputy mayor," said Dan. "Mansfield took a plane this morning to North Carolina for a vacation with his wife."

"How long will he be gone?" said Sharon.

"Indefinitely. And that's not the only strange thing. His wife left yesterday. Why wouldn't they be leaving together?"

Sharon said, "Maybe he had some unfinished business to take care of."

Birdsall said, "Sounds like you have an angle on this."

"It's starting to come together. First, you and I weren't so clever after all, *Special Agent*. Mrs. Streckfus just told us she'd intentionally left those e-mails on Frank's computer. She wanted us to find them so the FBI would catch Hagerty before he came back to Pueblo. He's the one who shot her and it's our fault."

"Wait a minute," said Birdsall. "Who's Hagerty?"

Sharon said, "Time for show and tell, Dan. Detective Birdsall needs to know."

Mahoney grumbled, extracted a photo of Hagerty from his briefcase and showed it to Birdsall. "This is the guy we need to nail." He continued with details of Hagerty's business activities in Afghanistan and his financial arrangements with Frank Streckfus.

Sharon added, "Gloria thinks Hagerty's going after the mayor. She wouldn't give him money so now he's after Mansfield for a big payday."

The foursome became silent for a moment until Birdsall looked at Eliot. "You've been rather quiet, sheriff. What's your take on all this?"

Eliot twisted his mustache. "I'm thinking Mayor Mansfield heard about Mrs. Streckfus and decided to make himself scarce for a spell. Maybe he had contact with Hagerty or maybe not. Probably not important now but the FBI should try to find the mayor in North Carolina and hear what he has to say. Shouldn't be too hard. No telling where Hagerty's off to but, Detective Birdsall, I reckon an APB should be put out. And Mrs. Streckfus is a big part of this. She should be questioned when she recovers."

Mahoney nodded and Birdsall said, "Right, I'll do the APB right away."

Eliot turned to Sharon and said, "I think we're done, Detective Hardcastle. You up for some breakfast?"

"God yes," she said, "I'm starving."

Eliot and Sharon left the hospital. They failed, however, to notice a woman wearing huge sunglasses, sitting in a silver BMW SUV near Eliot's vehicle, intently watching their departure.

CHAPTER TWENTY-FIVE

Eliot and Sharon weren't the only ones who slept poorly Friday evening. Chance Cullen tossed and turned, alone in his bedroom near the Masonic Cemetery, and troubled by the unexpected encounter with Muddy Waters and his cop girlfriend.

Shortly after seven o'clock the next morning, he called Stephanie. "We need to talk," he said, without letting her have the opportunity for a hello.

"Good morning to you," she said frostily.

"Good morning. When's a good time?"

"Have you had your morning run yet?"

"I just got up."

"Then come out to my place and we can do laps together."

"I'm on my way." He disconnected, changed into jogging gear and drove out to Pueblo West.

Stephanie saw him pull up, met him at her open front door, and gave him a tentative smile. "Hello again."

"Hi, Steph."

"Come inside and we'll talk. Or would you rather do some running?"

"Let's talk first. You may not want the rest."

She led him into the living room and sat on the couch while he pulled up a chair to face her. "So what's this all about, Chance?"

He cleared his throat and shifted nervously. "I do have some good news. Had a talk with Dorothy Dawson and she's going to give me a new schedule. Same hours as you, probably. Not right away because she has to juggle a few things around first."

Stephanie lunged at him, threw her arms around his neck and gave him a wet kiss. "*Fantastic.* It's wonderful, we'll have a lot more time together. Gives me goosebumps and all kinds of crazy ideas."

"Thought you'd like that."

"I do and I'm already thinking about our weekends. Aren't you excited?"

"Yeah, I guess so."

She leaned back into the couch, made a loud sigh and folded her hands in her lap. He fumbled around in his chair and crossed his legs.

"Quite a conversation we're having, Chance. Thought you wanted to talk."

"Last night, when I was leaving Parkview after my shift, I bumped into Muddy Waters."

She stared at him for a moment. "Sheriff Waters? From Leadville? What was he doing at the hospital?"

"I have no idea but we connected in the lobby as he was heading out. Had a few words and then it got physical."

"You assaulted a sheriff? What got into you?"

"I kind of lost it. All those years in the pen, thinking about what he did and what I'd do if I ever saw him again."

"You don't look too bad, considering. What did you do to *him*?"

"Nothing much. There was another cop with him, a Pueblo detective. I was kind of outgunned so the fight didn't get very far."

"How did it end? Are you and this Muddy fellow friends again?"

"No way. But he did have some words about my personal situation."

A serious look came over her face as she realized where this was heading.

"Yeah, he said I was sure lucky to have a job here at Parkview and somebody who cares an awful lot about me."

"He really said that?"

"How do you think he knew? Any ideas?"

She leaned forward and took both of his hands in hers. "All right, I did it. I talked to Sheriff Waters when I was up in Leadville for the Trails Marathon. Wanted to see if you two lunkheads could put aside all the old bitterness and be friends again."

"I never asked you to do that. And I'd never send a woman into the enemy's camp begging for mercy and forgiveness. You had no right to do that. This was serious business between the two of us."

"So what? It's all over now, isn't it? And why shouldn't I have talked to him? I care a lot for you, Chance, and I want a strong, open relationship with you for many years to come. Can't you understand that?"

"It was my responsibility to settle it. You blundered into something without knowing all the background. You could have been hurt."

"Sorry, I was just trying to help."

"It's a two-way street, Steph. You didn't want me going after the guy in Denver who beat up on you."

"You could't have. You didn't have a car and you're on parole."

He made a crazy grin. "I have a car now. We could spend our first weekend together meeting with your old flame, talking about the good old days."

"This has gone far enough," she said. "It's time you know the whole story. That guy often used me for a punching bag but I got back at him one night. We were at his place and he was so drunk he could hardly stand up. After he passed out I tied him up and got the hell out of there. When he woke up in the middle of the night and saw what I did, he cut the ropes and came after me. We had another scuffle in my kitchen and I jabbed him with a knife. My neighbor heard the commotion, called 911 and they took him to the ER but I wound up in jail, booked for assault with a deadly weapon."

"But you were defending yourself. That's a bum rap."

She smiled. "Sound familiar?"

"Sure does. What happened?"

"I got six months but the bastard got off scot free."

"All the more reason to go see this jerk."

"He's not in Denver anymore. Moved away, probably not wanting me to look for him when I got out."

"That's a helluva story, I'm glad you told me. Then you came to Pueblo?"

"Right, and you know the hospital's hiring practice for people with records. Let's keep it between the two of us."

"I won't tell a soul."

After several moments of silence she got up, came around behind Chance and rubbed the top of his head. "Time for a run.

When we get back I'll fix you a big breakfast and we can talk some more."

"Best offer I've had all week. Let's do it."

Sharon drove to her office on Sunday morning. She had cooked breakfast for Eliot and he'd left for Leadville. He pleaded having tons of paperwork needing his personal attention and she confessed to having the same problem.

She sat quietly in her cubicle and pondered her situation. *When are Eliot and I going to get over this Cassie crap and get on with our lives? Neither one of us wants to even talk about this problem now because there is no clear solution. And as long as she's out there somewhere, intent on doing me damage or destroying our relationship, it's not going away. Wonder if I could charge her with stalking?*

She swiveled her chair and turned on her computer. *The heck with all this agonizing. Let's get some work done.*

About ten minutes later she heard footsteps approaching and wondered if Cassie would be dumb enough to confront her in a police station.

"Good morning, Sharon," said Sgt. Hess. "I like it when people take advantage of overtime."

Sharon laughed at his customary bit of black humor; detectives could not receive overtime pay for extra hours. "Hello, David. Are you here for Sunday services?"

"Just catching up, same as you." He sat down in the lone visitor's chair. "I've heard about Mrs. Streckfus. Have you seen her yet?"

"Yesterday morning in the ICU. Three gunshot wounds, one serious, but I think she'll survive."

"Any clues on who did it?"

"Oh yeah, plenty. She knew the guy, an ex-Army sergeant who had a side business with her husband in Iraq and Afghanistan. I met with Ted Birdsall and Agent Mahoney right after I talked with her."

"You've been spending a lot of time on this, detective."

"I know, David, but it's all over now. For me, anyway. Birdsall's in charge of the assault case and Mahoney's chasing the international part. There's a good chance the mayor's involved in the overseas business."

"The mayor, huh? Well, I'm glad you're done with it. I've got a new job for you, something fishy going on at the Apple Store. Couple of banks and credit card companies have reported cases of fraud and ID theft. Multiple charges coming in for the same card being used in the store only several hours apart, some real and some phony. Check with the manager first thing tomorrow. He'll get you up to speed."

"Got it," she said. "I could use a change of scenery."

Hess stood up to leave. "Send me a report on your latest with Mrs. Streckfus."

"You read my mind, David. That's what I was working on."

He gave her one of his trademark exaggerated grins. "Have a wonderful day."

She worked steadily for the good part of an hour. She was nearly finished with her report on Gloria Streckfus when the desk phone's ring startled her. "Hardcastle," she answered.

"Hi, Sharon. Thought I'd catch you there."

"OK, Daniel, you got me. What's up?"

"More news about our favorite case."

"Your case, Mahoney. I'm off the hook, as of an hour ago."

"Don't you want to hear the latest?"

"All right, tell me."

"No. It deserves something better than a phone conversation. How about a lunch break?"

Sharon glanced at her watch. "Fine. Tell me where and I'll meet you in thirty."

"Let's do IHOP again. I'll get us a table."

Sharon finished her report ten minutes later, e-mailed it to Sgt. Hess and shut down her computer. She drove to IHOP and found Dan sitting in a booth, intently reading *The Pueblo Chieftain.* She slid quietly into the booth, punched the paper with her fist and said, "Wake up, Dan, your date's here."

He put the paper down and touched her hand. "I knew it was you. Got all engrossed in Doonesbury when you came in but had to finish it."

"You're reading the comics?"

"Sure. Good relief from the reality of our chosen profession."

"So what's your big news?"

"Uh uh, let's order something to eat first."

The waitress took their orders, sausage and eggs for Dan and a club sandwich for Sharon. When she left, Sharon said, "You look pretty pleased with yourself."

"I'm happy for two reasons. You're here and I have an exciting trip later today."

"Aha. Where to?"

"George Town."

"Back to your headquarters? What's exciting about that?"

"No, not D. C. It's two words, the capital of the Cayman Islands and named after King George III. Why don't you come along with me?"

"Now *I'm* getting excited but you're going by yourself. Tell me more."

"Our good mayor, Brian Mansfield, flew to Raleigh yesterday morning but he didn't stay there long. We've tracked him to George Town and he's staying at a hotel near Seven Mile Beach."

Sharon was momentarily speechless as several aspects of the Streckfus case whirled around her brain. "Wow, it's all coming together."

"Yes, *finally.* The Bureau has a man down there now. They asked me to join him because of my familiarity with Mansfield and Streckfus."

"Are you going to arrest him?"

"This is a tricky situation. The Caymans are a British Overseas Territory and we have to be careful not to create an international incident. They have a treaty with the U. S. for mutual legal assistance that covers various criminal offenses equally punishable in both countries but not U. S. tax evasion. The Caymans are the fifth largest banking center in the world and a popular tax haven. No income tax, no capital gains tax and no wealth tax."

"And Frank and Gloria Streckfus vacationed there every year."

"Probably visiting their money while having a fun time."

"What are you and the other agent going to do?"

"Bottom line, prevent Mansfield from making a big withdrawal. We think he'll be heading for one of the banks tomorrow and claiming the assets of his partnership with Frank Streckfus."

"Can you stop him from doing that?"

"Good question. We'll have to convince the Caymanian authorities and the bank that those funds were not deposited to evade taxes but were gained because of a criminal enterprise, selling U. S. military equipment on the black market to questionable organizations in Iraq and Afghanistan. Smells like treason and that's the way we'll present our case to them."

"If they go along with you, what happens to all the money?"

"Probably returned to the U. S. Treasury Department."

"I'm thinking of Gloria Streckfus," she said. "She won't be too happy if it comes down like that."

"Too bad. She'll be lucky to avoid prison."

Sharon sipped her iced tea. "Guess Hagerty is the only loose end."

"We'll get him, sooner or later."

After their lunch, they talked in the parking lot for several minutes. Sharon turned to her car and said, "Have a nice trip, Dan, and call me when you get back."

He deftly slipped his arm around her waist, pulled her into a close hug and kissed her. Sharon offered no resistance; she actually enjoyed his spontaneous and public display of affection.

"Sure you don't want to come with me?" he said.

"Mmmm, don't tempt me, Dan."

"Then take care of yourself. I'll see you in a couple of days and we can start exactly where we left off."

Sharon got into her car and drove from the lot. She was so excited, thinking about her close encounter with Dan Mahoney, she didn't remember a thing about the trip home.

CHAPTER TWENTY-SIX

Sharon was in her kitchen Sunday evening when Eliot called. "Just checking in," he said. "How's your day going?"

"Not bad. Just finishing a chicken pot pie."

"You were planning to spend some time in your office this morning after I left. Did you get a lot done?"

"I wrote a final report for Sgt. Hess on Mrs. Streckfus."

"So you're all finished with her?"

"Absolutely. Hess was also in the office today and he gave me a new assignment starting tomorrow. Fraud and ID thefts at the Apple Store. It'll be good to get back to some *normal* work again."

"Got a question for you. Have you seen my ring anywhere?"

"Your ring?"

"Yeah, the one with the diamonds on top. Grand prize for Top Cowboy at the Santa Fe Rodeo. Can't find it and thought I might have left it at your place."

"I don't recall seeing you wear it recently."

"Maybe it fell out of my bag when I was unpacking, or packing up this morning. Might have rolled under the bed or something. Could you look around for it?"

"Sure, I'll do that."

"Thanks, Sharon. I'll let you get back to your dinner."

She paused for a moment and thought about how mundane and almost pitiful this conversation was going. *He's grasping at straws and doesn't know how to talk to me anymore.* She snapped out of it and said, "Hey Eliot, something I forgot to tell you. I talked with Dan Mahoney and he's flying off to the Cayman Islands today. Mansfield is there and another FBI agent from D. C. is going to join him and—I don't know—maybe take him into custody and bring him back."

"Whoa, you lost me. I thought the mayor was going to meet his wife for a beach vacation in the Carolinas."

"He did fly to Raleigh but kept on going. We think he's after the money Frank Streckfus made overseas and hid in a Caymans Island bank."

"Can he get his hands on it?"

"Not sure. He'd probably need authorization from Frank."

"Partners in crime. Maybe they had a joint account. Hope your agent friend has some good luck down there." He paused. "Have to believe that Mrs. Streckfus plays a role in their operation. And the Hagerty guy. Any news on his whereabouts?"

"Not a word."

"Are you going to see Mrs. Streckfus again?"

"Not if I can help it. Ted Birdsall and Dan Mahoney are the chief bag-holders on the case. And Sgt. Hess was very clear; he doesn't want me spending any more time on this business."

"When do you think Mahoney will get back to Pueblo?"

"Have no idea but I'm sure he'll let me know."

"Yep, I guess he will."

"Don't worry, Eliot. I'll keep you in the loop."

They chatted for a few minutes. Before ending the call, Eliot mentioned a shakeup of the editorial staff at the Leadville *Herald Democrat*. It was more interesting to him than her but she listened with patience.

Sharon finished her kitchen cleanup, searched the house for Eliot's ring with negative results, and decided to take a walk. The sun was setting, the temperature had dropped to a pleasant 75 degrees, and she wanted the exercise. *Great opportunity to clear the head and think some pleasant thoughts.*

About an hour later Eliot polished off his own makeshift dinner of beef stew he'd scooped from a hot metal canister in Leadville's largest supermarket. He was about to watch a TV episode of *Longmire* but decided to check his e-mail first. His composure was shattered when he opened an e-mail with capital letters in the subject line reading MISCHIEF IN PUEBLO. A high resolution color photograph in the text block showed Sharon in a close embrace with Dan Mahoney, clearly enjoying the experience. The only text to accompany the photo was a question: **Think you can really trust this bitch?**

Eliot immediately called Sharon. "Have you checked your e-mail lately?"

"What's wrong, Eliot? Suffering separation anxiety?"

"Just answer the question, please."

"All right but I don't like the tone of your voice."

"Sorry, but there's something you need to see."

Eliot listened patiently and soon heard the sound of her computer being turned on. "OK, I'm downloading my e-mails." The next several seconds seemed like hours. "Damn you, Eliot, and damn that stupid slutty woman."

"My sentiments exactly."

"It's not as bad as it looks," she said.

"Think I've heard that line before."

"This is all your fault. The woman belongs in an institution, like our jail or the big house in Canon City."

Eliot let her vent. When she paused to take a breath he said, "Let's think about this for a minute. We know Cassie's in Pueblo and watching you."

"Stalking me."

"She has a camera and knows both of our e-mail addresses. Probably knows where you live."

"I don't like this, Eliot. Being a sitting duck and easy target for your deranged girlfriend."

"I don't like it either, Sharon, and I think we need to work together and put her out of action."

"Agreed. So how do we do it?"

"She's probably staying in a Pueblo motel. We need to find her."

"Don't even think about checking all of them. Too many in town and she could be using an alias or wearing a disguise. Maybe staying in a different one each night."

"Is there some way you can check? You're pretty handy with the computer, checking out financial trails and crime records."

"I'd need some kind of unique identifier. Like her social security number or a credit card."

"A credit card?" Eliot paused to think for a moment. "I might be able to help with that. She paid for dinner with a credit card at Quincy's the first time she was up here. Stayed at the Silver King Inn that night and probably used a credit card to pay for her room."

"Can you check with those places?"

"I'll head over to Quincy's right now, catch them before they close. Then I'll try the Silver King."

"Will they hand over that kind of information just like that?"

"They know me pretty well so it shouldn't be any trouble. I'll tell them I'm investigating a stolen credit card and a possible identity theft." He chuckled. "Taking a page out of your notebook, Detective Hardcastle."

"Call me when you have something. Even when you don't."

"It could be late."

"You think I can sleep with this crap going on?"

"I'll call you as soon as I can. And lock your doors, Sharon."

Eliot drove to Quincy's and explained the situation to the duty manager. He was in luck; the restaurant's copies of credit card receipts for the last three months were stored in a cardboard box. They found Cassie's dinner receipt after several minutes of leafing through all the paper. Eliot jotted down the card number, thanked the manager and went out to his SUV. Just to be sure, he drove to the Silver King Inn and went through a similar drill with the night clerk. It took longer this time but they found a receipt for Cassie's one night stay. She had used a different credit card this time and Eliot wrote its number in his notebook.

It was after nine o'clock when he got home and called Sharon. "Struck pay dirt," he said with triumph, and proceeded to read off the credit card data to her.

"Wonder why she used two cards?"

"Have no idea," he said. "She probably has a wallet full of 'em and pulls one out at random whenever she needs to."

"You did good, Eliot. I'll get right on this."

"Call me if you find anything."

"You'll be the first to know."

Sharon disconnected and returned to her computer. She worked steadily for a good half hour and soon became frustrated with the results. She found Cassie's charges which Eliot had identified in Leadville, a ticket on Southwest Airlines from Denver to Phoenix, and numerous charges in the Scottsdale area for gasoline, pharmacies and department stores. After that, nothing. There were no charges for anything in Pueblo. *This is not making any sense. Either she's using cash or other credit cards. Another dead end on this stupid search for an idiotic and dangerous woman.*

She was about to call Eliot when her phone rang. The caller ID displayed the words PVMedCntr. She thought of letting it roll over to voice mail but decided to answer it since it could be an emergency. "Detective Hardcastle."

"Oh Sharon, I'm so glad to hear your voice."

"Gloria? I'm surprised it's you. No, I'm relieved, you sound much better."

"A bit, I'm in a private room, still doped up with pain killers. Have you caught that Hagerty guy yet?"

"Look, I know you've been through a terrible experience, but I'm off the case now. You need to talk with Detective Birdsall."

"The heck with him. What about your FBI pal? Is he off the case too?"

Sharon hesitated, wondering how much she could divulge. "He had to leave town, back to the east coast. I think."

"Where's Brian Mansfield? Why hasn't he come to see me? Someone must have told him what happened."

"I understand he's in Raleigh with his wife. Something about a beach vacation along the Outer Banks." *I don't like where this is heading.*

"Very strange. Told me he wasn't going to do that. Let her do the hobnobbing with all the Cary socialite snobs without him."

"Guess he changed his mind."

"Do you know when he's coming back?"

"Sorry, I have no idea." The line went dead, prompting Sharon to stare at her phone. *Guess we're done here.*

Sharon called Eliot and summarized what she'd learned about Cassie's credit cards. "Nothing for Pueblo?" he said. "That is weird."

"Do you think she's *that* clever? Covering her tracks so we can't find her?"

"Frankly, no. Probably just our bad luck."

"What now, Eliot? Sit around and twiddle our thumbs?"

"I'm coming back down so we can twiddle together."

"Don't do that. It's late and you wouldn't get here until after midnight."

"No problem, I'll have a thermos full of coffee. I'm the one responsible for this mess and I want to see it cleaned up once and for all. Besides, I have a plan."

"A plan?"

"Yep, we know what her vehicle looks like and it probably has Arizona plates on it. So we drive around town, cruising through motel parking lots. We can do it quickly and with no risk on our part."

"We? You have a mouse in your pocket?"

"We're a good team, Sharon. I'll need another pair of eyes along while I do the driving."

"OK, let's say we spot her SUV parked at a motel. What's the next step?"

"We go into the front office and find out what room she's in.

You'll probably have to show your ID to get it."

"Then we break down the door? Drag her outside and beat her with rubber hoses?"

He laughed. "Sure would like to. Having you arrest her would be better."

"And what's the charge, sheriff? About the only bad thing we know about is her sending that photo to both of us. But we'd have a hard time proving it came from her."

"Guess we'll have to play that part by ear. Maybe provoke an incident, make her do something to justify picking her up."

"Hope I can stay awake until then."

"I'll poke you if you get sleepy."

"You do and I'll poke you right back."

He chuckled. "See you in a couple of hours."

"Drive safely. I'll keep my door locked. Call me when you get close to the house."

Chapter Twenty-Seven

Sharon answered her cell phone immediately. "Where are you, Eliot?"

"Just turned into your street."

"I'll unlock the front door."

Five minutes later he walked inside and Sharon greeted him with a warm hug and an enthusiastic kiss. "I know I told you not to come but I'm glad you did."

"Me too. That kiss was worth the trip."

"Come inside for a sec and tell me how you want to do this."

"Let's head out now and check a few places while we're both awake."

Sharon locked up and they got into Eliot's SUV. She glanced at the dashboard clock that read 11:50 P.M. "Is that the right time?"

"Yep."

"Did you put wings on this vehicle?"

Eliot chuckled. "I might have exceeded the speed limit once or twice. Not too much traffic on the highways so I was able to make good time."

He backed out of the driveway and headed towards

downtown. "Where would you like to start?" she said.

"That picture of you and Mahoney. You recall where it was taken?"

"Unfortunately, yes. Right outside of IHOP."

"Aren't there some motels around that place?"

"A Ramada and a Hilton Express, I think."

"Let's try them first."

They came to the group of motels and drove slowly through different parking areas next to each establishment. Eliot said, "We're looking for a silver BMW SUV with Arizona plates."

"Right, I remember."

The parking areas were well lighted with no motorized or pedestrian traffic in any of them. They searched until each motel in the immediate area had been checked out. Eliot pulled over and let the engine idle. "You need gas?" she said.

"I still have plenty."

"Shall we keep looking?"

"Let's try a few more places. Any ideas?"

"There's a big Marriott Courtyard over on First Street. A place like that may be more her style. What *is* her style, Eliot? You know her better than I do."

"Any port in a storm would be my guess." He shifted into drive and the vehicle lurched ahead.

They entered the Marriott's parking lot and, as they began a slow looping path, Sharon called out, "Bingo."

Eliot tapped the brakes lightly. "Where?"

"Back up, Eliot. On my side, we just passed it."

He put it in reverse and inched backward several yards. "Yep, there it is." He maneuvered the SUV to park directly in back of the BMW, making it impossible for an escape. He shut off the engine and both went over to look inside the vehicle. "It's not saying much to me," she said. She took out her notepad and wrote down the license plate number.

"Let's go inside," he said. "I'll let you do the talking for us."

A young woman behind the front desk greeted them with a smile. "Welcome," she said, "how may I help you?"

Sharon showed her ID. "We're looking for a woman who may be staying here. Mrs. Cassandra Hume, an Arizona resident."

"She may be registered as Cassandra Maugham," said Eliot.

The receptionist's smile disappeared. "Let me check." She sat down in front of her computer and worked the mouse and keyboard. "Sorry, no one here by that name."

Eliot and Sharon exchanged disappointed looks and she showed her notepad to the receptionist. "A vehicle outside in your lot has Arizona plates with this number. I'd like you to check your registrations and tell us who the driver is."

"This could take some time."

"'We can wait," said Sharon.

The receptionist went to a back room while Eliot and Sharon took seats in the lobby. Fifteen minutes later she came back and they joined her at the front desk. "OK, we have three different parties from Arizona staying with us right now." She spread three registration cards out on the counter for their inspection. "Sometimes they forget to fill in the license number."

They looked over the three cards. Two showed the names of man and woman couples and the third listed a Ronald Springer from Prescott. The space for a license number was blank in the last card.

"Hold on," said Eliot, "I'll be right back." He went outside and came back in less than five minutes.

"What were you doing out there?" said Sharon.

"Checking that plate again. It has a plastic frame with the name of a BMW dealer in Prescott. Must be Mr. Springer's BMW we were looking at."

Sharon glanced at Eliot and back to the receptionist. "Looks like she's not here. Thanks for your help."

Back in Eliot's SUV, she said, "I should have noticed that."

"Easy to overlook. What's next?"

"Home. I have to get up early."

"Sounds good. Maybe I can snoop around tomorrow while you're working."

On Sunday evening, the 737 touched down at Owen Roberts International Airport in a light rain. As the aircraft taxied toward the gate, the senior flight attendant made the customary announcement. "Welcome to George Town, capital of the Cayman Islands, where the local time is 11:45. On behalf of Cayman Airways, we wish you a pleasant evening and thank you for flying with us."

After the all clear was given for passengers to deplane, Dan Mahoney grabbed his carryon bag and raced to the immigration and customs stations. It was a quick process; getting his passport stamped, stating that his trip was for business purposes and having nothing to declare.

He immediately spotted his FBI contact when he entered the greeting hall for arriving passengers. Heavyset and a good ten years older than Dan, he had salt and pepper gray hair. The man walked over and extended his hand. "Special Agent Mahoney? I'm Bruce Fielding. Have a nice flight?"

"Hi Bruce, please call me Dan. The flight was OK but we

had a delay getting away from the gate in Miami."

"Probably because of our weather. Had a nice storm blow though a couple of hours ago. Ready to roll? I've got a rental parked outside."

"Lead the way, Bruce."

As they approached the car he told Dan, "They drive on the left here, just like England."

Dan had been heading for the car's right side but quickly changed direction to enter on the left where the passenger sits.

Bruce started the car and they drove from the airport through George Town's light traffic. "You're pretty good with this wrong-way driving," said Dan.

"Nothing to it. Had my baptism of fire in London and a later refresher course in Tokyo."

"What's the situation with Mr. Mansfield?"

"He arrived yesterday and is staying at the Ritz-Carlton. Quite a posh place out there along Seven Mile Beach."

"Sounds expensive. He must be feeling prosperous."

"All the places out there are pricey. We're staying at the Coral Stone Club right next door. Their usual nightly rate is $595."

"Good God, my boss will never approve that."

"Don't sweat it. They give us Feds a steep discount. We'll be OK."

"How about tomorrow. How do we handle it?"

Bruce chuckled. "Very carefully. We check you in, we get a good night's sleep and meet for breakfast in the hotel's coffee shop."

"And Mansfield . . . do we invite him to join us?"

Bruce laughed out loud. "I like your style, Daniel. No, we're going to tail him to the bank of his choosing when he leaves the

Ritz. I've got a guy over there, a native who works part time, and I've hired him to be our lookout. When Mansfield starts to move, he calls me and we're on him like flies on horse manure."

"All right, we track him to a bank. I don't think we can arrest him or take him into custody just yet."

"Correct. We'll need probable cause before we do something like that. He'll recognize you immediately and then it's hardball time for all three of us."

"You can't expect him to walk out of there with a sack full of cash."

"Of course not. But a cashier's check is a possibility. Or a wire transfer receipt for moving his money to another country."

"Then what?"

"Exactly."

The conversation paused until they reached the Coral Stone. Mahoney checked in and accompanied Bruce to the elevator and up to the third floor where they had adjacent rooms.

At the door to Dan's room, Bruce said, "Tomorrow's weather will be hot and humid, not like your Colorado Rockies. *Do not dress like a fibbie.*"

"Got it. Cool and comfortable, just like one of the natives."

Bruce laughed, patted Dan on the back and said, "Sleep well, my friend."

Brian Mansfield sat on the beach-side patio of the Ritz-Carlton, enjoying the elaborate breakfast buffet. He'd consumed copious amounts of food: eggs benedict, fresh tropical fruit, warm flaky pastries, and three glasses of champagne. As he sipped his coffee, he thought about the history of his partnerships with Frank Streckfus and Ed Hagerty. *We had some rough patches along the way, serious disagreements on how to transact our business in Iraq and Afghanistan, and whether we should continue our troublesome relationships with certain members of the royal family in Saudi. No matter, it's all in the past now. With the big prize in sight, I can forget about all their treachery and start a new life. After today, only two final obstacles remain: Hagerty and Gloria. Too bad his bullet missed her heart. If he'd been a better marksman, I would have set him up for a special meeting with that Hardcastle bitch.*

He finished his coffee, strolled over to the lobby and went out the front door. At the taxi stand, he got into the back seat of the first one in line. "UBS House, please. It's on Elgin Avenue."

"Yes, sir, I know exactly where it is."

Fifteen minutes later they arrived at a white seven story building in the center of George Town. Mansfield went inside and was greeted by a woman receptionist.

"I have a ten o'clock meeting with Monette Gilbert."

"And your name, sir?"

"Brian Mansfield."

She made a phone call and said to Brian, "Someone will be with you promptly, sir. You may wait here in the lobby. Would you care for some tea? Coffee perhaps?"

"Thank you, no." He found a comfortable seat on a leather sofa and found copies of *The Economist, Forbes* and the *Wall Street Journal* on the facing coffee table. He didn't have time to read any of them.

A well-dressed young man suddenly appeared. "Mr. Mansfield? Please follow me. We shall ascend to Ms. Gilbert's office."

They took an elevator to the seventh floor. Brian's escort led him to a corner office with magnificent island views in two directions. A woman about thirty-five with a dark complexion welcomed him. "Please come in, Mr. Mansfield. Would you like tea, coffee or water?"

"No, thank you. I'm fine."

Brian first noticed her slight British accent and then the spaciousness and well appointed office furnishings. *The mayor of Pueblo doesn't have it this good.*

Both took seats, she behind her desk and he in front. "How may we be of service today?" she said.

Brian fiddled nervously with his slim briefcase and had difficulty opening it. He found several papers clipped together and handed them to her. "It's about our account with your bank. I'd like to close it."

Ms. Gilbert examined the papers intensely and looked up at Brian with a confused look on her face. "This is most irregular. I don't understand."

"You don't understand? It seems clear to me. I'm the joint owner of this account with Mr. Streckfus and I want it closed." He found his passport and showed it to her. "I can accept a cashier's check or have the funds wired to another account, whichever is more efficient. The quickest way possible, that is."

Ms. Gilbert placed the fingertips of both hands on Brian's papers and carefully pushed them aside. "I'm afraid we cannot honor your request, Mr. Mansfield. You see, this account has already been closed out."

"That's impossible," he said, his voice louder and strained. "I don't believe it."

"It was closed only three days ago by Mr. Streckfus. I handled the entire transaction myself."

"How can that be? What happened to the money?"

"It was transferred to another account at our headquarters in Basel. I assure you this action was one hundred percent legitimate."

Brian stood. "That's impossible, Frank Streckfus is dead," he shouted. "I saw his body at the funeral home."

"When did Mr. Streckfus pass?"

"Couple of weeks ago. You've stolen our money, my money. I demand you get it back. I'm not going anywhere until I get all of it."

"Sit down, Mr. Mansfield. We will deal with this problem in a professional and civilized manner. I will not be threatened."

"No, I will not." He pushed his chair back an reached across her desk for the papers, knocking over her lamp in the process. "You people are out to cheat me . . . I've worked hard for this money . . . taken serious risks . . . No, I'm not leaving this place until you get it fixed."

Ms. Gilbert picked up her phone and spoke only two words. Within seconds two burly men wearing black uniforms entered her office, each touching one of Brian's arms. "These men will escort you from the premises, Mr. Mansfield. I advise you not to return until you calm down or we will ask the police to take you into custody."

"This is robbery and I'm going to sue your lousy bank."

Ms. Gilbert stuffed Brian's paperwork into his briefcase and handed it to him. "Let me know your mailing address and I will send you a complete record of your account. You would be well advised to closely examine its recent activities before initiating any legal proceedings. It will save you considerable time and money. Good day, Mr. Mansfield."

The security officers accompanied Brian down to the lobby.

As they approached the main entrance, two men were blocking their exit. Brian recognized one of the men and made a silly grin. "Well, well," he said, "isn't this just icing on the cake?"

"Good morning," said Dan Mahoney while pointing to his companion. "Mayor Mansfield, this is Special Agent Fielding."

Fielding nodded. "Mr. Mayor. We'd like a few words."

The two uniforms sensed what was happening and left.

Mansfield burst into delirious laughter. "You want some words? I've got some words for you. *You're screwed. I'm screwed. We're all screwed.*"

CHAPTER TWENTY-EIGHT

Sharon was about to leave her office for lunch with Eliot when she heard her cell phone jingle. Special Agent Dan Mahoney was calling.

"Hi, Dan, having a good time down there in the tropics?"

"You would not believe it. I'm at the George Town airport."

"Got everything wrapped up already?"

"Far from it." He told her about meeting Brian Mansfield in the UBS Bank lobby and the mayor's revelation that there was no money to be had.

"I'm not processing this, Dan. A dead man sent a transfer wire and the money was sent to Switzerland? You think Mansfield is lying?"

"Afraid not. While Special Agent Fielding sat with him, I went up to see Ms. Gilbert, the bank officer who met with Mansfield. She handled the wire transfer herself and, when she did, had every reason to believe it was legit. Now she's having second thoughts and major indigestion. And because the FBI has made its presence known by yours truly, her bank will have to treat the matter as possible fraud."

"The international incident you were hoping to avoid."

"Exactly."

"Where's the mayor now?"

"Right here with me and Fielding."

"Have you arrested him? Are you bringing him back to Pueblo?"

"No, to both questions. We're flying to Miami and then going our separate ways. Mansfield to Raleigh for a hookup with his wife and Fielding back to D. C. How about a late dinner with me tonight so I can fill you in?"

She ignored his question. "So he's getting off scot free."

"We don't have any solid evidence at this point that would lead to a conviction. But we're not going to forget about him. We'll watch him and keep digging until we find evidence that will put him away."

"This is crazy, Dan. After all the work we've done."

"There's still one more loose end, something we may be able to work."

"That inclusive *we* again."

"OK, think for a minute. Gloria Streckfus was pretty handy with her husband's computer, setting us up with those e-mails in the trash can."

"Keep going."

"So UBS in the Caymans gets wire transfer instructions from Frank Streckfus, or somebody acting like Frank, who just happened to get himself killed a couple of weeks ago. Like, maybe his wife? Couple of days before Hagerty catches her?"

"It's possible, I suppose."

"I'll bet there's more to this story on that same computer."

"What's your point, Dan?"

"Maybe you could drop by the Streckfus place and do some more snooping. She'll be in the hospital for a while and nobody will be looking over your shoulder."

"You're asking me do to something patently illegal while you're at 30,000 feet sipping a vodka martini? Don't think so, Special Agent."

"All right. I admit we're on a slippery slope here but I had to ask."

"Gotta go. See you around, Dan."

"What about dinner? I didn't catch your answer."

"I didn't throw it."

"More police work, huh?"

"As a matter of fact, an old problem has resurfaced just in time to haunt me. An e-mail, a short one with an attached photo of you and me. Standing in the IHOP parking lot and hugging each other before you head for the airport. My friend Eliot also got the same e-mail. Bottom line, that crazy woman is back in Pueblo. She's intent on doing serious damage to me and my relationship with him. Eliot came down last night and we've been cruising around town trying to find her."

Dan thought about it for a moment. "Kind of like looking for a needle in a haystack, isn't it?"

"Just about. We know what kind of vehicle she's driving but only Eliot knows what she looks like."

"OK, Sharon, I'll let you get on with it. I'll try to visit Parkview tomorrow and see if Mrs.Streckfus has anything to say."

"He wants you to do what?" Eliot was about to take a big bite of his sandwich when Sharon mentioned Dan Mahoney's snooping suggestion.

"Pretty risky, huh?"

"You could lose your job doing something like that."

"I know."

"And if you did find some incriminating information, the prosecutor couldn't use it in court."

"Right again. I think he's grasping at straws, just like the rest of us." She paused for a sip of iced tea. "Anyway, he's coming back tonight and plans to see Gloria tomorrow."

"I went by there this morning. Talked to a nurse but didn't see Mrs. Streckfus."

"What did the nurse have to say?"

"Not much. Her daughters have been in and out with the grandparents, probably staying with them for now. Other than that, the medical folks are concentrating on her recovery. Which is starting to look better, she said."

"Glad to hear that."

"Oh, and an interesting coincidence. Happened to see Stephanie White in the hallway and we talked a bit. Chance told her about meeting up with me and being overpowered by two policemen."

"And you set her straight?"

"Sure did. She laughed because Chance didn't tell her that one of the police officers who subdued him was a woman detective."

"He's kind of selective about giving her information."

"She also said he was pretty unhappy about her meeting me in Leadville."

"Probably hurt his macho pride."

"Right on target, Sharon. Doesn't want her fighting his battles."

"So they're a happy couple now?"

"Appears that way. Said his work schedule will be changed soon and they'll have more time to spend together."

Sharon took a last bite of her club sandwich. "What are your plans for this afternoon?"

Eliot grinned and twirled the end of his mustache. "Depends on your availability."

"I'll be at the Apple Store working on a new case. Does that interest you?"

"Afraid not. I'll do some cruising instead and see if I can locate that woman who's been causing so many problems."

"That should keep you busy. Call me if you see anything suspicious."

"I've also been thinking about something you said last night about Cassie's style. You know, The Broadmoor would be more like her style than the places we checked last night. We should take a look-see there tonight."

"That's up in Colorado Springs."

"True, but it's only forty-five minutes away. Maybe she's thinking we'd never look there and she'd be under the radar."

"Oh well, what the heck. Let's give it a shot."

After lunch, instead of driving to the Apple Store, Sharon went to Parkview Medical Center. She had two motives for doing this: visiting the sick was a corporal work of mercy, something she remembered from her catechism classes back in Creve Couer; the other was an ulterior one connected to the Mansfield-Streckfus money problem.

The duty nurse asked Sharon to keep her stay as short as possible and not cause the patient any undue stress. Gloria was still hooked up to an IV tube and not allowed any solid food.

When Sharon entered the room, she noticed Gloria was dozing. She sat in a chair next to her bed and looked around the room.

Three large floral arrangements were set on a table and a half dozen get well cards lined a window sill. The blinds had been partially drawn to diffuse the bright sunlight.

Gloria opened her eyes slightly and said, "Hi, Sharon. Been here long?"

"Not at all. Didn't want to wake you."

"Doesn't matter. About all I do is sleep, not much else going on." She shifted her body to become more comfortable which prompted Sharon to get up and adjust Gloria's pillow. "Any news on Hagerty?"

"Detective Birdsall put out an all points bulletin. But no, we haven't got more on him than that."

She sighed. "He's long gone, maybe even out of the country by now. What about our mayor? Is he back in town yet?"

Sharon hesitated. "I think he's still on vacation with Mrs. Mansfield. Right now his deputy is looking after city business."

"When's he coming back?"

"Not sure, probably by the end of this week."

"You're just a bundle of information today, detective."

"Wish I had more." She paused and said, "I've been thinking of Kate and Joanna. Are they OK? Is there anything I can do for them?"

"They came to see me last night with my folks. Been staying with them since I was brought here."

"Living with grandparents probably isn't going to be much fun for teenage girls."

"They make do with their iPhones, iPads and all the other iCrap things they have. Gotta keep connected with all their friends or they'll lose their place in the teen hierarchy."

Sharon laughed and Gloria made a hoarse and visibly painful

giggle. They chatted for several minutes and when a nurse came in to check Gloria's IV and the electronic monitors, Sharon decided it was a good time to leave.

She waited outside for several minutes, thinking about her next move. Instead of heading to the Apple Store she drove to the Streckfus residence. She parked about twenty-five yards away but still had a view of the front door.

She sat quietly in the car, content to watch the house and the surrounding neighborhood. The house looked unoccupied but there was plenty of activity nearby. During the next quarter hour of Sharon's stakeout, a woman came out of the house next door to water her rose garden, a mail truck stopped at every house on the block, and a UPS truck dropped off two boxes at a house immediately next to Sharon's car. When the UPS driver spotted Sharon and smiled, she quickly drove away. Bad idea, she thought, trying to do undercover spying in broad daylight. Kills all chances of plausible deniability.

Sharon worked until seven o'clock that evening and called Eliot before leaving for home. She found him putting hamburgers on the lighted outdoor grill when she arrived. He had everything ready for dinner, allowing them time to relax with vodka tonics before sitting down to eat.

Eliot's afternoon activity, he said, was driving around Pueblo looking for Cassie Maugham. The only thing accomplished was burning up plenty of gas.

Sharon talked about her detective work at the Apple Store. She'd interviewed the manager and three younger employees, two women and a man, who worked at the Genius counter fixing devices and otherwise helping customers learn how to operate their phones and computers. She felt the criminal activity was being done by people posing as customers rather than any of the store's employees. She only mentioned the Parkview visit as a minor event and conveniently omitted her informal stakeout of the Streckfus residence.

After dinner and cleaning up the kitchen, Eliot and Sharon got into his SUV and headed north to Colorado Springs on I-25. They arrived at the sprawling Broadmoor grounds at sunset and began a slow and methodical cruise through the hotel's many parking areas. After nearly an hour had passed with no sighting of the silver BMW SUV with Arizona license plates, Eliot pulled over to park. "Guess this place isn't her style after all," he said. "Think we should go around one more time?"

"Before we do that, let's check with the people in the registration office."

"Good idea."

They drove to the spacious circular driveway and entrance for arriving guests, parked the SUV and went inside. Two clerks were on duty, a man and a woman both wearing dark blue jackets, white shirts and blue ties. Sharon whispered to Eliot, "Must be nice to have enough money to stay in a place like this."

The woman clerk was working on a computer terminal but the young man greeted them with a flashy smile. "Welcome to The Broadmoor."

They showed him IDs but Eliot did the talking. "We're looking for a woman who might be one of your guests. Cassandra Maugham or possibly registered as Cassandra Hume."

"Has she done something wrong?"

"We just need to talk with her."

"Let me check." He went to a computer terminal and came

back several minutes later. "Sorry, sheriff, nobody here by either of those names."

"Thanks for trying." He turned to Sharon and said, "Guess we can head back."

"You know, I'm getting sick and tired of this, chasing all over hell's half acre."

The desk clerk spoke up. "Detective . . . tell me your name again please."

"Hardcastle. Sharon Hardcastle."

He smiled. "Excuse me for a moment." He went over to his female colleague and they looked through a short stack of cards and envelopes. He found something, brought it back and handed it to Sharon. "I thought your name was familiar."

She took the envelope and stared at the front. DETECTIVE HARDCASTLE was printed on the front. "What the heck is this?"

"Better open it and see," said Eliot.

She ripped it open, pulled out a single folded sheet of Broadmoor stationery and began to read the jagged and barely legible handwriting.

Hello, you stupid bitch. As you can see, I'm not here anymore. Where do you think I am? You call yourself a detective when I've been right under your nose all this time? I can't believe you're missing all these clues I've worked so hard to create and drop where you had to find them. Well, here's one that's really simple, something you should have no trouble understanding with your feeble brain. I'm in the Land of Oz so all you have to do is follow the Yellow Brick Road. Ta Ta for now. Big C.

Sharon crumpled the paper into a ball and shoved it into Eliot's hand. "Here's something for your scrapbook."

Chapter Twenty-Nine

Conversation was sparse during Eliot and Sharon's return to Pueblo. He concentrated on the highway while listening to country western music on the radio. Sharon kept turning over in her mind the two items troubling her: Cassie's vendetta and Gloria's financial wrongdoing. As they got closer to Pueblo, the Cassie problem faded and Sharon became more certain that she could and should do something about the Streckfus problem.

On reaching the first Pueblo exit Sharon said, "Get off here, Eliot."

"This is not the one for your place."

"I know. Humor me, please."

He exited the freeway and Sharon gave him a series of left or right turn prompts. Ten minutes later they were well inside an upscale residential neighborhood. There was no traffic and only a few houses had lights on.

"Thinking of upgrading your living quarters?" he said.

"Pull over next to the fire hydrant and turn off the engine."

After doing so he said, "Would you like to tell me what we're doing here?"

"Look to your left, Eliot. The big place with the double two car garage."

"Nice place. Pretty expensive, I'd say."

"*Very* expensive. It's the Streckfus home."

"Hmmm. All of its residents are elsewhere, I suppose."

She extended her arm and massaged his neck. "I need you to do me a favor. I'm going inside and have a quick look through Frank's computer. I'll have my cell phone handy so you can call me if you spot anybody coming."

"So I'll be aiding and abetting."

"Let's not get too technical about this. It's more of an extension of the search, like the one Gloria allowed before. The one we never finished because Mansfield showed up and interrupted us."

"You should have been a lawyer, Sharon."

She sighed. "You know the old saying, desperate times call for desperate measures."

He chuckled. "Think I've heard someone else say that recently."

"I won't be long and the risk is small."

"If you find something, what then?" he said.

"Then we'll go home, with or without it."

"I must be crazy."

She pulled his head closer and kissed him. "Two of a kind," she said, got out of the SUV and walked briskly to the house's front door. It was locked, as expected. She looked around the front porch for places to hide a key and found a doormat, the most logical place. There was no key under it but she did find one tucked under a flower pot sitting to the side of the front door. She put the key into the doorknob's lock, but before turning it, said a silent prayer that the alarm wouldn't go off. She'd given it a lot of thought before this moment, concluding that when Gloria was taken to Parkview's ER, Kate and Joanna would have been too stressed to think of setting it.

Here's hoping, she thought.

She stepped inside, closed the door and spotted the alarm panel. The green light was on and she exhaled a huge sigh of relief.

She turned on her pen flashlight and walked directly to Frank's office. She sat in his chair, placed her cell phone on his desk and turned on his computer. Her eyes became more accustomed to the darkness as the computer came alive and the software was booted up.

Becoming familiar again with the screen icons, the e-mail folders and the files was easy because she remembered the previous searches when Gloria was in the room. But she was taken aback when she started browsing the e-mails. Many were missing, that much she could tell, and there were only a few e-mail folders. *Someone must have deleted a lot of them.* When she clicked on the internal hard drive icon and saw only a few plain vanilla file folders, she became even more agitated. *There's nothing worth looking at on this machine. It's been sanitized and she's covering his tracks.*

She turned off the computer and walked to the front door. Before opening it, she had another idea. *As long as I'm here, I'd better make sure I didn't miss anything.*

Sharon made quick searches of the living room, dining room and kitchen and saw nothing suspicious. She took longer to rummage through the master bedroom and found another laptop computer sitting on a corner desk. This was a newer machine than his and would probably require a password to gain entry.

For the ordinary computer user, this would have presented a near impossible situation. However, because of Sharon's extensive experience dealing with property-related crimes and her detailed knowledge of Gloria's financials and personal data, the odds were significantly in her favor.

She went to work and within minutes had determined Gloria's password, a combination of Kate and Joanna's names plus the year Gloria was born. She pulled up the e-mail program and was reviewing the names of file folders when the nearby landline telephone rang loudly. It was such a shock that Sharon jumped from the chair and made a loud *Gah* sound. She felt a nervous pressure but went back to work.

Over the next several minutes she browsed e-mails addressed to people with Western and Arabic names and with subjects diverse as combat vehicles, furniture, field rations, desert clothing and equipment, and weapons of different caliber. She also discovered files identified by countries such as Iraq, Afghanistan, Yemen, Egypt, Libya, Syria and Israel. The more she found the greater her level of anxiety over the sheer volume of information and the scarcity of time to examine it.

The sound of her cell phone jolted her back to the present. "What's up?"

"You've been in there for quite a while. Everything OK?"

"There's a lot and I need more time."

"Don't think we have it. One of your town's patrol cars just made a sweep and I had to scrunch down so he wouldn't see me."

"Aw crap, what am I gonna do?"

"Better wrap it up, Sharon. We need to make some long tracks."

She disconnected and sat still for a good thirty seconds before making a decision. She shut off the computer, tucked it under her arm, locked the front door on the way out and climbed into the SUV. They were a block away when Eliot turned to look and noticed the computer on her lap. "Adding larceny to your bag of tricks, eh?"

"Not at all. Only a temporary loan for a very short period of time."

Eliot kept silent for the rest of the trip to Sharon's house, fearing his line of questioning wouldn't ease the escalating tension.

When they arrived she asked him to make some coffee while she took the laptop to her office. He made a small pot, brought two cups to her office and found her hard at work. "Thanks for your patience, Eliot. Almost finished with this part."

"What are you doing there?"

"I've hooked up an external hard drive and I'm transferring everything relevant from Gloria's machine to that device."

"And after that?"

"The computer goes back home and we were never there." She took a tentative sip of coffee and looked up at him. "Would you like to run me back?"

He grunted a hmph. "A little double jeopardy this time?"

"I'll be in and out of there before you can say Jumpin' Jack Flash."

Eliot sat down next to her and sipped his brew. "Don't forget to wipe your prints off the computer case."

She laughed. "Gee whizz, sheriff, I would have never thought of that."

An hour and a half later, Eliot and Sharon were back in her home and getting ready for bed. Gloria's computer had been returned to its original desktop position, prints wiped clean and the front door locked. Even a CSI team would have difficulty finding clues that someone had recently gained unlawful entry.

Sharon crawled into bed and Eliot followed after turning off the light. She cuddled up close and he eagerly embraced and kissed her. "Thanks for helping me tonight," she said. "I knew I was over the line but I could never live with myself if those people got away with stealing millions of dollars from their own country."

"We're a good team, Sharon, in so many ways."

"The varsity."

He kissed her again. "What are you going to do with all that iniformation on your hard disk?"

"Good question, sheriff. Tomorrow I'll hook it up to my computer and import all the stuff I transferred from Gloria's machine. Then I'll burn two CDs with all that data and give one CD to Dan Mahoney. The other CD goes into a safe hiding place, like a bank safety deposit box. I'll delete all that stuff from my own machine and then be free and clear of this whole mess, now and forever. Mahoney and his Bureau cronies can get their jollies investigating all of it from now to kingdom come."

They became silent, content to enjoy their familiar intimacy. After a few moments Eliot said, "I'm not sleepy. Guess I should have skipped the coffee."

"Neither am I." She stuck her hand inside the waistband of his pajama shorts. "You recall the last time you made love to me?"

"Have to think about that one. Seems like it's been awhile."

"Still remember how to do it?"

"Well . . . you know what they say."

She punched him playfully in the chest. "You'd better not mention broncos or you're sleeping on the couch."

He chuckled. "Riding a bicycle was closer to what I had in mind."

She pushed him over, sat on top and bent over to kiss him. "Close enough."

Eliot woke suddenly the next morning. He was lying on his stomach with his head facing the clock on the bedside table. It read 8:32. He rolled over to face in the opposite direction and wake Sharon so she wouldn't be late for work but her place in bed was empty.

He stretched hard while lying on his back and sighed, mentally replaying last night's lovemaking. *We are really good together but we won't have any kind of future unless we take care of this Cassie thing once and for all.*

He padded to the kitchen and found a half-full pot of coffee that was still hot. He poured himself a cup and took it to the kitchen table where he found *The Pueblo Chieftain* but figured on reading it later when his brain cleared up. Feeling restless and not sure what to do next, he wandered into the living room to look out the front windows, hoping to find some kind of divine inspiration that would guide him to Cassie's whereabouts and give him the golden words that would persuade her to abandon her lost cause. Instead of receiving a heavenly manifesto, the sight of two vehicles in the driveway sent him another message. *She's still here.*

Eliot went directly to Sharon's second bedroom, the one doubling as an office, and found her sitting at the desk busily working her computer. "Morning, sweetness. Thought you left for your other office."

She turned her head toward him. "That can wait. Wanted to get this CD ready for Mahoney and not lose our momentum."

He moved closer, put his cup at the desk's corner and gave

her a kiss on the neck. "When did you get up?"

"About seven. Pull up a chair, I want to show you some things."

He sat close to her side and looked at the computer screen. "Lay it on me."

She opened a file and clicked on a document. "This is something Gloria sent to the Cayman Islands bank. She's telling them to close the account and transfer all the funds to their bank in Zurich."

"So she's pretending to be her husband?"

"I think they've been partners in this deal all along. She was probably the brains of the operation while Frank did all the heavy lifting overseas."

"And the bank followed through."

"They sure did." She clicked on another document. "This is a bank transfer order and a receipt for the transaction."

He stared at the screen for a few seconds. "Good Lord, I'm having trouble with all those numbers. Is that dollars or Swiss francs?"

She laughed. "It's dollars, just a shade over twelve million."

"And now it's gone forever, hidden away in a Swiss bank."

"Maybe not forever. We'll have to let Special Agent Mahoney work that problem with Justice or the State Department."

"That should keep him busy for a while." *And stop him from trying to interest Sharon in all his romantic bullshit.*

"Here's another interesting thing," she said, clicking on a different document. She kept silent, allowing Eliot to read the text.

"That guy Hagerty again," he said, "wanting a bigger slice of the pie. Who did she send this to?"

"A guy called Younis, Frank's contact in Saudi. I've seen something like this before in one of those e-mails that Gloria planted for Mahoney and me. He thinks it's a code name for one of the Saudi princes. Did you catch the part about cutting Hagerty off the payroll?"

"Yep, on a permanent basis, I'd reckon. Can you tell when she sent it?"

"About two days before Frank was murdered in his Kabul hotel room, give or take because of the difference in time zones."

"Hmm. Sounds like Hagerty knew something was up and got there first." He stood, picked up his coffee cup and drained it. "This is all well and good, Sharon, but what happens next? The only locals still alive are Mrs. Streckfus and Mayor Mansfield. You or Mahoney can't take any of this to the DA, especially since you got it without a search warrant."

"I know, I know. But it's Mahoney's problem, not mine, and certainly not yours."

After a pause he said, "Want some more coffee?"

"No, thanks, I've had too much already."

"Then I'll fix us some breakfast. You about finished?"

"Pretty much. I'll be out to the kitchen in a couple of minutes."

A short time later they sat down to a bacon and egg breakfast. "You have a busy day ahead?" he asked.

"Top priority will be seeing Mahoney. I'll give him a call when I get to the office and set up a meeting. Other than that, the usual financial skulduggery. What are you going to do with yourself?"

"More cruising around your fair city. See if I can pick up Cassie's trail."

"Sounds like a good opportunity to burn up a lot more gas."

"I'm open to ideas."

"I'm fresh out, Eliot. And I think this waiting around for her to make a move is part of her strategy. Scaring us and making us wonder what kind of crap she's going to try next."

"Agreed."

Sharon got up and took her plate to the dishwasher. "Maybe you could think of some counter-terrorist moves before putting your SUV into DRIVE."

CHAPTER THIRTY

Sharon sailed into her office about 9:30, feeling nervous about her late arrival but relieved when there were no colleagues waiting to speak to her or urgent messages lying on her desk. She turned on her computer and started to get herself organized for the day's activities. There were several routine e-mails in the INBOX and she answered them promptly.

The first order of business was to call Special Agent Mahoney. He recognized her ID and answered his phone after two rings. "Hi Sharon, good to hear from you."

"Hello, Dan, how's your day going?"

"Same old, same old. What's up?"

"We need to have a meeting today. I have something important for you."

"Business or intimately personal?"

"You never give up, do you?"

"Can't afford to with so much at stake."

"It's information about the late Mr. Streckfus and his finances."

"All right, I'm listening."

"Can't tell you more than that on the phone."

"How about lunch then?"

"I can do lunch, but not IHOP, please."

"I understand. How about Cactus Flower? 12:30 then?"

"See you there, Dan."

Sharon disconnected and began working on the Apple Store fraud and ID theft case. After several minutes passed, Detective Wasserstein planted herself in the cubicle entrance.

"Hey Hardcastle," she said, "another date with your oh-so-special agent?"

"He's not *my* agent, Deborah, and he sure isn't anything special."

"Whatever. I like your style, though, cozy lunches masquerading as an official business meeting."

Sharon had been looking steadily at her computer screen, trying to send her a message, but it wasn't working. She turned towards Deborah and said, "This will be my last meeting with Special Agent Mahoney. After that, he's all yours."

"You have his phone number handy?"

"It's in the book." She turned back to her computer and Wasserstein drifted away, humming a lively tune.

Sharon worked steadily and lost track of tme. About 12:15 she realized that she'd better scurry if she wanted to be on time for her lunch meeting. She picked up her personal items and started to leave the cubicle when Detective Birdsall suddenly appeared and blocked her exit.

"Just got some fantastic news, Sharon. Hagerty's been arrested and they're bringing him back to Pueblo."

"No kidding," she said. "Where'd they find him?"

"Bozeman, Montana. The dumb bastard got all tanked up in a saloon, started a fight with a bunch of ranch hands and got himself thrown in jail for disturbing the peace. An alert deputy sheriff matched him up with the APB I sent out after Mrs.

Streckfus was shot. A real break for us and the D.A. is working on the arraignment as we speak. We'll charge him with attempted murder and maybe a few other things after we interrogate him."

"That's great, Ted, a big feather in your cap. I'm meeting Special Agent Mahoney for lunch and I'm sure he'll be excited to hear about this."

"Tell him to give me a call and I'll fill him in with the details."

"Will do. He'll probably want to question Hagerty when he's back and safely locked up."

Sharon entered the Cactus Flower close to 12:45 and found Dan sitting at a corner table. He saw her coming, got up and gave her a hug when she came closer. He tried to kiss her but she turned her head. After relaxing his arms slightly he said, "Something wrong?"

"It's not that. I'd just like to keep it strictly professional right now and we've got a lot to talk about."

"Fine." He backed away, pulled out a chair for her and they sat down. "I was starting to worry . . . that you changed your mind and weren't going to show."

"Sorry I'm late," she said, "but I have the best of reasons. Detective Birdsall stopped at my office with some good news. A Montana sheriff recognized Hagerty from the APB. He was already in the Bozeman jail and they're extraditing him back to Pueblo. He'll go to trial for attempted murder for sure and possibly several other charges for good measure."

"Amazing. And it washes away all kinds of sins you might have committed, Sharon, even showing up late for lunch."

She gave him a brief scowl and said, "Birdsall said for you to call him if you want more info."

"I'll do that. I've got some questions for Mr. Hagerty as well.

Like . . . did you kill Frank Streckfus?"

"Which he'll surely deny."

"Of course he will. You know, this presents an interesting legal situation with local and Federal jurisdiction involving separate cases. Birdsall on the extortion attempt and shooting Mrs. Streckfus, and me with all the stuff Hagerty was doing overseas. And figuring out what to do about Mayor Mansfield."

"Should keep you and Ted pretty busy for a while."

"Plus all the lawyers."

A waitress had been standing patiently next to their table waiting for a pause in the conversation. "Think we'd better order, Dan."

He ordered a beef burrito and margarita and she opted for a taco salad and iced tea. After the waitress left he said, "So what's this mysterious thing you have for me?"

Sharon pulled a small plastic case from her purse and handed it over. "Information. The most precious commodity of our trade."

"Such as?"

"Everything you always wanted to know about selling U. S. military equipment to the locals in Iraq and Afghanistan."

"May I ask where you got this?"

"No, you may not."

Mahoney gave her a wide grin. "You did it after all."

"My lips are sealed. And you never got that CD from me."

"So what do I do with this? I won't be able to use it in court."

"Oh, you'll think of something. But it's pretty clear that Gloria Streckfus has been playing us for fools and she needs to stand trial when she recovers. She's the one who sent the transfer instructions to the Cayman Islands bank only a couple of days before Hagerty shot her. It's there on the CD."

"This gives me an idea. Bruce Fielding, the guy who was in

the Caymans with me, is working with Justice and the State Department to recover the money sent to Switzerland. We could use this information to pressure the Caymans bank, make a strong case the money was gained illegally. They wouldn't know where this info came from and couldn't tell if we were bluffing or not."

"There you go," she said. "I thought about this while I was driving over here. You've got Gloria, Hagerty and the mayor, all of them guilty as sin. You might be able to parlay a plea deal with one of them, maybe Mansfield, testifying against the other two for a more lenient prison sentence."

"Good thinking. I'll certainly enjoy working this angle with you."

"You'll be working with Birdsall, not me. I'm off this case as of now. You need to get that through your thick skull, Agent Mahoney."

He laughed. "This case is like the tar baby in the Uncle Remus stories. Once you touch it, Sharon, you can't let go."

"Just watch me."

The waitress brought their food and the conversation moved on to more pleasant topics. When they finished lunch, Dan tried to pick up the check but Sharon insisted on paying her share. He got up and said, "I'll walk you to your car."

"Sit down, please. Can you wait five minutes to give me a head start?"

"Why?"

"I don't want any more pictures taken of you and me together."

He sat down. "Oh, that."

"Yeah, that. Crazy Cassie is still out there, stalking me and playing stupid mind games. Eliot's down here from Leadville and we've been trying to catch her."

"How long will he be in town?"

"As long as it takes, I suppose. Or until he runs out of vacation time."

"He must care an awful lot for you."

Sharon was speechless for a moment, not expecting such a sensitive comment, and made a weak smile. "Yeah, I guess he does."

It was Dan's turn to be quiet for several seconds. "OK, I think the handwriting is on the wall and I'd better stop to read it."

"Sounds like a smart thing to do, Dan."

Sharon started to get up but Dan reached out and touched her hand. "Before you go, a quick question."

"Shoot."

"Would you mind if I asked Wasserstein out for dinner sometime?"

"What?" She pulled her hand back smartly and simultaneously caused her chair to make a loud scraping noise. "You want a date with Deborah?"

"You don't want me to?"

"Good Lord, Dan, it's not what I want. You're a grown man, a supposedly mature adult. You can do whatever you like. And certainly not ask my permission to date another woman."

"Guess I'm not doing this very well."

"She's Jewish, Dan. And you're Catholic, remember?"

"What does that have to do with it?"

"Nothing . . . I just thought . . . never mind."

"I'll stay away from your office. Don't want to make you uncomfortable."

Sharon began to laugh nervously. "Go ahead and give her a call. I think she'll like that." She made a half turn to leave and added, "I do believe you two deserve each other."

CHAPTER THIRTY-ONE

Sharon left the Cactus Flower and drove to the local office of a nationally known bank. She met one of the vice presidents, a woman about sixty, and spent a half hour discussing the recent identity thefts at the Apple Store. A number of debits had been registered for non-existent purchases of iPads and iPhones. The VP was cooperative and eager to put a stop to these activities. Sharon suggested the bank put a computer-generated flag on all future debit card transactions at the Apple Store but the VP agreed only to consider it since it would cost the bank money to process such transactions. Sharon was disappointed but chalked it up to the practice of today's banks to pay strict attention to the bottom line. She also wondered if the automated flag wouldn't save them money in the long run.

She returned to her office in mid-afternoon and was immediately joined by Detective Wasserstein. "Quite a long lunch you had there, Hardcastle." After a cackling sort of laugh she added, "Or maybe it was a short lunch followed by a quickie? You do look a bit flushed."

Sharon made a disgusted grunt. "Sorry to disappoint, but it was just a quick lunch. No more, no less."

"That's too bad. You're uptight, need to get your bell rung

more often."

"Speak for yourself, Deborah. Who knows, maybe your Prince Charming will ride in soon on a white horse and scoop you up for a magic ride into the Kingdom of Love."

"Hoo ha, I'll drink to that."

Sharon sat down at her desk, turned on her computer and proceeded to ignore Deborah. Wasserstein got the hint and returned to her own cubicle. Sharon looked around her desk, hoping to find a message from Eliot but there was none.

She worked for several hours and went home about six o'clock. Eliot was still away so she poured herself a glass of Chardonnay and made an omelet with bacon, onions and cheddar cheese. After cleaning up, she called Eliot's cell phone but it rolled over to his voice mail. "Call me," she said and disconnected.

Sharon had nothing to read and wasn't interested in what was on TV so she went to her home office and switched on the computer. After a few minutes, a thought occurred to her about Cassie and the credit cards she'd used for dinner and the motel room in Leadville. She decided to run another check and was excited to find that one had been used only a couple of hours ago. She'd checked in at The Broadmoor again.

She picked up her cell phone and called Eliot. "Please answer this time, please answer," she said while the phone was ringing.

"Hi Sharon, sorry I missed you awhile ago."

"Eliot, I ran a check on Cassie's credit cards. She just used one and is back at The Broadmoor."

"You sure about that?"

"Absolutely."

"Pretty clever, something I'd never thought of. But that's her style all right, doing the unexpected."

"Where are you? Are you still in Pueblo?"

"Yep, I've been cruising around town, with no luck. Now I know why."

"Come back here and we'll go up there together."

"Be there in a couple."

Fifteen minutes later Eliot and Sharon were in his SUV and heading north on I-25. "All right, Eliot, how do we handle this?"

"Carefully," he said. "We're dealing with an emotionally disturbed person and anything can happen."

"Something unexpected, like you said. I brought my weapon, just in case."

"Let's hope it doesn't come to that."

"Where's yours?"

"In the glove compartment."

Several miles before their exit she said, "You know I'm out of my jurisdiction in Colorado Springs. And you sure don't have any legal authority there."

"I know that but she may not."

"So we do the big bluff?"

"Long enough to get her in my vehicle and back to Pueblo where you can put her away for a long time."

"What do we charge her with?"

"Stalking, for starters. I have a feeling there will be others."

Ten minutes later as the sun was about to disappear they arrived at The Broadmoor's main entrance. Both went inside and found the same desk clerk who'd been on duty last night. Sharon flashed her ID card and said, "Detective Hardcastle."

"I remember," he said, "you were looking for somebody."

"We think she's back again. Registered as Cassandra Hume."

"Let me check." He tapped his keyboard and eyed the

monitor. "Yes, she's a guest. You can use the desk phone to call her."

"Just tell us how to find her room," said Eliot. "We'll take it from there."

The clerk placed a small map on the counter and showed the location of Cassie's room and their present location. "Thank you," said Sharon as they left.

When they came close to the room Eliot said, "There's the silver BMW we've been looking for."

He parked his SUV, they got out and walked cautiously toward the BMW. "This isn't it," said Sharon, "the damn thing's got Colorado plates."

"Hold on." Eliot went to the rear bumper, knelt down and fiddled with the license plate. It almost came off in his hand. He got up and said, "My guess is that she stole this plate. Doing the unexpected again."

"No wonder we couldn't find her. Probably drove by this vehicle several times and never noticed it."

"Think you could call it in?" he said.

"It would take time to run it through and the owner may not have noticed it missing. We can do that later. Let's grab her now."

They walked over to the room. When Sharon pulled her pistol out from a hip holster Eliot gave her a nervous look. Once at the door, she took a position on his left. He knocked hard three times and called out, "Cassie, open the door."

Several anxious moments passed until a woman's voice called out from an open window on his right. "Eliot, is that you?"

"It is. Now open the door."

They heard a jiggling of the lock before the door flew open

and Cassie bounded straight into Eliot's arms. She gave him a series of rapid-fire kisses, squealing out frantic words like someone rescued from a hostage situation. "You did it," she cried out, "you came back, I knew you would, I never—" She spotted Sharon who was holstering her weapon. "What the hell is *she* doing here?"

"She's going to arrest you and we're taking you back to Pueblo."

Cassie backed away from him, fists clenched and raised in the air. It was the first moment Eliot and Sharon noticed Cassie was wearing only panties and a pink T-shirt.

"This is bullshit," she shouted, "I haven't done anything."

"Wrong," said Sharon, "you've been stalking me and we have your photos to prove it. There's also another matter about your license plate."

Eliot turned Cassie around, grabbed both wrists and gave her a firm nudge back into the room. "Let's get you dressed before we leave here."

"What about my things? My vehicle?"

"Toss them in your suitcase. We'll have your SUV towed back to Pueblo and you can pay them when you get out."

Cassie started crying. "I want a lawyer. I don't deserve this kind of treatment. You know me, Eliot, I wouldn't do anything against the law."

"Get dressed," said Sharon, picking Cassie's suitcase up off the floor and spreading it open on the bed. "Throw in everything you want to keep and let's get going."

Cassie grabbed a wad of tissue, dabbed her eyes and blew her nose, and dressed hurriedly in jeans and sandals. "You two are going to regret this," she said. "I'll sue you both for false arrest and get your asses thrown out of the department. You'll be out on the street begging for handouts."

"Just get on with it," said Eliot.

Cassie started throwing clothes and toilet articles helter skelter into the suitcase. She opened a top dresser drawer, scooped out several items of jewelry, and tucked them under several items of underwear already in the suitcase.

Sharon spotted a brightly shining object and said, "Stop right there." She called Eliot over and pointed into the suitcase. "Think you need to look at those things, sheriff."

Eliot stuck his hand under her folded panties and pulled out a ring. "I'll be damned. My rodeo prize."

"You think that ring is worth more than five hundred dollars?"

He snorted a laugh. "Are you kidding? More like five thousand."

"Cassandra Hume, you're under arrest for grand larceny." She went on to recite the Miranda rights spiel which now accompanies all arrests in the U. S. Eliot only smiled and put a finger to his lips advising her not to say anything.

However, Cassie couldn't contain herself and started blubbering again. "It's all so unfair. You gave me this ring a long time ago . . . "

"So you took it back when you stayed in my cabin that night?"

"Sure, I knew you wanted me to have it again."

Eliot put the ring back in her suitcase. "Pack it up, Cassie." He turned to Sharon and said, "It's evidence now, Detective Hardcastle. We need to protect the chain of custody."

"Right you are, sheriff."

The trio arrived at Pueblo's police station an hour later. Cassie was booked, her suitcase was inventoried and turned over to the desk sergeant, and she was led by a matron to a cell while still screaming threats and demands for her attorney.

It was almost midnight when Eliot and Sharon returned to her home. With little conversation, they made themselves ready for bed. In the cool darkness of her bedroom, they rested quietly and enjoyed the familiar intimacy of each other's body. Eliot said, "Quite an exciting day we had."

"I'm still too agitated for sleep but I'm relieved that woman is behind bars. Takes a big load off my mind."

"Me too. Now we can focus on more important things."

"Hey, I forgot to tell you what happened today. Hagerty was caught by a Montana sheriff and they're bringing him back to Pueblo."

"How about that? Hagerty and Cassie in the same jail."

"And my lunch meeting with Mahoney turned out well. He was happy to get that CD. Told me his Washington pal is working to have all the money sent back to the Caymans bank from Switzerland. Gloria Streckfus won't be so rich after all."

"What about the mayor?"

"He's part of this whole operation. Lots of legalities for the Feds to sort out. But Hagerty shooting Gloria, that's Ted Birdsall's case. The whole thing's a jurisdictional nightmare. A ready-made situation to work some plea deals with suspects testifying against each other."

"I'll bet the mayor is sorry he sent you that text message."

"Right, and that's just one thing he's regretting right now."

"You have to wonder why he got you started on that track."

"I think he had some idea that I'd uncover what Frank and Gloria were doing and have them indicted. Kind of a dumb move on his part."

"You and that FBI fellow make quite a team."

"Made. It's all in the past tense, Eliot. Now get this. He had the nerve to ask me if it was all right to invite Wasserstein out for a date. Can you believe that?"

Eliot broke out laughing. "The man has finally revealed his true colors. He's nothin' but a hound dog."

His laugh was infectious and Sharon joined in with some giggles. Her vision had become used to the darkness and she detected a smile on Eliot's face. "What are you thinking?" she said.

"When's the last time you had a vacation?"

"Hmm. Last year right before I met you. Why?"

"Same for me. It think it's high time you and I went off somewhere together."

Sharon rolled over to be closer. "Any place in particular?"

"As a matter of fact . . . yes. Had my road maps out today, looking at our country's great west and southwest. We could make a big loop trip, driving north up into Wyoming and heading west. Absaroka County is along the way and we could pay a courtesy visit to Sheriff Longmire, have a drink with Walt, Branch and Henry Standing Bear at the Red Pony."

"*Eliot.* You're crazy, there is no such county. It's all fiction."

"Yeah, I know, but we could pretend. Jackson Hole, the Grand Tetons and Yellowstone are real enough though."

"That's more like it. Where to from there?"

"Heading in a southwestern direction. Stopping in Vegas for a while, take in a show or two, play some blackjack."

"Sounds like fun. Any other attractions in that town?"

Eliot sang an old tune, " . . . goin' to the chapel and we're gonna get . . ."

Sharon sat up. "Is that a proposal I'm hearing?"

"Should I get out of bed and down on my knees?"

"*No. Yes.* No, not on your knees and the answer is *yes—yes—yes.*" She gave him a dozen kisses. "Oh my, this is exciting, I won't be able to sleep tonight."

"When can you break free for the trip?"

"By close of business tomorrow. I'll spend the day getting organized, get Debbie to take over my cases. I'll work it out somehow with Dave Hess, make sure I don't burn any bridges behind me."

"You want to keep your job, I take it."

"Yes, don't you?"

"I'm up for reelection in several months. Maybe we could wait until then before deciding anything. See how it pans out."

"Oh, I think you'll be reelected all right. And we could keep doing what we've been doing. Up in Leadville one weekend and down here the next."

"It's workable, at least for the short term. With five work days followed by a passionate weekend, our marriage will never get dull."

"It's a deal, cowboy." She cuddled up closer and both were soon fast asleep.

RICHARD C. ("DICK") REYNOLDS was born in East St. Louis, IL and raised mainly in St. Louis, MO. In 1953, he enlisted in the Marine Corps as a private and retired twenty-four years later as a Lieutenant Colonel.

From 1977 to 1994, Dick was a Systems Engineer for Hughes Aircraft Company in Fullerton, CA and Brussels, Belgium. During this time, he worked on command and control system programs for Greece, Norway, and Denmark, and on air defense projects for NATO, the Arab Republic of Egypt, and the Kingdom of Saudi Arabia.

After retiring from Hughes, Dick began a fourth career—fiction writing. His forty-plus short stories have appeared in such publications as *Timber Creek Review, Skyline Magazine, Barbaric Yawp*, and *Imitation Fruit Literary Journal*. Author of five earlier novels, *Averil, My Anchor, Mayhem in Mazatlan, Nightmare in Norway, Filling in the Triangles*, and *Shattering the Triangle,* a collection of short stories titled *Around the World in 80 Years* is also available from Valentine Press or Amazon in soft cover.

Dick and his wife Bernadette currently reside in Santa Fe, New Mexico.